"*Song of the Tree Frogs* is a POWERFUL story of brotherly love, forgiveness, healing, and resiliency of the human spirit, that is so beautifully written by J.W. Kitson."

—**Karen Abercrombie**, SAG actress, and award-winning Dove and Movieguide star, best known for her lead role in *War Room* (also a national and international speaker and CEO of Earth Mother Entertainment)

"*Song of the Tree Frogs* is a novel with appeal to both teens and adults. The book's unflinching arc takes the world of child abuse and abandonment thoughtfully, invoking both the pain, and the faith path of two young and tormented brothers. We meet human devils and angels along the way toward a satisfying resolution about perseverance, forgiveness, and unconditional love.Wonderfully evocative, *Song of the Tree Frogs* is being brought to film in 2020. This novel and its film will set a new high bar on this serious, societal issue."

—**Richard Cutting**, writer, SAG actor, producer, and screenwriter (*National Treasure: Book of Secrets, House of Cards*)

"J.W. Kitson has created an emotional triumph in *Song of the Tree Frogs*, which speaks a lot for the best qualities of the human condition, especially kindness and a sense of duty and service to others. Although these themes are brought about by its Christian morality, I believe that anyone of any faith can enjoy the heroism of Samuel and his wife…I'd highly recommend this novel for fans of heart-wrenching family drama and tales of hope through adversity."

—**K. C. Finn**, Reviewer from Readers' Favorite (making this novel a 5-Star rated, award-winning book)

"A roller coaster of epic emotions: fear, joy, sadness, redemption. *Song of the Tree Frogs*, now a major motion picture, is a journey into the deepest and darkest parts of the soul, testing your resolve in both faith and forgiveness."

—**Tom Dutta**, International Best-Selling Author of *The Way of the Quiet Warrior*, Founder and CEO, and radio and film producer

"I love the dimensions the characters bring to the plot. Each one is so complex, and the story pulls you into their lives and makes you want to be an advocate for the boys."

—**Meggie Jenny,** a Best and Best Supporting SAG actress with Treasure Coast Talent Agency

"This is more than just another novel to read. It is a can't -put-it-down story of the awful truths of family secrets, youthful endurance and hope. Expect to have your life's perspective jolted, shaken, and returned to you in a new wholesome approach to what one can do with personal faith and persistence. Can't wait for the next work from this author!"

—**C. Russell-Reese**

"An emotional page-turner! The story of Michael and Phillip is so well written that you feel like you are there with them. The author truly makes the reader connect and care for the boys, especially Michael. You'll have a hard time putting this book down and will experience an emotional roller coaster. I highly recommend it!"

—**D. Sherman**

"A book that held me in suspense from start to finish. I have read well over a thousand books and when I started this one, I found myself rooting for the boys from the very beginning and wanted to protect them from the obstacles that they faced. I give this book 5 stars and would recommend it to anyone from their mid-teens and up. He is a very talented storyteller."

—**Amazon Reader**

"I could hardly see the words on the pages of the last few chapters because of the many tears rolling down my face."

—**Eloise Y. Lott,** Christian author (and 89-year-young fan of *Song of the Tree Frogs)*

"The story will stay with you! This book is a testament to how forgiveness can create joy after tragedy. The author has provided a page-turning account of the real life struggles that many people go through in their way to find the ultimate peace that only forgiveness can provide. Highly recommended!"

—Amazon Customer

"*Song of the Tree Frogs,* surely a sad tale, prevails in its desire to express love between siblings…the instinct for the elder to protect the younger…the strength to overcome and survive regardless of the cruel hand life has dealt. First time author Kitson gets his point across that, no matter the circumstances into which we are born, love endures the struggle."

—D.A. Dysert, freelance writer, Boston, Massachusetts

"I honestly hate reading, but I couldn't stop reading this book!"

—Michael, high school student

"Michael and Phillip's story is tragic and beautiful, and should be required reading for teens and adults. As a teacher and lover of realistic fiction, I urge everyone to read this important book."

—Brooke Tier Harman, high school English instructor

"This story leaves the reader with a tremendous sense of admiration for the young boys' bravery throughout a traumatic upbringing. It keeps you engaged, especially with an unexpected ending! The therapist in me encourages all to read."

—Mallory R. Wines, PhD, LPCC

"Absolutely amazing! It has been a long time since a book has so completely captured me as this book has! The author so accurately captures the experiences of these young boys. This is definitely a must read!"

—Wendy, Amazon Reader

"“I couldn't put it down. My emotions were everywhere. The boys just felt like family to me. I fell in love with both of them."

—**Lori Haustman-DeMarco,** junior high teacher

Song of the Tree Frogs filled me with overwhelming emotions, causing me to shed many tears. I haven't experienced that from a book in a long time. I found myself endlessly pondering what would unfold in the chapters to come."

—**Mrs. Tiffany Moses,** school counselor

"This book takes you on an inspiring journey through the life of two brothers, and it makes you want to dive right into the book and save them!"

—**Anonymous** female high school student

J.W. KITSON

SONG OF THE TREE FROGS

A NOVEL

NEW YORK

NASHVILLE • MELBOURNE • VANCOUVER

SONG OF THE TREE FROGS

Published in New York, New York, by Morgan James Publishing. Morgan James is a trademark of Morgan James, LLC. www.MorganJamesPublishing.com

ISBN 9781683506058 paperback
ISBN 9781683506065 eBook
Library of Congress Control Number: 2017908671

Cover Design Concept by:
Flor Figueroa and Josh Menning
Menning Films

Interior Design by:
Megan Whitney
Creative Ninja Designs
megan@creativeninjadesigns.com

Front Cover Actors:
Cameron McKendry - top left (adult)
Matthew Ketchum - top right (adult)
Erich Schuett - bottom left
Mark Henne - bottom right

For William Wallace Smith, my father, who also loved to write;
for Gladys Frye and Helen Smith, my grandmothers, who taught me
to find peace while listening carefully to the song of the tree frogs;
and to the countless victims whose lives have been impacted
by hatred and abuse.
"Love endures all things!"

CHAPTER ONE

I dug my fingernails even deeper into Michael's arm when I heard my brother's bedroom door slam against the wall with a deafening thud. "Where are you, boy?" Dad hollered. He was after Michael, and I didn't know why. "Don't you dare be hidin' from me!"

My brother and I scurried from my bed like frightened mice and hid between the mattress and dresser. I frantically yanked my camouflage blanket from my bed, thinking it would hide us from Dad.

"What did I do, Phillip?" Michael whispered.

I started to say something, but ceased when unknown objects exploded against the walls in Michael's room. "You better answer me right now!" Dad shouted.

Seconds later, I heard his booming footsteps approaching my door. After he stormed into my room, he tore the blanket from us and hurled it through the air, knocking over several items from the top of my dresser. When Dad lurched toward us, Michael tightened his grip on my arm, while pressing his cheek forcefully against mine. His face was sticky from his sweat and tears.

"What did I do, Dad?" Michael cried.

Dad grabbed my brother's arm and violently snatched him away from me. Mucus was clinging to my hands, causing my fingers to lose their grip on Michael. I reached out for my brother's outstretched arms, but Dad thrust his finger into my face and demanded, "Stay right there! I mean it!"

I slid back into the corner and curled my legs up against my throbbing chest.

"I'll beat your—"

The ear-piercing screams of my brother forced me to press my clenched fists against my ears, blocking out Dad's threat. After he dragged Michael into the hallway, I started to get up, but after hearing Dad yelling at Michael to lift his feet, which must have been dragging across the floor, I quickly slid back into the corner beside my bed and wrapped my arms around my trembling legs. I rocked back and forth—hoping the chaos would end.

A determination to protect Michael forced me to accept no other option than to leave my room and go after him. Even with the warning of a beating still echoing in my ears, I tiptoed to my door and peered into the hallway. I could hear Mom hollering from downstairs, but her words were garbled, and I was unable to understand what she was saying.

"Let go of the railing!" Dad hollered.

Sickening slaps on bare skin were followed by even more shrieks from Michael. I crept down the hallway and looked around the corner just in time to see Dad latching onto my brother's shirt, which began to tear when he lifted him from the floor. Mom helplessly tried to free Michael, but Dad violently pushed her away, causing her to stumble into the living room and topple over the arm of the sofa. I immediately disappeared into the shadows at the top of the stairs. When I peered around the corner again, I saw Dad pull an envelope from his pocket and wave it in Mom's face.

"Stop this, Tony! You're going to break his arm!" Mom pleaded.

Dad's voice erupted with explosive anger, while his hand was still welded to Michael's elbow. "Tell me who this Samuel guy is, or I'll *really* break this little bastard's arm!" Michael whimpered, begging Dad to release him.

"You need to stop this, Tony! *You're scaring him over nothing!*" Mom latched onto Michael's other arm and yanked him toward her.

During their ruthless tug-of-war battle, my brother's head thrashed back and forth.

Dad raised a fist high into the air, while crumpling the letter in his other. Mom's shoulder and elbow jerked upward. "You never said nothing about no guy named Samuel before!"

"I don't remember *anyone* named Samuel!" Mom insisted, while lowering her arm.

"Don't lie to me!" He thrust the creased envelope into her face again. "This is a letter he wrote to you, ain't it?"

"Tony, I'm telling you that I don't know anyone named Samuel!"

Still grasping Michael's arm, Dad shoved my brother closer to Mom and shouted, "So, how do you explain *this*?"

"Momma, I'm scared!" Michael cried.

Dad unexpectedly released my brother, and he fell to the floor, almost striking his head on a wooden end table. Michael sat up and massaged his arm before crawling over—like a wounded animal—and hiding behind a green swivel chair in the corner of the living room. I lurched forward, wanting desperately to rush down the stairs and save him, but I didn't dare let Dad know I had disobeyed him by leaving my room. When I heard muffled cries drifting out from behind the chair, a sickening, dull ache shot across my stomach, twisting it into knots. I covered my mouth quickly after realizing a loud gasp had escaped my lips.

When Dad stormed over toward my brother again, Mom jumped in front of him. "Don't you dare lay a hand on him! I mean it, Tony! He doesn't understand *any* of this!"

Dad took the envelope and pushed it forcefully into Mom's face again. "I wanna know who this Samuel guy is!" he demanded.

"If you'd just tell me where you got that letter, I'm sure I can explain," Mom reasoned.

"Don't act like you don't already know, Ellen!" He shoved Mom into a chair and snatched Michael up by his arm. More tears flowed from my disbelieving eyes when I witnessed Dad grabbing the back of Michael's neck and thrusting his head into Mom's face. He snatched a handful of Michael's hair and jerked his head upward. "So, who does this little bastard *really* belong to?"

Mom's mouth was sealed.

"Well?" he asked accusingly. "Now it's all making sense! You let me believe he was my kid all along, didn't you?" He smashed Michael's head violently into Mom's chest. "You made me look like nothin' but some pathetic joke all these years!"

"Dad, you're hurting me!" Michael pleaded. "I won't be bad no more! I promise!"

"I said to leave him out of this, Tony!" Mom struggled to lift Michael from her chest while crawling out of the chair. "He doesn't understand why you're doing this to him!" My brother fell backward onto the floor and curled into a ball. Mom stood and pointed down at him. "This has nothing to do with Michael!"

"Are you kiddin' me?" Dad yelled. "It's got *everything* to do with him!"

As the appalling memory swirled in my mind like leaves stirred up from a brisk, cool wind, I was unexpectedly startled by the blowing of a car horn behind me. I accelerated through the intersection, embarrassed I hadn't noticed that the traffic light had already turned green. Sweat was clinging to my forehead, and I quickly wiped it away with my shirtsleeve. I reached over and turned the air conditioning up and inhaled the cool, welcomed breeze, which quickly chilled my clammy skin. Those awful memories of Dad, the letter, and Michael's abuse were chiseled into my conscience like an engraving on a monument—a memorial to some tragic historic event never intended to be forgotten.

As I drove by somewhat familiar but aging landmarks, my thoughts continued to conspire against me, slowly robbing me of the courage I needed to carry on with my quest to visit my brother that day. I even began to doubt whether my love for Michael was strong enough to bury in my mind all of the inexcusable, evil things I had allowed Dad to do to him. I've always heard people say that love can endure anything, but I'd learned early on in my life that such an expression was nothing more than some false hope embraced by naïve people who had never experienced real pain like us. Michael and I had no choice but to learn that hatred was the most powerful weapon any human could ever use to eradicate others. I watched as Dad successfully used hatred against those he once cared about—including himself.

I shook my head vigorously as I turned slowly into the large, paved entryway to my remote destination. Almost with a sense of relief, my attention was immediately focused on how the ivy-covered stone walls and the huge wrought iron gates towered over my car. I hadn't noticed any of it several months ago when I had left Michael there in the care of strangers.

A small stone building, which looked like a guard shack, was positioned just off to the left of the gate, but I didn't see anyone inside. I wasn't exactly sure when visiting hours began and ended, but since the gate was already open, I assumed it was okay to drive onward. I was kindly motioned forward by a gentleman in a blanched gray uniform. I waved at him before squinting my eyes, trying to veil the late afternoon sunlight blinding me through the car's windshield.

Once I drove through a patch of shade, which darkened the interior of my car, I suddenly realized that I was only minutes away from confronting

Michael—alone. A sudden, sharp pain jabbed against the wall of my stomach, causing my foot to lift slightly from the accelerator when I flinched. Regardless, I knew that I simply had to talk to him, even though I wasn't sure he would be able to fully grasp all that I had to say. *Would he even acknowledge me?* It had been months since I'd been close to my brother, and his current condition did not warrant such neglect, especially from me. Shamefully, I wasted most of the day battling myself over pathetic excuses as to why I shouldn't visit him.

I was able to examine many unfamiliar things along the way to my destination, especially the large red brick building sitting like a fortress on the lush, emerald hill in the center of the vast property. Mammoth trees stood as guards along the narrow, winding road, and dispersed throughout the freshly mowed lawns, several people walked about aimlessly as if they were in some sort of drug-induced trance. A few of them were in uniforms, which brought back the oppressive feelings I'd had moments earlier. Several stared at me as I drove by, but they soon went back to their activities as though I had never disturbed them in the first place. My fingers became a tourniquet around the steering wheel when I spotted one man who reminded me of my dad. His dark, disheveled hair, the withered, scrawny body, the gaunt cheeks, only reminded me of the man I hated more than anyone in the entire world. Thankfully, Michael and I had each other, and Dad vowed to get even with us if we ever joined forces and retaliated against him. Nothing would please him more than to see Michael in such a place, surrounded by iron bars. Dad pledged to ruin Michael's life no matter how long it took him, and shamefully, I almost let him do it.

I reached up and wiped my face, smearing a tear across one of my flushed cheeks. If only I had picked up the ax in the garage, and used it sooner to stop Dad, I might have spared Michael the agonizing nightmares that stalked him so often in the darkness of his room. I wondered how Michael would ever forgive me for abandoning him, especially after the murder that changed everything.

After arriving at the red brick building, I turned off the car. At first, I could only hear the clicking noises coming from the engine as it started to cool. Stalling again, I reached over and picked up the newspaper from the passenger's seat. As my heart rapidly pounded against the inside of my chest, I scanned the headline: "More Clues Leading to Possible Suspects in Westview Murder Case." I dropped it back onto the seat and leaned my head against the headrest. My sigh seemed to echo accusations all around me. With no further excuses left, I knew what I had to do, so I unbuckled my seatbelt and opened the door. My brother would be expecting me to show up sooner or later.

Today was that day.

CHAPTER TWO

I had a special gift in the trunk for Michael, which I *needed* for our visit. Its nostalgic value would be something familiar—something that would reconnect us, and hopefully ease the constant anxiety possessing my thoughts. My real fears were hidden behind a mask of contentment I tried to wear every day, and I was afraid that Michael would see through the disguise—easily discovering the guilt and grief I'd openly pretended never existed. My regrets had become a kind of disease that sought to destroy my body, and a full dose of my brother's forgiveness was about the only cure I thought I needed. In spite of my neglect at protecting him so many times, Michael always seemed to be able to say what I needed to hear—heroically relieving *my* anguish, while disregarding his own. My hope was that the gift would be the bridge that might span the deep chasm of regret separating us—at least in *my* mind.

As I nervously walked toward the front of the brick building, I couldn't help but wonder again what I would say to Michael. There were already too many times when I did nothing, especially when we were younger and practically held captive in our rooms. I still can't bear to look at striped wallpaper in a bedroom without thinking of the many nights I would lie on my bed, violently shaking from the sensation that I was languishing behind the bars of some secluded prison—sealed up with nowhere to go, and no way to get to Michael as he cried out into the suffocating darkness for any rescue from Dad's torment. Before I was eight years old, the lines embedded into my wallpaper were just that—lines—but when Dad came home with the letter, the lines forever became iron bars, much like the ones surrounding Michael's new home. When I did try to protect Michael, Dad would often force me back into my bedroom. He would then punish Michael even worse for my interference. Dad somehow interpreted my pathetic attempts at defending my brother as some sort of act of treason against *him*.

After setting my gift on the ground, not far from the building, I was overcome with disturbing images, which had somehow embedded themselves into my conscience like someone's handprints left to harden in cement. I squeezed my eyes shut and did everything I could to stay in the present, but with little resistance, the humiliation of the past ensnared me, briefly forcing me to resurrect the remembrance of being nothing more than a confused, naïve seventeen-year-old boy left alone with his dying brother in a melancholy hospital room years earlier.

Nearly paralyzed by the sudden memory, I quickly opened my eyes and gazed at several trees huddled closely together like frightened children in the dark. My lungs screamed for air, while I attempted to find any distraction that might rescue me from the carnage I was still hoarding in my mind from that night I watched my brother dying from his overdose in the hospital.

Thankfully, the color of the red brick building reminded me of my favorite crimson sweatshirt my grandmother had given to me during our last Christmas together with her. For several years, it was perfect for the chilly Alabama nights when Michael and I sat together and talked on the old fallen tree at the edge of our property. The soothing melody of the tree frogs helped to shield us from the hatred that sought to invade our thoughts and cheat us out of the few good memories we'd secretly hidden from our parents.

The tree frogs always reminded me of Grandma Gladys, (whom Michael often called Nana Gladie). She would take us outside at night onto her porch so that we could listen to those familiar creatures nestled in the forest behind her house. Grandma would even tell us how she could pick out specific tones coming from particular frogs, which she then began to name for us. Being a realist, I didn't really believe her, but Michael swore that he could identify certain *voices* as well. To our amusement one evening, Michael yelled out, "Nana! I can hear your favorite frog! It's gotta be Franklin! I know it's him!"

Grandma chuckled and dotingly pulled Michael close to her chest and hugged him snugly. In the glow of the citronella candles, I watched my brother's face turn a darker shade from the force of her embrace. Grandma gave the best hugs! Her arms were a cozy security blanket—the only sense of real peace and comfort we'd known during our early childhood.

From her back porch, we would rock on the old metal glider while she sang some of her favorite church songs to us. The feel of the artificial green carpet sent tingling sensations across our bare feet as we pushed off with our toes in order to keep the glider moving in a kind of perpetual motion. While rocking endlessly together, Michael would burrow his bare shoulder into Grandma's abdomen and eventually collapse into a deep slumber—often using one of her breasts as a cushion. Meanwhile, Grandma and I would continue to listen to our nightly serenade. Maturity eventually taught me how important and sacred those special moments truly were with her. Like a priceless family heirloom, those moments with Grandma eventually become a kind of treasure that she had implanted into my memory—a kind of legacy she somehow knew I might need in the future.

One night, Grandma rested her cheek on the top of my head, while gently rubbing my arm. "You know, Phillip," she whispered, "Grandma loves both you boys, but there is something *really* special about you that I've been wanting to mention."

"What's that, Grandma?" I whispered.

"Well, it's about the way you look for details in things that no one else really sees."

"What do you mean?"

"It's just that I see you looking at things, Phillip—common things like clouds, pictures, and people. It's like you're always studying them, trying to figure them out like a puzzle."

"Do I really do that, Grandma?"

"Yes, honey, you do. Even my best friend, Eloise, noticed you doing it the other day. Honey, you are so smart, and Grandma is so proud of you."

I grinned and snuggled even closer, despite the warmth pouring from her body. "You know, I bet you would be good to take to an art museum. You would probably see special patterns in the artwork."

"Hummm . . ." I mumbled, "I guess maybe I do look at things harder than others."

"You certainly do, honey," she whispered. "God made you so special."

She gently lifted my chin and kissed me on the forehead before standing. I helped her carefully lift Michael into her arms. After tucking us into bed that night, she knelt beside Michael's bed, recited a prayer, and kissed both of us before retreating to her own room. From that point on, I became more aware of the times I studied objects and people in more detail, looking and listening for patterns that others might not see or hear. That night, Grandma also opened our window in the spare bedroom, which Michael and I often did at home, and I even tried to identify certain *voices* echoing from the woods. I think I actually heard Franklin that night!

With the echo of tree frogs still resonating in my ears, I looked up at the huge red brick structure again, wondering if it was still possible for me to face Michael alone. Perhaps my visit would finally let me know how to feel—or how to move my life forward once again. I looked down at the gift I'd brought, and instead of resurrecting the special moments I'd cherished between Michael and me, I was plunged into an abyss of disturbing images I'd hoped to avoid that day. Tears rolled down my face as I knelt, resting my knees upon the manicured lawn. With my eyes stinging with pain, I had no choice but to face the stone cold reality of my brother's existence—the remnant of a crime I knew I could never erase.

My eyes closed abruptly, but in the darkness, a faint image soon appeared, and hidden within it, I saw Michael and me getting ready for school many years ago. I also saw my brother, later that night, lying on a hospital bed with a brave couple standing close by. Thankfully, that couple refused to walk away from two desperate boys left wounded on yet another one of the battlefields of our lives—one that neither of us could have escaped on our own.

CHAPTER THREE

"You look like crap," I said to my brother that morning.

Michael rolled his eyes. "Gee, thanks a lot, Phillip."

"Seriously, Michael, did you stay up too late watching 'The Arsenio Hall Show' again?" I took a bite of an apple I had grabbed earlier from the kitchen.

"I'm fine," he replied. "Just hurry up and eat your breakfast. I don't wanna miss the bus. You remember what happened the last time we did!"

"You didn't have another nightmare, did you?" I asked. "They seem to be getting worse lately, aren't they?" My brother was silent.

"Michael!" Dad yelled. "Get in here right now, boy!"

I almost choked on the piece of apple I was chewing. "What did you do?" I whispered.

"Who knows," Michael replied, shaking his head, "but I better go see what's wrong." He sighed and shuffled his feet toward the kitchen. I stepped forward and grabbed his arm because I wanted him to stop, but I also knew my effort would be futile. "I better go," he whispered.

My brother's eyes started to glisten in the early morning sunlight beaming through the dining room window. My stomach erupted into spasms, and I dropped the apple onto the dining room table.

When my brother walked into the kitchen, with me close behind, Dad was leaning against the counter—his glare saturated with hatred. Michael stopped near the refrigerator and looked back at me. I saw his throat straining as he tried to swallow. Michael shoved his hands into his pockets. He remained silent, as if waiting for the verdict in a murder trial. I could clearly see my brother's back and broad shoulders heaving with each breath after he'd turned back toward Dad. That's when Dad stepped aside, revealing the reason for his anger.

Without uttering a word, Michael rushed to the counter and sealed the peanut butter jar. Once he put it into the cupboard, he turned and stepped toward me.

Suddenly, Dad reached out and grabbed Michael by the back of his neck. He spun my brother around and thrust his forearm into Michael's throat before pushing him violently against the refrigerator door, causing several boxes of cereal on the top to cascade to the floor.

Michael's eyes narrowed. "Dad . . . *please*!"

"How 'bout you skip breakfast for the next couple days! I told you, boy, I ain't gonna let you mess up *my* house."

"Come on, Dad," I pleaded, thoughtlessly stepping forward. Dad jerked his head toward me. I swallowed, nearly choking again. "He at least put it away," I timidly responded. Dad's menacing eyes narrowed, reminding me of a deadly viper, ready to strike.

"Shut your mouth, Phillip! This is between me and him." Dad turned again toward Michael. "So, no eatin' breakfast until Monday, Mikey!" Dad grinned. "What do you think about that?"

Michael's face was flushed from the surge of blood rushing to his head. My brother grabbed Dad's forearm, probably trying to ease some of the strain on his throat.

"Get your stinking paws off my arm, boy! Dontcha dare touch me!"

Michael grimaced while lowering his hands. The discomfort was evident by the tightening squeeze my brother's hands soon had on the edges of the refrigerator door. Dad was a lion, clamping down on the jugular of some innocent prey. He grinned before saying, "Awww, Mikey's a little upset, Phillip."

I noticed a tear gliding down my brother's face.

"*I think he's gonna cry*. Is that what you're gonna do, boy?"

"Come on, Dad," I begged, "just let him go!"

Dad never looked at me.

"Dad . . . *please*!"

He continued to stare into Michael's eyes, acting as though he could read my brother's most intimate thoughts.

"He can't breathe, Dad!" I pleaded.

After he glanced toward me, Dad's stern expression caused me to lower my head slightly to the floor. My heart pounded at the thought of what he might do next.

He turned back to Michael and whispered, through clenched teeth, "This ain't over, boy!"

As I slowly raised my head, I saw Dad wink at him, right before looking my way again. He paused, smirked, and then slammed Michael against the refrigerator again. I knew my interference had made things worse.

Dad looked at Michael, and then at the cereal boxes scattered on the floor. "Get that cleaned up too."

He meandered toward the doorway—confident in his victory over us—but he stopped and glared at me. His black, threatening eyes twitched with anger.

I really did it this time! I thought. The sensation of his warm, putrid breaths striking my face caused me to turn my head slightly.

As he started to leave, he forced his shoulder into my chest, knocking me into the wall. I could hear him chuckle once he left the kitchen.

After he stomped up the stairs, I heard his bedroom door squeak open. "Hey Ellen," he yelled, "do you know what that little bas—" The door suddenly slammed shut. Somehow, it was Mom's fault that Michael neglected one of Dad's ridiculous rules.

I quietly stepped over to Michael and stabilized him as he reached out for my hand. "You okay?" I whispered.

Michael gasped for air as he massaged his throat. "Yeah," he said, "let's get outta here before he comes back."

"Yeah," I said, "but what about Mom? He's gonna hurt her again."

"Who cares?" Michael said.

We picked up the cereal boxes and put them back on the top of the refrigerator before retrieving our backpacks from the dining room floor.

"Come on, Phillip!"

As if dealing with Dad wasn't bad enough, it was always embarrassing having the bus pull up in front of our house, because our yard was cluttered with several rusty junked cars and piles of useless things Dad thought he might need some day. I hated that we had to put up with the degrading comments we often heard on the bus. Then, there were the worthless idiots my parents invited over to our house on the weekends. Their shameless, lewd behaviors often extended way into the early morning hours until the furniture and floors were covered with bodies. Their contorted carcasses were sometimes lying around like corpses that had been dead for several days. The toxic fumes of stale cigarette smoke, pot, alcohol, and vomit saturated the air. Michael did everything he could to get away from the house, but I often stayed, trying to do what I could to protect Mom.

By the time we made it to school that Friday, the difficult, daily task of trying to avoid even more conflict was only compounded by the realization that I was also going to fail two tests. The fight between my parents the evening before prevented me from studying. After first period, my friend Gwen informed me in the hallway that she had been invited to a party that evening. She wanted me to go, but I just rolled my eyes when she walked away. It was at the home of this rich kid who never bothered to acknowledge my existence in the first place. I could stay home and get that same treatment.

I never really understood why I had such concern for Mom, especially since she didn't seem to care about my brother or me. It's hard to understand, but there was a loyalty I had for her, regardless of the pathetic existence she chose to live. Mom was needy, uncaring, neglectful, and somewhat defenseless against an addict like Dad. Regardless of logic, I still felt obligated to protect her. Michael, on the other hand, didn't seem to care what happened to Mom.

CHAPTER FOUR

At dismissal, I was nearly crushed by a stampede of rowdy, anxious teenagers trying to leave school that afternoon. While sorting through a mound of trash in my locker, I knew my next dilemma would be telling Gwen about my real desire to skip the party that night. I suddenly heard her coming down the hallway, and when I turned my head, we made eye contact. I knew it was too late to escape her forthcoming interrogation, and since she demanded my undivided attention every time she spoke to me, the thought of missing the bus did cross my mind.

"Well, did you decide to go with me to the party, or am I going to have to go by myself *again*?" I knew what I wanted to say, but her intimidation caused my stomach to churn.

"I'll have to see what my parents have planned tonight before I can give you an answer," I said. Disgust shot across her face, and her glaring eyes made my breaths stick to the inside of my lungs.

"Michael already said you would be taking him," she insisted.

I cleared my throat and lowered my head. "I'll . . . ahhh . . . have to call you after dinner."

She slammed my locker shut. "You better, *Phillip Alexander Williams!*" She knew I hated it when she said my full name.

Exasperated, I rolled my eyes, tossed my backpack over my shoulder, and bolted for the parking lot. A few minutes later, I was walking up the aisle, nearly exhausted from the sprint to the bus. Getting safely to an empty seat is a lot like running through a field of landmines. Making eye contact with the wrong person; saying hello to someone another student hated; or accidentally bumping into a kid with anger issues, could easily bring on an explosion of fury, likely to cause verbal humiliation and bodily harm. I quickly managed to spot a vacant seat midway through the bus, and thankfully, I also saw Michael sitting with one of his classmates near the back. I cherished the protective feeling of having a seat full of nothing but isolation. I slid across the seat and rested my head against the cool glass of the window, hoping for a little relief from the headache I'd been fighting since lunch. I let the vibration of the slowly moving bus sooth my head. Sadly, anxiety threatened to take my mind hostage at the thought of returning home.

As the bus pulled out onto the main street, I wondered again how I might break the bad news to Gwen. Trying to figure out some lame excuse wasn't as easy as I'd first thought. After all, hiding the truth about a lot of things was getting harder with each passing day. Like so many other regrets in my life, I figured I would end up making the wrong decision not to go with her. Then again, I thought about how our choices can sometimes be the right ones, even if we can't quite understand the outcome until much later.

Surprised that I still had the energy to think, I entertained the idea that my life was just a giant jigsaw puzzle, and unfortunately, there wasn't a clear picture available to help guide me in assembling the pieces into the right order. It would take someone far greater than me to figure it all out in the end. For some odd reason, the letter that Dad brought home that one night seemed to find its way into my thoughts as well. After all, it was a huge piece that left me wondering how it fit into the puzzle of my life. For years, Michael and I had been curious about the man who wrote it, but we didn't dare mention the name *Samuel* around our house.

When the bus stopped at a traffic light, I lurched forward, jolting me back to another familiar dilemma. I realized that our home was just a few minutes away. The thought of spending the evening with my parents, in the midst of a bunch of inebriated idiots, sickened me. Dad often enjoyed using Michael as an opportunity to show off his cocky, arrogant sense of humor, especially when there was a room full of his friends. One time, Dad put his arm around Michael as he hastily passed through the family room on his way to get something from the laundry room. I was behind my brother, but I stopped in the doorway once I saw Dad grasp his arm. Sarcastically, Dad smirked and asked, "Hey everybody, don't I have a handsome bastard for a son?" Michael froze when Dad yanked on a handful of hair on the back of his head. "So, guys," he asked, "who does Mikey *really* look like more?"

Someone raised his beer can and shouted, "Definitely ain't you, Williams!"

After further childish taunts from others, another guy shouted, "Mike's a lot better lookin'."

Mom slammed her beer can down and stormed out of the room, leaving a vortex of smoky, pot-filled air swirling behind her. Dad shoved Michael and told him to hurry up because he was interrupting their *good time.* My brother was still shaking when we made it back to my bedroom.

Those were also the nights when Michael and I would sneak out and escape to the fallen tree near the woods. While sitting peacefully—listening to the tree frogs—we talked about everything from running away, to living with a nice family who made us feel like we mattered. Those were our secret desires—born solely from the notion of wishful thinking on our part. Of course, we had no clue where we'd go if we did take off. After Grandma Gladie died, Mom and Dad isolated us from anyone who might have truly cared about us. Then again, even if we did escape, we always worried they'd find us and drag us back home.

Sitting with my brother alone on the tree trunk was sacred to me. The gentle sound of his breathing was almost as comforting as the embrace of Grandma Gladie during those serene nights when we sat together on her porch. If it was a rainy night, Michael and I would stay in my room. We would still open the window far enough for us to hear *nature's soundtrack* coming from the forest. Either place was fine, because my brother—my best friend—was next to me.

As the bus pulled up to the stop before mine, it hit a pothole, causing my head to bounce against the window. I rubbed my temple while looking slightly to the left to see if anyone had seen me hit the glass. No one reacted, so I was safe. As Bonnie McIntosh walked by me on her way off of the bus, she timidly said, "I'll see you Monday in history class, Phillip."

A few people chuckled around me when I replied, "Huh? Oh yeah, I'll see you . . . Monday." Like me, Bonnie was one of those shy students who just wanted to someday fit in with the crowd. Regardless of her social status, I noticed her—even if no one else did.

Someone took great pleasure in reaching over two seats and hitting me on the back of my head. "Hey Williams, is that your *new* girlfriend?" he taunted.

Apparently everyone knew about the slight crush I had on Gwen.

Another insignificant jerk shouted, "Hey Phil, ya better hope Gwen doesn't find out. She'll tear ya a new one."

I just shook my head and cautiously placed it against the window again. I suddenly noticed that the glass looked as though it hadn't been cleaned in years. I could still see the remnants of the words *bite me* smeared onto the surface with someone's finger.

After we arrived at our stop, Michael slowly shuffled toward the front of the bus. With an alarming sense of dread, I grabbed my backpack and trudged ahead.

Someone yelled, *"I'll see you Monday in history class, Phillip."*

I never bothered to look back. I had other concerns.

An explosion of fear surged through my body when I stepped off of the bus and saw Dad extinguishing his cigarette on the bottom of his shoe. The fact that he was standing near the garage—his sacred shrine where he often communed with friends—told me that something ominous was at hand. Michael took off in the opposite direction toward the back door of the house. He didn't get very far when Dad pointed at him and shouted, "Get over here—now!"

At that moment, I remembered Dad whispering to Michael that morning in the kitchen: "This ain't over, boy!"

CHAPTER FIVE

Michael was suddenly immoveable, as if his feet were firmly sealed in cement. I wanted to tell him not to go to Dad, but the acid rising from my stomach seemed to burn away my words.

"You ugly bastard, I told you to get over here right now! I mean it!"

I was sure that Dad had already been drinking, and I didn't know how much control he had over himself.

Like the shuddering motions of a deer sensing danger, Michael cautiously approached Dad and mumbled, "I'm really sorry I forgot to—"

With a force that could have smashed a boulder into rubble, Dad backhanded Michael and screamed, "Didn't I tell you to straighten up the garage yesterday?"

Michael's head jerked violently backward, and he stumbled from the intensity of the blow. His backpack dropped to the ground like a brick. I wanted to shout at Dad to stop, but my lungs were being squeezed by my tightening chest, and there was no air left in me to form any words. I was shocked that Dad had actually risked hitting Michael out in the open. I looked back to see if the bus was still in front of the house, but its red taillights were already at the next drop off farther down the road.

Michael regained his balance and attempted again to tell Dad how sorry he was for forgetting his chore, but Dad grabbed the back of Michael's shirt collar and pushed him violently into the garage. I could see the exposed skin on Michael's back when his shirt was nearly forced over his head. The garage slowly darkened as the huge door closed with a thud. My parched throat caused me to cough with each attempted swallow. I dared to take a few steps toward the garage, but I knew there was nothing I could do to prevent Dad from finishing what he'd started that morning in the kitchen. I *hated* him for what he was about to do to my brother. I squeezed my eyes shut and clenched my hands. "Come on, Phillip," I whispered to myself. "Move your feet! You gotta save him!"

I flinched when I heard an explosion of glass shattering against the wall—followed by a loud slap. "Owwww! Come on, Dad! I said I was sorry!"

"Don't you dare try and get away from me, boy!"

I paced several times in the yard, not far from the side door. My shirt was dampening from perspiration. Just ten feet separated me from the side door—*yes, ten stinking feet*—and I couldn't force myself to go in and save him. I was a witness to yet another merciless crime, and I did nothing to prevent it!

I chose to pick up our backpacks and head toward the house like a coward. I started to sprint when I heard something slamming into one of the garage walls. It could have been Michael. When I arrived at the back door of the house, I wondered how I would face my brother later—knowing I'd abandoned him once more to that cruel, soulless pig.

Mom was sitting at the kitchen table, casually smoking when I rushed in, dropped the backpacks, and told her that Dad was beating Michael for not cleaning the garage.

She smashed the cigarette butt into the ashtray. "Well, what do you want me to do about it?"

"Mom, you gotta stop him!"

"Just how do you think I can fight off your dad? Why didn't you try when you were out there?"

Her words slapped me in the face.

"Seriously, Mom, Michael really needs you! Dad will only take it out on him even more if I get involved, just like he did this morning."

"Yeah, Phillip," she said, as she stood, "and who do you think he came after as soon as he was done with your brother this morning?"

I rubbed my forehead and sighed. "But, Mom—" My skin felt hot. "Dad's really gonna hurt him. I know he is!"

Mom walked over to the sink and gazed out the window. Without looking my way, she mumbled, "It's me he's after. He uses Michael to get to me."

"What?" I asked. "What are you saying?"

She didn't answer.

"Mom!" I leaned against the refrigerator and rested my throbbing head against its cool surface. "Is this all because of that letter from years ago?"

Her head slumped toward the sink. "You just don't understand," she said—her voice quavering.

I walked over and stood behind her and placed my hand on her shoulder, causing her to cringe. "Mom, we gotta stop him. Why can't we all just leave him behind?"

She stormed toward the doorway leading into the dining room, but she suddenly stopped. Facing away from me, she said, "You have no idea what he's capable of doing. He said he'd make sure I never—"

She suddenly got silent and took a deep breath.

"Never what, Mom?"

Her shoulders sank. "I'd never get custody of you boys, because he would—"

She quickly retreated toward the living room. I locked my fingers behind the back of my neck and closed my eyes briefly. It finally made sense. When I opened my eyes, which were stinging with tears, I retrieved the backpacks from the kitchen floor and headed for the stairs.

I dropped everything on my bedroom floor, collapsed onto my bed, and buried my face into my pillow. I wanted to scream! Sweat rolled down my temples, and my jaw started to ache from the grinding of my teeth. Moments later, I sat up and decided to walk over to one of the windows and stare out at the garage. My emotions were a noose around my neck, squeezing the life out of me. I leaned my head forward and rested it on the glass. A small trace of dust wafted into the air from the windowsill, stirred up by the blast of air from my flailing nostrils.

I gazed around the room. It had become a prison—a resurrected memory triggered by my gaze at the wallpaper. I had to escape, so I hurried from my room and rushed through the hallway and down the stairs. I paced throughout the dining room, waiting for Dad to come into the house.

Mom walked in from the living room. "How was school today?" she asked.

Dazed at first, I replied, "O . . . kay . . . I guess?" My right eyebrow shot upward. I never mentioned anything about the tests I'd likely failed. "Gwen asked me to a party tonight," I said.

"I see that little manipulator just can't seem to leave you alone, can she?" Mom headed for the kitchen. "I'll mention something to your dad after dinner."

After she disappeared, my arms shot outward in disbelief about her sudden change in the conversation.

When the front door slammed shut, I retreated out the back door. My walk to the garage was like being led to an execution chamber on the last day of my life. Images of Michael's condition bombarded me, causing my muscles to stiffen with each step. When my fingers touched the cool metal handle of the side door, I yanked them away. *What could I possibly say to him? How could I even attempt to apologize?* I thought. I almost turned and darted back to the house in order to hide in my room, but I knew there was no way I could live with myself if I did.

I slowly opened the side door and walked in. The pungent, oily odor of the garage ambushed my nostrils. At first, I didn't look at Michael. *I couldn't!* I stood and gazed at the shards of broken glass on the floor, which the overhead lights reflected into various patterns on the walls and ceiling—like looking into a kaleidoscope. When I did glance over at my brother, I saw one of his hands trembling uncontrollably. He appeared to be struggling as he crawled around on his hands and knees searching for nails that had scattered from the jar Dad had apparently thrown. Michael never looked up at me, but I did notice blood dripping onto the floor directly from his face.

I walked over and stood by him. "Michael, you're bleeding. Are you okay?"

He took the back of his hand and wiped it across his mouth. Without looking up, he answered, "What do you think?"

I saw a coating of mucus and blood smeared across the back of his hand. Michael had been dealing with this type of brutality for nearly ten years. *How much longer could he resist the violence before he decided to shed some of Dad's blood as well?* I wondered. I walked over and grabbed a roll of paper towels from the shelf and returned. After squatting on the floor next to him, I lifted his head toward mine and wiped the blood from his lips and chin. At first, he grimaced from the touch, but he still allowed me to help him with the injury.

Tears glided down his cheeks, and when I reached around and patted his back, he flinched.

"Ouch!" His body contorted, and he quickly pulled away. "He slammed me against the car after he pushed me into the garage. It's not like my back wasn't already sore from this morning," he complained.

I shifted my weight and sat on the floor. Tears flowed from my eyes. "I'm so sorry I left you, man!" I pleaded.

While gazing at my brother, he placed his hand on *my* shoulder in order to comfort *me.*

"I can't . . . I mean . . . I don't know how to stop him, Michael. I just don't know how!" I cried.

"Phillip, I don't know how much longer I can take it, man." He sniffled. "I mean it!"

My shame had flooded my conscience, and I somehow knew my apologies—my pathetic, hollow words—would mean *nothing*! I placed my hand on the back of Michael's head, which was drenched with sweat. "Hey man, I'm . . . God, Michael, I'm . . ."

Michael pulled his knees up to his chest and folded his arms over them. "There was nothing you could have done," he said. "You know he would've done the same thing to you." He dropped his head onto his arms. After sniffling a few times, Michael looked up. "Stop blaming yourself, Phillip. I'll be okay. Besides, Dad will probably blame the marks on me playing soccer or football again." I handed him a paper towel and he wiped his face. "I gotta get this done," he said. We both started crawling around, searching once more for nails. I soon noticed that Michael kept groaning while moving across the cement floor. Without looking up, Michael mumbled, "Nobody cares about us, Phillip! If they did, they woulda done something to help us by now."

"Who can we tell without Dad knowing we said something?" I asked.

"No one," Michael responded. "We don't have anybody since Nana died."

"Yeah, I know," I replied. Michael slowly shifted his weight and rested his hip onto the floor. "I really am so sorry for—"

I squeezed my eyes shut, refusing to allow my tears to escape again.

"I told you, man, there was nothing you coulda done," Michael said.

I looked at him. "Michael, what did Dad do to you? Why do you keep moaning when you move?" An appalling silence swept through the garage. "Please tell me," I begged.

After a brief pause, Michael replied, "I need to finish cleaning up before he comes back out here."

He tried to move, but the pain caused him to rest back onto his hip again.

I grabbed his upper arm. "Michael, what did he do to you?"

He thrust his thumb and finger into the corners of his eyes. Tears still escaped. Without looking up, he pointed over to one of the side walls of the garage. A wooden board was leaning against a ladder.

"Oh my God, Michael! Did he beat you with that?"

Michael nodded his head and sighed. Tears continued to roll down his flushed cheeks.

I stood and leaned over the workbench and buried my reddened face into my hands. "I'll find a way, Michael. I'll get us outta here for good, even if I gotta ki—"

Michael's eyelids widened. His gaze shot straight through me.

I suddenly pushed away from the workbench and walked over and retrieved the broom. When I returned, I said, "You stay there and just rest. I'll take care of the garage."

Michael complied by scooting over to the wooden frame of the workbench and resting until I almost finished sweeping. He coughed several times from the dust I'd stirred up.

I wanted to tell Michael about Mom's conversation in the kitchen, but then, I realized she didn't deserve any sympathy at that time. As I worked, I wondered how I could truly apologize for what I had allowed Dad to do to Michael that day. I simply didn't know.

CHAPTER SIX

I felt as though the garage was gleaming with the brilliance of polished brass when we finished. Even the shelves were organized neatly for convenience. I thought about putting some of Dad's things in places where he couldn't find them, but then I realized my brother was ultimately the one responsible for cleaning, and I knew the consequences would be dire.

As I was putting the broom against the wall, Mom came out to tell us that dinner was ready. Mom glanced around the garage, and I wondered if she would notice the red mark on Michael's face. Whether intentional, or out of pure ignorance, Mom never acknowledged the huge red blotch on his cheek. Eventually, I realized that people likely knew the truth about the abuse, but they just didn't care, and probably didn't want to get involved. Mom was an accomplice to it as well.

"Wow, the garage looks great you guys! Your dad will be so happy."

Resentment ignited my emotions like a bomb, and I glared at her, hoping she would feel the same agony—the same pain and humiliation Michael always had to endure. *She* wasn't the one who sat up with him at night until he fell back to sleep after one of his terrifying nightmares. *She* wasn't the one who helped him change his bed sheets when his sweat soaked them, especially the nights after Dad left his room with an evil grin plastered across his face. Unbridled contempt directed my eyes to a shimmering object just beyond her shoulder.

The ax.

My pulse soared as I tried to process the deviant scheme now taking shape in my mind.

"Phillip?" Mom paused, cocking her head. "Phillip!"

I was a million miles away.

Michael nudged me, and I blinked several times. "Mom's talking to you," he whispered.

"What?" I replied.

"Did you hear what I said?" she asked.

"About what, Mom?"

"How nice the garage looks. Your dad will be really happy."

Michael turned toward me and rolled his eyes. "Oh . . . thanks. I'm sure he will." I said.

"Well, dinner's ready. You better hurry into the house before your dad has a fit."

As I walked with Michael over to the door, my eyes were still captivated by the ax seemingly begging me to pick it up. *Would I ever go that far?* I wondered. I shook my head, turned off the lights, and closed the door.

After washing up in the bathroom, I glanced in the mirror and saw Michael's eyes squinting while turning his head from side to side, comparing one cheek to the other. "I'm so sick of this!" He sighed. "My cheek is pretty red, isn't it?"

I handed him a towel. "Not really," I said. "It'll go away by Monday. It always does."

I wanted to apologize again, but he headed for the dining room before I could think of exactly what to say. When I looked into the mirror, I wanted to punch the deserter and coward I saw in the reflection. I slammed my hands on the counter and shook my head before turning around and heading downstairs.

As Michael reached for the bowl of mashed potatoes, he didn't get to take his first scoop before Dad turned and said, "Did you get that garage cleaned up?"

Without looking up, Michael timidly replied, "Yeah."

Dad reached over and grabbed Michael's chin and jerked his head as if trying to snap it off his neck. "You better look at me when I'm talkin'!"

"Yes sir," Michael replied.

"And I suppose you decided to help the little crybaby again," Dad said to me.

Holding back a torrent of anger, I said, "I just thought I should. I kinda made some of the mess in there too."

"See Mikey," Dad responded sarcastically, "you really don't deserve someone nice like Phillip. He looks out for you. Did you at least have the decency to thank'm?"

Michael's watery eyes glistened, but I knew he wouldn't let any tears escape. "Yes, sir."

Dad loved it when either one of us broke down in front of him and bawled like frightened kids petrified by a raging thunderstorm. It was always the assumption of what Dad *might* do to us that caused our bodies to writhe with terror. Quite often, he never had to lay a hand on us. The fear was enough punishment.

After warning Michael again about remembering his chores, Dad never spoke another word directly to him that night at the table.

Mom, on the other hand, had the audacity to say, "Yeah, Tony, you should see how nice the garage looks."

Dad sneered. "Who do you think you are?" he yelled. "I don't need no cleaning inspector around here!"

He slammed his hand on the table, causing all of us to jerk. I saw Michael's chest heave for some much needed air, and he never took his eyes away from his plate. Mom folded her arms and said nothing.

As I waited my turn for the mashed potatoes, a shiny reflection caught my attention. With my head also tilted down at my plate, my eyes were suddenly fixed on the object slightly to the right. I reached over and ran my finger along the grooved handle of a stainless steel knife. Its handle seemed to be an extension of my fingertips. My eyes closed, and I envisioned how I could end our miserable existence with one swift plunge into the flesh of Dad's chest. It would all be over, and Dad would be out of our lives forever!

"Phillip!" Dad bellowed. "Pay attention!" He slammed the bowl on the table. "Here's the potatoes."

My eyes sprang wide open, and the lofty image of murder was quickly buried by the tone of the repulsive man sitting next to me. I gazed at the bewildered expressions etched onto the faces of the people staring back at me.

I looked down at my trembling hand, which was still clenched around the handle of the knife. "Sorry. I didn't see you hand me the bowl." I released my grip on the knife and quickly pulled my hands up to my temples and rubbed. "Just fighting a headache."

After putting some potatoes onto my plate, I looked up at Michael. He lifted his eyebrows and jerked his head slightly back, obviously curious about my bizarre behavior.

Unexpectedly, Dad looked up and asked, "Phillip, did you clean your room like I told you?"

"Yes, sir," I said. "I just have a couple things to put away from school this afternoon."

Knowing that their company was due to arrive soon, Mom tried to hurry us along. When I stood and began clearing the table, I was surprised to see her bringing in dessert, which she rarely did. Dad had requested German chocolate cake that night. She put a piece of cake in front of him before she handed one to me.

As Mom began to place a piece in front of Michael, Dad reached over and violently stabbed the cake with his fork. The small plate crashed onto the table's surface. "What do you think you're doin'?"

Mom's face turned red. He actually made Michael sit at the table while we ate in front of him. I was too afraid not to eat the cake, since it would provide Dad with even more incentive for taking his anger out on my brother, much like he did that morning when I spoke up and pathetically attempted to defend him.

Could this miserable day get any worse? I wondered. Choosing to eat in front of my brother was such a lousy way of protecting him from Dad. Once again, I had abandoned my brother earlier in the garage, and here I was doing it again at the table. I tasted nothing but shame with each bite. I did my best to avoid looking at Michael.

Dad scooped up the last morsel of his cake, shoved it into his rotten mouth, and slowly removed the fork between his taut lips, savoring the final remnants of sweetness. "Mmmmmm, this cake was so good tonight, Ellen."

He dropped his fork onto his plate and grinned at Michael—almost daring my brother to react. My whole body became possessed with hatred.

As Dad stood and sauntered from the room, my hand tightened around the fork I was holding, and my cheeks exploded from the burst of air rushing from my pounding chest. I wanted him dead!

"No!" Michael whispered, shaking his head.

Mom told us to clean off the table before she rushed up the stairs and entered her bedroom. Michael leaned forward and rested his elbows on the table. His forehead eased into his hands as he mumbled, "I really thought you were gonna do it."

I forced my chair back against the wall, grabbed the remaining plates and silverware, and stormed into the kitchen.

As Michael and I finished washing the remaining silverware, we heard Dad yelling. "You need to get that goofy braid outta your hair too. Look decent for our friends for once, will you!"

I heard a loud boom from an object hitting the door, followed by a shriek from Mom. It was her turn to face Dad's wrath. I knew then that I couldn't leave the house that night, regardless of how much I despised both of them. I collapsed onto one of the barstools as my stomach twisted like the violent winds of a tornado. I agonized over the brutal events of the day, and I just wanted it to end.

Moments later, we heard him yell, "And I want those two lazy idiots outta here tonight. They don't need to be snoopin' around. Now get dressed! My friends will be here any minute."

I knew I still couldn't go with Gwen, but I thought it might be a chance to get Michael safely out of the house.

Their bedroom door opened and suddenly slammed shut.

"Stop it, Tony!"

I heard something slam against the wall with a forceful thud. Her frail, thin body was no match for him.

Further responses were muffled by the ringing of the phone. I knew it had to be Gwen. After my nervous greeting, Gwen blurted out, "Well, are you going or not?"

"Hey, Gwen," I replied. "Well . . . I'm not allowed . . . 'cause I forgot to . . . umm . . . clean the garage."

"You idiot!" Gwen screamed. "Now who am I supposed to go with?"

"I think Michael still wants to go, so take him with you tonight," I suggested.

At least I thought he was allowed to go. Deep down, I knew Gwen didn't really care if the biggest nerd in school took her to the party. Showing up alone is what likely bothered her the most. She agreed about Michael tagging along, but she also demanded that I better be *more responsible.* I knew Michael wouldn't contradict my story about the garage. She ordered me to have my brother ready by 7:30 *sharp*! I jerked the phone away from my ear when she slammed hers down without saying goodbye.

Nearly four hours later, my brother was lying on a hospital bed—dying.

CHAPTER SEVEN

Death hovered over Michael's hospital room like a vulture. The absurdity of the situation that Friday night forced me to consider leaving Michael's hospital room for a break, just to escape the thoughts of doom clamoring inside of my aching head. I honestly didn't want to leave him alone, but if I didn't venture away from that depressing room for a few minutes, I thought I'd start ripping out my hair.

Hopelessness was my companion, dragging me down the hallway. My dry mouth craved the cool, wet sensation of a drink, laced with a near-lethal dose of caffeine. On my way to the lobby, I thought about my brother and wondered what it was that he'd taken that night at the party. I suspected that he might be experimenting with some of the same narcotics I'd witnessed my parents taking at home. Perhaps his drink was spiked with something? I didn't know for sure.

Unexpectedly, I realized that part of the tragedy I was facing might actually be *my fault.* Unable to avoid it, I found myself entertaining one horrifying question: *Was I the one to blame if Michael died?* My shaking legs managed to carry me the rest of the way to the lobby where I abruptly dropped into one of the chairs. An intense wave of nausea stirred in my gut, forcing me to thrust my fists deep into my stomach as I leaned forward. *I should have gone to the party to watch over him!* I thought.

Conjuring up the energy to stand, I walked over to the soda machine. After I slipped my hand into my pocket, I found only lint, which drifted to the floor after I released it from my fingers.

No money.

I shoved my other hand into the other pocket.

Nothing.

"I can't believe this!" I gazed up at the ceiling and rolled my eyes. *"Seriously?"*

In utter frustration, I leaned forward and rested my head on the clear plastic covering on the front of the machine. When I opened my eyes, only inches from my face were rows of refreshing soda cans all lined up perfectly—taunting me.

"This really sucks!" I mumbled.

A soft, friendly voice interrupted my moment of self-pity. "Did it steal your money?"

I tried to quickly recover from the barren hand that poverty had dealt me. I managed to smile. "No, I just forgot to bring some money."

The woman tilted her head slightly and grinned.

"I really don't need the soda anyway," I said. "Too much sugar and caffeine."

I turned and walked back to where I had been seated earlier. My defeated body seemed to absorb right into the chair. I dropped my head back and stared upward—drained of almost all of my dignity.

Moments later, I heard a can of soda banging against the front covering of the machine as it plummeted to the bottom tray. I looked up as the woman was retrieving it. She walked over and handed it to me. "Nope, I guess it didn't steal your money after all," she cordially said. Her pleasing smile was medicine to my ailing soul.

I grinned and replied, "My grandma always told me that we should never take things from strangers." My face was beaming with embarrassment.

"Well, then," she chuckled, "I guess I should introduce myself to you. My name is Sarah." She extended her hand. The touch of her skin seemed cool at first, but she gripped my hand tightly and asked, "And you are?"

"Phillip, ma'am," I said, trying not to make eye contact.

"It's a pleasure meeting you, Phillip," she replied.

Suddenly, when I gazed up at her, I pointed and said, "Wait a minute! You're the nurse helping out with my brother, aren't you? He's Michael Williams in Room 422."

"Yes, I know," she said. "Now, don't you worry. Your brother's in good hands." She pushed the soda even closer to me. "Now that we are no longer strangers, would you please not hurt my feelings and take this soda? It has way too much sugar and caffeine for me." She winked.

Salivating, I couldn't resist. I accepted it. "Thank you, ma'am." Before opening it, I asked, "Ma'am, is my brother *really* going to be okay?"

She reached down and put her hand on my shoulder. A peace seemed to flow right through me like a refreshing cool breeze on a hot summer day. It had been a long time since someone had touched me so tenderly. "Your brother is strong. The doctor is having us keep him sedated for right now." She looked down the hallway, and then at the elevator. Hastily, she glanced at her watch and said, "I'd better get back to work." She walked toward the hallway leading to Michael's room, but then she turned and said, "If you need anything, don't hesitate to ask. It was really nice meeting you, Phillip. Michael is so blessed to have you as his brother."

Relieved, I replied, "It was nice meeting you too, ma'am. And thank you for looking out for my brother."

She smiled once more.

"Oh, and thanks again for the soda! I really did need one."

She waved and walked down the hallway and disappeared around the corner once she reached the nurses' station.

I opened the bottle and took several gulps. The carbonation tingled in my parched throat. The absence of the kind stranger suddenly left me feeling isolated again. Thankfully, the abstract paintings on the wall caught my attention. Their gaudy mixture of colors appeared to have been done by a group of kids doing finger painting in an art class. I guzzled more soda and slid farther back in the chair.

As I sat there, I tried to think of someone I could call for help. It was really late, and my parents were in no condition to come to the hospital. If I called my best friend, Andrew, how would he explain to his parents why he had to leave so late in the night, especially after being summoned to a hospital? Dad's parents had died, and I didn't know my mom's parents at all. I knew who they were, but they wanted nothing to do with us. And calling

Aunt Sylvia was out of the question. She always called Mom immediately with any news that might create drama. Besides, I didn't want Mom to come right away, especially in her usual weekend condition. The one person I could trust and rely on the most was unconscious down the hallway, and Gwen was out of the question because of what she said to me when I picked up Michael earlier that night.

I shook my head, realizing how pathetic it was that I had no one I could trust—no one to reach out to. It was actually the first time I fully realized how successful Dad was in isolating us from decent people. I also wondered if my parents had heard from someone about Michael's condition and his location, and perhaps they were already on their way. I rested the soda on my knee because I could feel my hands trembling again at the thought of them stepping off of the elevator and seeing me sitting there alone—defenseless. My legs twitched with spasms, and I could hear a fizzing sound erupting from the can. I decided to place it on the table in front of me just so I wouldn't spill it.

I pressed my hands against my eyes, unable to block the memories of how I had ended up in this situation in the first place.

When Gwen had called me earlier from the party, she seemed upset that something awful had happened to Michael, so I rushed over to check on him. He was passed out on the floor in this kid's living room. The disgusting odor of his vomit had infiltrated the air, and no one could get him to wake. An upperclassman helped me carry him to the car, and surprisingly, Gwen went back to the party after telling me to just keep my mouth shut. She warned me that no one wanted the police showing up.

After placing Michael into the front seat, he fell forward and hit the dashboard. That's when the blood started gushing from his lips and nose. I did everything I could to get him to wake up, but he barely had a pulse. I rushed home so I could get someone to help us. After pulling into our driveway, I ran in to tell Mom and Dad that I thought my brother needed a doctor, but no one seemed interested. I was even threatened by some of their friends for bothering them. Mom, whose eyelids sagged from whatever she was intoxicated or high on, told me that Michael was probably drunk, and Dad ordered me to ". . . throw the drunk bastard in his bed."

I pleaded once more with Mom, and I even told her that Michael was bleeding, but she told me to settle down and just do what Dad had ordered. That's when she tossed me a box of tissues and threatened, "You guys better not get any blood on my carpet or furniture!"

When I tried to explain again, Mom told me to stop being so melodramatic, while at the same time, Dad started removing his belt. I had no choice but to follow my instinct, so I took Michael to the hospital on my own.

I ran back to the car, where Michael was still unconscious. *Should I really go?* I thought. "Come on, Michael," I pleaded, "you need to wake up!" I tapped his cheek several times, but he never responded. *Come on, Phillip! Think, man!* After a lengthy sigh, I started the engine and backed out of the driveway. *What are you doing, Phillip? Dad's gonna kill you for this!*

Fifteen minutes later, I pulled into the parking lot at the hospital. I turned the motor off and tried feverishly to rouse Michael. "Come on, man! You have to wake up!"

Nothing was working, so I got out of the car and retrieved a wheelchair from a small area just off to the side of the automatic doors at the entrance. After some careful maneuvering, I managed to get Michael safely into the emergency room.

With the remembrance of the muffled words, "May I help you, young man?" spewing from the mouth of the lady at the registration desk earlier that night, I blinked my eyes a few times and rubbed them vigorously. I looked around the lobby once again, and it didn't take long for me to remember that I probably couldn't hold off the hospital staff forever with the story about my parents being out of town that night. I had to give our address to them in the emergency room, but I told the staff, and the police—who had stopped by briefly—that my parents went shopping and out to eat, so they weren't expected home until late. I knew my parents were doing drugs at home, so I had to keep the police away from them as long as possible. "I left them a message on the answering machine," I claimed.

Not wanting to cope with the thought of police getting involved, I quickly switched to something else to preoccupy my mind. If I couldn't sort things out correctly, I might slip and say something I knew would cause even greater suspicion from the staff. I grabbed a magazine from the table in front of me and started flipping randomly through the thin pages. A photo of a family standing on their green manicured lawn, in front of a gleaming white house with black shutters, instantly distracted me again, but the sting of sadness forced me to wonder if such a life would have ever been possible for us, especially if the letter would have stayed hidden forever. I leaned my head back and gazed up at the ceiling. I began recalling the night that Dad, along with a single sheet of paper, had changed our lives forever.

CHAPTER EIGHT

It was a beautiful, crisp October afternoon, and Michael and I ran off of the bus because we couldn't wait to show Mom a picture of a pumpkin my brother had colored in his first grade class. We also couldn't wait to jump into the pile of dried leaves Dad had raked for us the night before. Grandma Gladie constantly reminded Dad that he had two sons who desperately wanted to spend more time with him, so he sometimes did nice things for us just to appease her.

We raced to the door, knowing Mom was fixing a special meal that day, because Dad had recently been promoted to a shift leader's position at work. It only paid a couple dollars more an hour, but to us, it was a huge deal worthy of a celebration. He'd been working really hard around the house, too, clearing out some old boxes stored in the basement for years, which he'd been taking to work to throw in the dumpsters. That night, he came home earlier than expected, and while Michael and I were watching Mom frost the cake, he slammed the front door and bolted for the kitchen. We all jumped off our seats. He charged through the kitchen doorway like a raging bull and ordered Michael and me to go to our rooms.

"Tony, what's the matter?" Mom asked. "Did something happen at work?"

"So, how long did you think you could keep everything a secret?" The interrogation had begun. We scurried up the stairs when Dad barked, "Answer me!"

Michael decided to stay in my room, but it wasn't too long before Dad had come looking for him. Michael ended up becoming the collateral damage from their fierce battle over the letter in the living room that evening.

After he yelled, "It's got *everything* to do with him!" I raced back to my room when Dad looked up and saw me staring down at them from the top of the stairs. Several minutes later, I heard Dad and Michael coming down the hallway. There was a sickening thud on Michael's bedroom floor, which was followed by ear-piercing screams. "Stay in your room, you little bastard," Dad shouted. After he slammed my brother's bedroom door, various objects plummeted to the floor in the hallway. "I'm done with you!" Dad yelled.

Moments later I heard the front door bang shut. Dad likely retreated to the garage. I tossed my camouflage blanket off of me and sneaked over to the door. When I peeked out, I saw several pictures scattered down the hallway. Assuming they had been kicked by Dad, I stepped out of my room, intending to retrieve them. One of them was Michael's kindergarten picture, and while I stood there examining his innocent face through the fractured glass, the beat of someone's footsteps coming up the stairs forced me to dash back to my room with the cherished photo. Not wanting to be caught with it, I hid it under my dresser. It was the last school photo Dad allowed Mom to purchase of Michael.

"Dr. Lowers on line four."

I jerked from the sudden announcement over the intercom. I sat up straight and wiped the sweat from my forehead with my shirt. Still panting, I eased back in the chair and sighed. Sadly, I fully realized that such horrid memories were permanently seared into my conscience. Dad had managed to scorch a mark on my mind and soul so deep that I doubted it would ever heal.

Looking for any distraction again, I scooted up in the chair and looked at the colorful artwork on the wall. Instead of haphazard splotches of paint, a blueprint of sorts started to manifest itself. Just as the painting seemed to have no purpose or design—the very essence of chaos—neither did my existence. Regardless of the artist's intent, the paintings were simply a metaphor describing my life: confusing and messy, certainly abstract, and with no real chance of ever being a masterpiece worth more than the canvas it was painted on.

Unexpectedly, a vile thought pummeled my mind: Michael's life was also the embodiment of chaos, just like the paintings. Hopelessness had once again entombed me in fear, forcing me to accept the fact that I couldn't live without my brother, and I knew I couldn't live with Dad knowing that Michael wasn't by my side. I remember Grandma Gladie saying something about God working all things out for us, but a life—without Michael—was *never* going to work out!

Just as my mind entertained the horrible idea of self-annihilation, the rumbling sound of an elevator door startled me. *Was it Dad?* When I dared to look up, I saw a tall man stepping off of the elevator. He immediately looked familiar for some reason, but I couldn't quite place where I had seen him before. His despondent expression revealed nothing but grief, and the disheveled appearance of his clothing reminded me of the messy splotches that emerged from the paintings. His eyes widened when he saw me. The stranger turned quickly and headed down the opposite hallway from where Michael's room was located.

I decided to walk back to Michael's room. The whole way down the hallway, I wondered how I might end my life, or perhaps, how my parents would end it for me.

CHAPTER NINE

As I entered Michael's hospital room again, I looked at the monitor to see if anything had changed. It hadn't. I really wanted—I needed—to see Michael sit up and be my healthy, active brother again. I approached him and began counting each breath that he took, and before too long, my breaths were synchronized with his.

After my pulse seemed to settle, I walked to the window and inserted a couple fingers into the blind and pulled the thin aluminum slats far enough apart so that I could peer out into the darkness. The only activity taking place several floors below me happened to be a small group of people smoking cigarettes outside of the emergency room and a security guard leaning up against a newspaper box, drinking what I assumed was a cup of coffee. The solitude of the moment was a change of pace from the onslaught of emotions weighing on my mind. As far as I was concerned, though, time could stay right where it was, because at that moment, Michael was alive—and so was I!

Weakened from fatigue, I decided to sit in the chair at the foot of my brother's bed. After I sat in silence for a few moments, I meticulously began studying Michael's face for the first time in a while. He looked so peaceful for once, even with the breathing tube and IV fluids keeping him stable. It seemed a little awkward thinking this at first, but I really noticed how handsome

Michael was. The soft overhead lighting revealed some aspects of his athletic physique, defined by husky shoulders and a stout chest. His strong jaw line looked as though it had been chiseled from stone, and although swollen many times, he still had a distinguished shaped nose. Swooping almost down into his eyes was his chocolate brown hair. I remembered how some of the girls took great pleasure in brushing it to one side for him. He attracted the attention of a lot of different girls, but getting too involved was definitely out of the question—for either of us. I blushed when I thought about some of the intimate conversations that took place on the old fallen tree in our backyard.

Our classmates never seemed to suspect that anything was abnormal about our lives—a kind of hushed acceptance, perhaps—and they didn't hassle us over being a bit standoffish at times. Besides, most of the kids we did talk to had parents similar to ours. I guess they assumed that my dad was a lot like theirs—fathers just trying to make tough southern men out of their sons. Sometimes I wondered if maybe that's how Dad saw his treatment toward us. If people suspected any abuse, they never mentioned it. My best friend acted as though he thought something was wrong at times, but my brother and I knew the consequences if anyone had reported their beliefs to authorities, so we were willing participants in Dad's deception—silencing any suspicions with clever excuses.

As I continued to gaze at Michael, I thought about how much I wanted him to open his eyelids just so I could see life restored into his striking, sapphire blue eyes. People always complimented him over something he simply inherited. I was sometimes jealous that no one ever noticed the apparent lackluster genes that fate had somehow sewn into my DNA. Anyway, I hated seeing him so lifeless, so opening his eyes would have been such a relief to me, regardless of their color.

An explosion of absurd thoughts jolted me back to the dilemma I knew I couldn't avoid. Several ideas about how I could end my life seeped into my mind, but I tried desperately to prevent them from becoming authentic plans. *Would I dare go that far just to be with my brother if he died?*

With so many emotions pelting me like hail during a violent storm, I felt an irresistible desire to be by Michael's side, just like I had felt in the garage earlier that day. I got up from the chair and stepped closer toward Michael. As long as I was near him, I could keep my raw, untamed fears caged inside of me. I couldn't explain it, but Michael seemed so fragile all of a sudden, almost as though he would shatter if I applied the slightest amount of pressure to his motionless body. I simply couldn't touch him. It was so unfair to see his life possibly end in such a meaningless way. Dad, who probably hoped to be around for the final day of Michael's life, didn't even have the decency to show up for his ultimate victory at the hospital that night. With my mind being devoured by bitterness, the injustices of our past had been resurrected once more.

Mom had parents still living in our community, but Michael and I never knew them. She had told us they thought they were too good for trash like us. Grandpa Stewart was a wealthy business owner, and for years I couldn't understand why Mom never called on them for help. I remembered her telling us about the time she worked for Grandpa Stewart, which was prior to Michael's birth; however, I never knew why she suddenly abandoned her job.

For reasons I never completely understood, Mom started working for Grandpa Jack not long after she ran into him—literally—at the local grocery store. According to Mom, their carts crashed into each other as they were turning a corner in the frozen foods section. That was the first time Grandpa saw me, and I guess seeing his firstborn grandson up close and personal must have triggered something inside of him, but when he learned that Mom had become pregnant again, he was enraged, and they stopped speaking to each other once more.

Grandma Gladie, however, was there throughout our early childhood. Sadly, though, she had been widowed when Dad was twelve years old. Grandpa Williams had been killed when he wrecked his car into a utility pole one night. His blood alcohol level was over twice the legal limit. This left Grandma to raise Dad all alone. It had also been rumored that Grandpa Williams was abusive at times, and I often wondered if Dad was a victim of his own father's rage.

After Dad killed our sense of family when he found the letter, I realized that there was an obvious difference in the way he treated my brother. There were many times Michael and I would hide in my closet and embrace each other through the unimaginable terror of Dad's threats and tantrums. Oftentimes, Dad simply pretended that Michael didn't exist—at least until there was some reason to make a big deal out of something Michael had done wrong. Spilling a glass of milk, talking out at the table, and even forgetting to put things away, could easily end in a nasty beating, and a few days worth of verbal attacks that could destroy anyone's self-worth. When my brother was twelve years old, Dad beat him mercilessly, right before forcing Michael to sleep in a saturated bed that he had peed in that night. My brother wasn't even allowed to change his urine-soaked underwear. What kind of parent beats his kid for having nightmares, resulting in accidents in the middle of the night? Then again, I was just as guilty. As far as I was concerned, Michael had his terrifying dreams because of my unwillingness to stop the abuse.

I realized that Michael's treatment was nothing more than a sadistic form of pleasure intended to belittle and humiliate my brother into thinking that his life was nothing more than a curse to our family. The brutality of Dad's 'discipline' taught Michael one clear lesson: his life meant nothing to the only man he knew as his father. Mom's excuse for not getting involved was always that it would make things worse. It didn't take long for bitterness to fester like a cancer inside of me when I thought about the many times she had abandoned Michael, especially when he cried out for her help. What was stopping her from rescuing her son? Was it fear? Guilt? Perhaps a merger of the two? Too often, she sacrificed her son to protect the identity of a man we never knew.

As I stood beside Michael's bed, the notion of my parents being arrested materialized in my mind as some kind of hopeful fantasy. I entertained the idea that having them caught with drugs might lead to my brother and me getting away from them, especially if they were sent away to jail. Then again, if Dad ever found out that I'd sent the police to our house, there would be no telling what he would do to all of us.

I happened to look out into the hallway and noticed Sarah, the nurse I'd met earlier, staring at me while she was talking on the phone. *Did she suspect my story was bogus and was now talking to the police?* Panic caused my knees to buckle when I saw her hang up the phone and head toward my brother's room. She grabbed something from a cupboard on the way. I thought for sure that she had figured out I wasn't being honest about my parents being out of town.

When she stepped into the room, she had a blanket over her arm. She politely asked if I needed it. Even though I didn't, her smile was so pleasant that I decided to take it just so I wouldn't offend her. I realized how much I needed her maternal compassion.

I happened to look at the cream-colored blanket and then down at my shirt. "I'm sorry about the blood on my clothes, ma'am," I whispered. "I don't want it to touch the clean blanket."

"Just one minute," she said. A few moments later, she returned with a shirt. "One of our male nurses had an extra shirt in his locker. It should fit," she said. "I asked him earlier if he happened to have a spare one after I saw your shirt. I hope you don't mind that I asked him. I just knew that you had to be uncomfortable with having blo—well, some stains on your clothing. Sorry, though, he didn't have extra pants that looked like they would fit you."

I stepped into the small restroom near the doorway of Michael's room. I soon emerged and said, "Thank you, ma'am. It fits perfectly." Actually, the shirt was a little tight.

She smiled and told me to have a seat in the chair by Michael's bed. She gently unfolded the blanket and covered me. My own mother hadn't done something that nice in a long time. Not long after she left the room, I surrendered to the fatigue possessing my body.

CHAPTER TEN

The nightlight in the hallway casts a familiar and foreboding silhouette on the wall outside of Michael's bedroom door. I tap numerous times, but no one responds. I stretch forth my hand slowly and turn the knob ever so gently. With my fingers spread wide, I push, and the door eerily squeaks open. "Michael?" I hear nothing. I whisper again, "Michael, are you okay? I thought I heard you crying."

More silence fills the dreadful blackness of the room as my eyes try to adjust. I whisper my brother's name once more. I tiptoe over to his bed and kneel beside him. "I'm fine, Phillip," he whispers. "Just go back to bed."

"I thought I heard you crying." I reach out and touch his shoulder.

"Ouch!"

He whimpers and withdraws.

"Man, I'm sorry, Michael. What did Dad do to you?" I whisper. "I saw him come in here earlier."

Michael curls his legs up toward his chest and pulls his sheet close to his neck. His whole body shakes the bed. He sniffles once more. "Just leave me alone, Phillip. Go back to your room before he catches you."

"I'm sorry, Michael. I should have come over earlier to see if you were okay."

"I'm tired, Phillip. Please, just go back to your room before he hears you and comes back in. I don't want that drunken pig back in here."

Laden with guilt, I stand and walk to the door. Before I exit my brother's room, I look back, and the glow from the hallway light sends a thin beam across his face. His glassy eyes sparkle from the light. I gently close the door and return to my own bed. Once I pull the sheet up to my chest, I weep—my mind consumed with immeasurable shame. What had really happened to Michael that . . .

I jolted awake, and the blanket that Sarah had brought to me tumbled onto my lap. I sat straight up in the chair and looked at Michael. My familiar nightmare accelerated my breathing, causing the room to whirl around like a merry-go-round. When my eyes focused, I scanned the dreary room before settling my attention once more on Michael's tranquil body. I leaned forward and lowered my forehead into my quaking hands. "God, please . . . I can't take it anymore!" I took several deep breaths and slid back into the chair. I glanced again at the monitor above my brother's bed, and the numbers were nearly the same as the ones I had memorized before dozing off.

In silence, with just the intermittent chirping of one of the machines resonating throughout the room, I thought about the one and only solitary place in the entire universe where Michael and I could celebrate our brotherhood—our allegiance to each other. Had it not been for that old fallen tree, I wasn't sure he and I would have survived.

One summer evening, when Michael and I were younger, a fierce thunderstorm passed through our area and blew over one of the huge beech trees just at the edge of the woods near our property line. It became our savior—sacrificed by the wrath of nature—existing solely to provide us with a sanctuary from our personal hell. On Michael's thirteenth birthday, we carved something very special into one of the smaller limbs of the tree right around the area in which we always sat. The engraving was near two larger limbs, midway up the mammoth trunk.

With no one to help us through our struggles, we were at least able to find one place in the world where we could pretend that people like Dad never existed. We also entertained the possibilities of what it would be like to live a normal life, with a normal family. By the time I had turned sixteen years old, I was convinced that good people had somehow become extinct, or maybe they were on some endangered species list—almost too rare to find. Running away wasn't an option at that point either, but we still embraced the meager thought of it. Then again, I knew I couldn't leave Mom.

We soon learned that getting out of the house, and away for a while, was the best therapy we could afford. We headed to the woods where we could sit for a long time and just talk. Neither of us had realized, at that time, how special those private talks were for both of us. We listened to the tree frogs, which always seemed to bring tranquility to our restless spirits, and we also shared our personal dreams with each other. Most kids aren't afraid to tell their parents what they want out of life, but we didn't dare, because our dreams often excluded Dad from everything we'd ever hoped for in our lives. Michael and I made a pact that we would never allow Dad to kidnap our fantasies, like he did our childhood.

We relaxed on the old tree whenever we focused our attention on the familiar tunes coming from the forest. *Our* tree frogs became a sort of serene symphony, which somehow helped to calm the dissonance Dad forced into our existence. They also provided us with a soothing background for when we shared the happier memories, especially the ones where we spent long evenings on the back porch at Grandma Gladie's house. Ironically, after that violent storm one evening, I realized that nature's fury had provided us with a peaceful place to rest and escape from the madness of our cruel world. Dad's fury, on the other hand, never gave us such a safe haven. Our tree was the safe place where we could explore the idea of a better life. It was our place, because we engraved special words into one of its limbs, and no one could claim it as their own. The carving distinguished our tree from the billions of others scattered throughout the entire world. Yes, we tried to immerse ourselves into the peaceful solitude of the forest's earthy smells and other mysterious sounds, but there were too many times when the commotion in our minds needed to be purged.

Several months before Michael was taken to the hospital with a drug overdose, I could tell something was haunting his conscience. He started to tell me about the guilt he was experiencing because of his feelings toward Mom. We had been sitting on the tree for a while that night, and the lemony fragrance of the forest conifers, combined with the sweet smells of Magnolia and honeysuckle from the neighbor's yard, were beginning to relax me for the first time that entire day. Michael decided to interrupt the silence by explaining how Mom surprisingly tried to stop Dad from beating him earlier that day. Dad caught my brother drinking from the milk carton while standing in front of an open refrigerator door (a mortal sin in Dad's eyes). As usual, she eventually walked away, leaving Michael all alone with Dad in the kitchen. His belt flew through the loops of his pants and flung outward with the snap of a whip. "Phillip, I know I shouldn't feel this way, but I hate Mom so badly sometimes!" Frustration caused a puff of air to burst from his nostrils like the grunt of a deer when startled. "She always gives in to him."

I placed my hand on his back and gently rubbed in circular motions. "Yeah, she is pretty pathetic when it comes to Dad."

"I don't care, Phillip. She's worthless," Michael insisted. "Moms are supposed to protect their kids! All she cares about is getting high with that useless pig she's married to." My pulse was racing, because Michael's tone clearly echoed the cold, fierce hatred he had for our parents. "I wanna leave here forever! I want out before it's too late!" he insisted.

"I know, Michael, but we don't have any place to go. Besides, no one cares whether we're dead or alive."

Just hearing myself say that, caused my heart to sink into my gut.

Sparked by the hopelessness we felt that night, our attention focused once more on the mystery involving the contents of the letter Dad had found years earlier. We always had our suspicions about the man who wrote it, but we never had any proof as to who he was. Regardless of the answers, Michael and I knew what we had to do quite soon: *find it!* Past attempts rendered nothing, but we had to solve its hidden secrets, or we would never have the chance to embrace any kind of peace in our lives. Knowing how Dad could hold a grudge, I was fairly confident that he would never destroy the evidence the letter contained. No matter what, it had to be located. We needed answers.

I was startled by a soft tone interrupting my thoughts about the letter. "So, you seem really close to your brother," Sarah said. She had come into the room to check Michael's IVs.

I looked at my brother and sighed. "Yeah, he's kinda my whole world." I glanced at her and then back at Michael. He was still unresponsive to our voices. A single tear cascaded down my cheek and dropped onto the blanket. I wiped my cheek before she noticed it.

Sarah stepped over and placed her hand on my shoulder. "Your brother is very blessed to have you in his life. I really mean that, Phillip. You must really love each other."

"Yeah," I said, as my voice crackled like fire devouring wood. "People used to notice how much we seem to care for each other."

Another nurse came to the door and said, "Sarah, there is someone who needs to speak with you again."

"I'll be right there," Sarah replied. She patted my shoulder softly and said, "Phillip, if you need anything, feel free to call me back into the room." After taking several steps toward the door, she turned and said, "I can get you another soda if you'd like."

My face reddened. "No thank you, ma'am."

She smiled and nodded. "Maybe later then." Before leaving, she asked, "Phillip, you wouldn't happened to be related to anyone with the last name Roberts, would you?"

I tilted my head, and squinted my eyes. "No, I don't think so, ma'am. Why?"

"Oh, I was just wondering, because Michael kind of reminds me of someone with that last name." She grinned—her lips quivered. She hastily replied, "Oh well, no big deal."

She hurriedly left as I turned back toward my brother and resumed analyzing the numbers on the monitor.

A sudden urge to be closer to my brother again jolted my body like a static shock. I scooted the chair closer to his bed, daring to touch his hand for the first time that night. As if trespassing onto forbidden property, I slowly rested my hand on his. He felt cool to the touch, almost like he was filled with death. I gently picked up Michael's hand and held it for a few minutes. I noticed a few scars on his knuckles from fights he'd sometimes gotten into with bullies at school.

Worried that I might cause further harm, I delicately placed his hand back onto the mattress, as if I was returning a fragile, priceless heirloom to a secure place. I leaned forward and rested my head on the mattress next to his hand. I took several deep breaths. A sense of hopelessness wrapped its confining restraints around me like the tethers of a straightjacket. I looked up at my brother and cried out, "Come on, Michael, please open your eyes." I caressed his arm. "Please don't leave me! I need you!" My head collapsed onto the mattress again.

"*Michael, please . . .*"

CHAPTER ELEVEN

As I rested my head on the mattress beside Michael's arm, my heart fluttered like the wings of a bird suddenly taking flight. My mind couldn't escape the conclusion that the innocent discovery of the letter was ultimately the reason why Michael ended up in the hospital that night. It was almost as if someone had planned it that way all along. Perhaps if Dad had never discovered it, the abuse wouldn't have started, and Michael wouldn't have always been so anxious to get out of the house all of the time. Was this just another piece of the disastrous puzzle that life seemed to be assembling for us?

Knowing Dad wouldn't have gotten rid of such a valuable piece of evidence, we made our first real attempt to find the letter one night after our parents left for a bar to celebrate a friend's birthday. We decided to start our search in all of the usual places: the closets, the basement, dressers, but it wasn't until we searched Dad's *sacred* area in the garage that the letter emerged from the shadows. While we were sifting through boxes, several papers scattered across the floor like confetti and drifted under the *untouchable* workbench. Michael got on his knees and shined a flashlight under it. He happened to notice the rounded edges of something attached to the bottom. We both got as flat as we could onto the floor, and I reached under and pulled it loose. *It was the letter!* Remembering how protective he was over that area in the garage, I was amazed it took us so long to figure out that it was the perfect place for him to hide something with such personal value.

With the letter—the source of our misery—held firmly in my quivering hand, we both stood. I turned it over and saw Mom's name written on the front. I turned it back over and paused before removing its contents from the envelope. Sweat poured from my body, and my teeth chattered like I had been trapped out in a frigid snowstorm, suffering from hypothermia. Michael was standing close to me, but he was also looking toward the side door. Like me, he probably expected Dad to come bursting through it, wielding some sort of weapon.

My temples pulsated. They felt like they were about to leap from my skull. I looked at Michael—his bulging eyes were glazed over. Gasping for air, I mumbled, "Well . . . this is it." Michael didn't reply.

I slid the letter out and unfolded it. It was tattered around the edges and stained with small splotches of grease and dirt, and it was still crinkled from when Dad held it in his fist the night he'd thrust it into Mom's face several times. Even after ten years, the damage he did that awful night, to both the letter and us, was still evident—something permanent—like deep scars from a terrible accident.

Michael had moved over so close that I could feel his warm moist breaths on my neck. I chose not to say anything, even though it bothered me at first. Michael remained silent as I began reading the letter to him. My lips spewed forth the very words that had altered our lives forever.

Ellen, I can't believe the news you gave me in the card yesterday. I wish you would have told me in person. I want to talk to you about all of this, but your father is getting suspicious about all of the talking we're doing at his store. Maybe you can call me when he's not around! I wrote this letter in case we couldn't talk right away. When are you due? Please don't hate me for this, but how sure are you that it's mine? Could it be Tony's? I'd be lying to you if I didn't tell you how scared I am right now. I still can't believe this happened, but I will take care of things if it's mine. We can never let anyone know about this! You know how people are around here! See if you can get away for an hour, so we can talk in person about this whole thing. Please, Ellen, you have to call me soon! Samuel

Like a dead autumn leaf drifting aimlessly to the ground, the letter floated to the garage floor from my hands. Michael reached down and picked it up with one swift movement. My knees started to wobble, so I leaned against the workbench. I was shocked to find proof about the affair, which now led to even more unresolved questions. I never thought Mom would do such a thing, especially against someone like Dad. My fists squeezed closed as tightly as my eyes—almost as if they were controlled by the same muscle. My suspicions were confirmed: Dad had tried his best to destroy *the evidence* created from her secret romance! How could he do that to my younger brother? Then again, I did little to stop it.

Then the most devastating realization hit me like some rogue wave slamming into a defenseless ship, capsizing it. I realized that the young man standing next to me—the only person I had left in this miserable world—might not be my full brother after all! I looked straight into Michael's tearful, reddening eyes, and I knew it was only a matter of time before he came to realize the same frightening conclusion as me. I didn't know whether to reach out to him, or simply bust Dad's workbench to pieces with my bare hands.

"*She couldn't have!*" Michael insisted.

Any words of comfort I might have attempted to offer disintegrated as a surge of acid crawled up from my stomach.

As Michael scanned the contents of the letter once more, his head hastily popped up like a slice of bread in a toaster. "Phillip!"

I reached out to stabilize him.

"Do you think that Samuel guy might be my *real* dad?" He looked upward and locked his fingers behind his head. The letter was getting crumpled again. When he looked back at me, while lowering his arms toward the floor, he yelled, "What's all of this really mean?" He held the letter outward and pointed at it. "Mom got pregnant from this guy!" His head raced back and forth. "Is this letter about *me*?"

I grabbed his arm. "Michael, it's okay, man."

His face drained of color, and I felt his body weight shifting. I thought for sure he was seconds away from either passing out or punching something.

He yanked his arm away from me. "Phillip, does this mean—" He shook his head again. "It can't!"

"What, Michael?"

"Does this mean Dad beat me all these years just because Mom screwed some guy that we don't even know?" His arms were stretched out in disbelief. "Phillip, I might not even belong to Dad, and Mom knew it all along!" A crimson color had returned to his cheeks before he slammed his hands onto the workbench. "Why did he take it out on me, Phillip? I never did anything to him!"

I understood the seething anger that must have quickly kindled a raging fire inside of him.

"If I really belong to that Samuel guy, where has he been all these years? Why didn't he come and take me away from all of this?"

He looked around the garage, as if searching for something to throw. I shuttered when I realized that my search for a resolution to the curse of the letter might have opened up a completely new path for my brother. Could I lose my brother forever to a guy I never knew?

I was startled when Michael violently kicked a bucket full of empty aluminum beer cans. They slammed against a wall and spread out across the floor like shrapnel from a hand grenade. As he paced the floor, a bitter expression on his face made me think that Michael was about to destroy everything within his reach. He suddenly stopped pacing and yelled, "Oh my God, Phillip, does this mean—" His whole body stiffened. "Phillip, are we still brothers, man?" He started to gag.

"Not here, Michael!"

"Phillip," he cried out, "please tell me we're still brothers!"

I grabbed the sides of his face with my hands. His cheeks were tacky to the touch from his tears. "Look at me, Michael. Nothing's gonna change between us! You're my only brother, and that's the way it's always gonna be! Do you hear me?"

He squeezed his eyes shut, acting as though he was trying to process what I had said to him. "We don't know anything about this Samuel guy, so don't panic over something we can't explain yet. Besides, no matter what, we still have the same mom."

Michael sat down on an overturned five-gallon bucket and sobbed. His emotions were a pendulum—first anger, then fear—leaving me nervous and wondering what he might do next. He reached out and grabbed my shirt and pulled me closer. He tilted his head forward and rested it into the palms of his hands. "Phillip, what am I supposed to do now?"

I rubbed his shoulder and patted his back. For the first time in nearly ten years, I realized that Michael had possible proof that he might actually be the child of some other man. The tainted blood of Tony Williams might not be flowing through his veins after all!

"I can't believe this is happening!" he cried.

I attached the letter back under the workbench in the exact position we'd found it. Tampering with Dad's prized letter caused us to bolt from the garage. Michael raced into the kitchen and opened a can of soda, which he began to guzzle as he collapsed onto one of the barstools.

I sat beside him. "You need to calm down, Michael," I demanded.

"I can't believe what that letter said! I just can't believe it, Phillip! Now what? What am I gonna do?"

He started to gag again before quickly covering his mouth with his hand.

"Hurry!" I hollered.

I jumped up as my brother ran for the upstairs bathroom. He had only seconds to spare before the soda ejected from his mouth. I kept yelling for him to hurry, because I wasn't in the mood to clean up a trail of vomit from the kitchen to our bathroom. He almost missed the toilet. At one point, I thought he was choking, so I got down on my knees next to him and gently rubbed his back as he vomited and wailed.

"Dad's gonna find out what we did! I know he is!" He started to retch once more. He quickly hoisted himself up to his knees and thrust his face into the toilet again. Exhausted, he rested his head on his arm, which was draped over the toilet seat. As he tried to catch his breath, he mumbled, "Phillip, you gotta help me get away. He'll kill me if he finds out I know the truth about Mom and that guy! I know he will!"

He sat on the floor and sobbed. I realized that Mom had gotten away with her secret for at least six years before Dad found the letter, and Dad's anger and humiliation had to have eaten away at his pride.

As Michael nearly collapsed onto the bathroom floor, I grabbed a towel and wet it. I tried wiping the vomit that had splattered onto his face, but he kept pushing my hand away as if he was swatting at an annoying fly. Finally, he reached for the towel. I flushed the toilet before running to get him a glass of water to rinse his mouth. He said he just needed to sit there for a few minutes longer. He pulled his knees up to his chest and locked his hands behind his head. I put the toilet seat lid down and sat on it beside him.

Michael leaned over and rested his head against my leg. "What's gonna happen to me now?" he asked. "There's no way Dad can find out what we did. Promise me you won't tell him, Phillip!" he pleaded. "You can't tell anyone we found the letter! Dad will kill me, and then he'll go after you like he always said he would!"

Perplexed, I asked, "What do you mean he'll come after me like *he always said*?"

Michael looked away. "Just make sure he doesn't know what we did tonight."

I rubbed the back of his head, trying to lull him into a calmer state of mind. His hair was drenched with sweat, and his body radiated heat like a furnace. I dowsed another washcloth with cool water and placed it on the back of his neck. "I promise, Michael. I'll never tell anyone."

I helped him to his feet and guided him to his room. He sat on the bed and began to weep again.

"Michael," I pleaded, "you've got to settle down. We don't know when Mom and Dad will be coming home. They'll know something's up if they find you this way."

His shirt was stained with vomit, sweat, and tears, so I helped him remove it before retrieving another from his dresser. After I got another washcloth, he cleaned off his clammy face and chest before slipping on the clean shirt. I wrapped everything up in a hand towel from the linen closet and ran it down to the laundry room. When I returned, he had already crawled into his bed. I knew it wouldn't be long before he collapsed under the strain of the anxiety and shock. I pulled the covers up to his waist and stepped away from his bed.

As I turned toward the doorway, Michael said, "Thanks, Phillip."

That wasn't what I expected, but at least he sounded more in control of his emotions. "That's what brothers do," I replied. "Remember—*brother's forever!*" I turned out the light and closed the door behind me, realizing that what I had said was likely more for my benefit than his.

Fearing Mom would become suspicious of the vile smelling shirt and towels in the laundry, I decided to throw a full load of bath towels into the washing machine, along with his shirt. I ran back upstairs and finished cleaning up the bathroom and sprayed heavily to eliminate the odors. Remembering the empty beer cans, I ran to the garage to clean up anything we might have messed up. I even rechecked the letter several times. After about thirty minutes, I looked in on Michael, but he was turned away from me, so I didn't know if he was asleep or not. I didn't say anything.

After heading downstairs and opening a fresh can of soda, I headed for the living room sofa where I watched some television program that brought little interest to my mind. I wanted it to appear as though we'd had a boring evening at home, but my mind kept returning to the contents of the letter. I kept seeing those sickening words Samuel had written when he asked when

Mom was due, and of course, if she was sure *it* belonged to him. In one sense, I wanted Michael to belong to another man—one that might not resent the fact that my brother was ever born. On the other hand, I didn't want to see us split apart because of it. Eventually, my thoughts had devoured every ounce of energy I had left, and I drifted off to sleep.

Jarred from my torturous memory, I lifted my head from the mattress as someone entered Michael's hospital room. A different nurse came in to check the bags of fluids hanging beside his bed. She also asked if she could get me anything.

"No thanks," I whispered.

I decided to get up and walk out to the lobby again for a few minutes. I needed a different atmosphere besides the depressing surroundings of the grim, ashen room Michael was in that night. I needed another distraction—anything—no matter who or what it was.

To my surprise, the man from the elevator was sitting next to Sarah in the lobby when I entered. They were whispering, but as soon as they saw me, Sarah stood and hurried back in the direction of the nurses' station. She only smiled at me as she passed by. I expected her to say something kind, but she seemed to be in a rush, almost as if she had been caught doing something wrong. Her face was red. The tightening in my chest returned when I considered the possibility that she had called the police and was now afraid to look into my eyes because of some hidden betrayal.

The gentleman, now alone, seemed disoriented—somewhat agitated, like an animal sensing danger. His demeanor was nothing like Sarah's. He gripped the handles of his chair, just three seats away from mine. I had this strange feeling that somehow he knew something personal about the current dilemma my brother and I were facing, but I didn't exactly know why or how he knew. He looked even more familiar the closer I observed his features: the brown wavy hair, his bronze, tanned skin, which was wrapped firmly around his well-built frame. He attempted to look away, but he was obviously curious about me as well. I continued to observe his different traits as if meticulously trying to associate them with people I had already known from my life. I had seen him before, but I wasn't sure where. I was still intrigued over his peculiar behavior when he first stepped off of the elevator earlier that night. As we sat there, his inquisitiveness was obviously overpowering his manners, because he turned and stared at me. His forlorn facial appearance only seemed to emphasize his pitiful eyes.

His eyes!

I realized that I had made a connection. *It was those eyes!* Yes, his big *blue* eyes! I knew why he looked so familiar. I could swear that I was looking at an older version of Michael. Who was this stranger? Why was he there talking to Michael's nurse? How did he know her? My pulse surged, and my mouth dropped open. Was he the person I thought he was? Was I about to say something I never thought would spew from my own lips?

I cleared my throat, looked directly at him, and asked, "Excuse me, sir, but—" His body stiffened as I asked a very simple, but important question: "Are you Samuel?"

CHAPTER TWELVE

As I glanced away from the stranger—mortified that I'd asked something incriminating, I was almost too apprehensive to confront the reality that he might offer an answer I wasn't prepared to hear. *Had I just spoken to Michael's real father?* I wondered. I swallowed hard, nearly choking on my saliva. This stranger was a rigid-looking man at first glance, but after closer examination, I had a glimmer of hope due to his incredible resemblance to Michael. Even if he wasn't the man who wrote the letter, my brother could have easily passed as his son. His brown hair, although slightly highlighted with traces of gray, was the exact shade as Michael's. The bridge of his nose, the broad shoulders, and even his sturdy chin were a perfect match to my brother's physical traits. His eyes were as deep blue as Michael's, and sadly, I could see the same type of pain and sorrow covering his face that I had observed many times in my brother's. I saw the loneliness—the unending grief—likely from personal regrets (possibly stemming from the reality that he'd missed out on something crucial to his entire existence). Perhaps he had a missing piece to the puzzle of his life as well. *Was it Michael?*

I remembered that Dad was a pretty strong guy when he was younger, but the years of drug abuse had weakened him. Dad still liked to wear his sleeveless, plaid shirts just to show off the muscles he had left. Dad's gaunt cheeks showed the signs of rapid aging, and dark circles had formed around his menacing black eyes, which matched the color of his often greasy hair. After seeing this man in the lobby with me, I realized that Michael had very little resemblance to Dad.

"Umm," he mumbled. His gaze seemed to look straight through me, almost as if he was probing my innermost thoughts. "I understand you're Michael's older brother. It's Phillip, right?"

Shocked at first, I nervously replied, "Yes, sir." I licked my dry lips and asked again, "Are you Samuel?"

I could see his throat pulsating from his rapid heartbeat. It seemed we were both holding our breaths when he answered, "Yes, my name is Samuel."

Etiquette dictated that I should shake his hand; however, I couldn't seem to raise my arm to do so.

I asked, "Are you the guy who—" I suddenly wondered how I could ask a stranger about an affair he supposedly had with my mother. My boldness overshadowed my coyness, but I *had* to know the truth. "What I mean is . . . are you here because you think Michael might be your son?"

He lowered his head and sighed. When he looked up again, I saw that his eyelids were squeezed shut. Two tears escaped from the corners of his eyes and cascaded down his cheeks. "Yes, I believe it's possible," he whispered, opening his eyes.

Possible? I *needed* a definitive answer.

"Oh," I whispered.

"I'm sorry, Phillip, I just don't know for sure. That's probably what you didn't want to hear."

I placed my hands on my legs to keep them from bouncing. "How did you know my brother was here?" I asked.

"Well," he said, "my wife works here, and she phoned me as soon as his name appeared on the chart sent up from the emergency room." Samuel seemed to relax, as if he was elated to have someone else there with him. "Phillip, I heard Michael was in pretty bad shape, and I was afraid that if I didn't come here tonight, I might not get to—" Tears were clinging to his eyelashes, and he took a deep breath. "Let's just say that I had to see him."

"Can I ask you something, sir?"

"Well . . . yes," he replied, as he wiped his eyes.

"Why now? If you thought Michael might be your son, why didn't you try to contact him before tonight?"

Samuel's head slumped forward—likely weighted from guilt. I started to rethink my spiteful attitude concerning him. He wasn't what I expected: a narcissistic, egotistical coward. I could see that he felt shame for the years he stayed in the shadows and never revealed himself to Michael; however, that irksome idea about his intentions for being there that night wouldn't release its grip on my mind.

"Phillip, I've asked myself that question a million times. I was afraid of having to face the reality I'd abandoned my child, and I never knew for sure what your father might do to your mom and Michael, especially if he ever found out about the aff—well, my friendship with your mom."

Sensing caution in his wording, I knew that I couldn't upset the delicate balance of seeking the truth while trying not to offend and chase him away, especially since Michael needed someone else in his life besides me. After all, Samuel seemed to be there out of genuine concern for my brother. It wasn't as though my parents really cared. As for me, I was just happy to have company that night.

Samuel slid forward in his chair and asked, "Phillip, how did you know I was Samuel?" With both a sense of guilt and relief, I broke the promise I'd made to Michael by telling Samuel about our knowledge of the letter. However, knowing the dangers of revealing too many secrets, and the chance I might accidentally mention the abuse, I decided to change the subject.

"You know," I said, "you sure do look a lot like my brother."

He smiled. "That's kind of funny that you say that. My wife has always mentioned that same thing to me."

"Really? You guys actually talked about Michael?"

"Yes, Phillip. We often do."

"To be honest," I said, "it's your blue eyes that made me think that you might be the Samuel from the letter. I don't always see too many people with brown hair and blue eyes like my brother's. I know it doesn't make any sense, but you just look so much like him."

"Lots of people have blue eyes, Phillip, so I guess I don't completely understand how that made you think that I was the guy from the letter."

"Michael is the only one in our family with blue eyes, and I just thought you looked so much like him when I saw you staring at me. Your whole appearance just made me think I was looking at an older version of my brother."

"Oh, I guess I can understand that," he replied. He eased back in his chair and asked, "Did your father ever say anything about the possibility that Michael belonged to me and not him?"

I hesitated before answering. "No," I said, "I just remember that he was mad at my mom for a few days after he found the letter."

"Oh, I see," Samuel said. "I have always been afraid of what your father might do if he found out Michael might actually be *my* son."

"Sir, is your wife the lady you were talking to earlier?" His eyebrows stood at attention. "She's one of Michael's nurses," I said.

"Yes," he replied, "she's my wife."

Excitedly, I described how nice she had been, and about the soda she'd purchased for me.

"Wait a minute!" I exclaimed. His back stiffened. "Sarah asked me if Michael was related to someone with the last name Roberts. Is that your last name?"

Samuel snickered. "Wow, you're pretty good at figuring things out," he replied.

My chest swelled, recalling how Grandma Gladie had always said the same thing to me in the past.

"Yes, Phillip, my name is Samuel Roberts."

I grinned for some reason, perhaps satisfied that I'd solved a riddle that had haunted me for about ten years. I knew Samuel's last name.

"By the way," he said, "Sarah told me what an amazing brother you are to Michael."

My faced reddened. "Well, we kinda stick together a lot. Life gets sorta tough sometimes."

"Phillip, I truly never meant to hurt your mom, but since she never got in contact with me after I wrote the letter, I just figured that she was done with me simply because I asked if she was sure the baby was mine. I never forgave myself for putting that in there. It was a huge mistake that I will regret for the rest of my life. I guess I never fully realized the burden it likely put on you and Michael."

Was that an attempt at an apology? I wondered.

"Maybe my mom was afraid, or even mad like you said, but I just remember Dad being upset about some guy named Samuel," I said. "Your name has always been a big secret."

Samuel sighed.

"Sir, how did Sarah know for sure that my brother was the right Michael Williams?"

Samuel described the numerous times he'd pointed Michael out to her when they saw him around our town, but they never got too close. Samuel said he used to go to Michael's soccer games just to watch him. Secretly, he was looking out for Michael, and of course, we never knew it.

"Hey!" I snapped my fingers. "That's where I've seen you! You were the guy who always stood off to the side of the bleachers! That was you, wasn't it?"

Samuel chuckled. "Yes, that was me. There were times I just couldn't stay away, Phillip. I *had* to see him. He cocked his head. "You know, I can't believe you remembered me from his games." He smiled. "As I said before, Phillip, you really are an observant young man."

"I always wondered how you knew Michael," I replied. "To be truthful, sir, I thought you might be some kind of pervert, and I warned my brother to watch out for you."

"Oh," Samuel snickered, "I didn't think I was that obvious with my enthusiasm when he scored a goal. Besides, I always checked to see if your parents were there, which they never seemed to be, so I'd stay for the game."

Without thinking, I responded, "I actually kinda liked having someone else cheering for my brother besides me. Most of the time, people whispered rude comments about him because of our par—" I lowered my eyes, feeling guilty for what I was about to say.

"It's okay, Phillip," Samuel reassured. "I know what you were about to say. It's kind of all over the community about the partying that your parents do."

"Oh . . ." I mumbled under my breath, before looking back at him.

He reached out toward me before hastily withdrawing his hand. "Phillip, I just want you to know that I'm on your side," he kindly responded.

Unable to speak, I nodded and sighed.

"Speaking of your parents, Phillip, are they coming here tonight?"

"Well," I replied, "my parents are out of town. We've tried to get them, but no one has reached them yet."

Samuel's head jerked as he squinted his eyes in disbelief.

"When I drove over to the party, I was afraid that Michael might—" My eyes widened. "Michael!" I shouted. I sat up quickly. "I have to get back there and check on him!"

CHAPTER THIRTEEN

Sarah rushed into the lobby. "Michael's coming out of it! Both of you come with me!" My heart raced as fast as my feet as I darted toward Michael's room. Samuel waited in the hallway as I ran over to the chair I was sitting in earlier and somehow found enough strength to shove it aside with my leg.

"He's choking! Is he okay?" I yelled.

"Yes, Phillip. The ventilator isn't allowing him to speak, but he'll be okay. Nurse Lori's been here with him the whole time."

I grabbed Michael's hand while he was convulsing. "He's not okay!" I insisted. "You need to get that stupid tube outta his throat!" My brother's fingernails dug into my skin, and the force of his grip was crushing my fingers.

Sarah leaned over and put her face close to his. "Michael, my name is Sarah. I'm your nurse. You're in the hospital right now, and the tube is to help you breathe easier, so don't fight it."

His grasp tightened on my hand.

"Michael, please listen to me. Don't fight the tube. Just relax." She looked up at the other nurse assisting her. "Go ahead, Lori." The nurse injected something into his IV.

Michael's eyes frantically scanned the room. "Michael, please just relax like she said," I begged. "*Please!*" His grip weakened suddenly. "It's okay . . . just calm down . . . Sarah will make everything better. I promise, Michael!" Tears rolled down my face and over the curvature of my chin before falling onto the bed, soaking immediately into the sheet. I nodded to help reassure him. "Yes, that's it, Michael!" I caressed his hand. "You're gonna be okay." His breaths soon harmonized with mine. "That's good. You're doing it . . . you got this!"

A solitary tear escaped from the corner of his right eye and glided down to his ear. Taking the path of least resistance, it dropped onto his pillow and disappeared, leaving only a small trace of its brief existence. I reached over to the nightstand and pulled a tissue from the box. I gently wiped his eye as I smiled and whispered, "Yeah, you're gonna be okay, Michael." I looked up at Sarah, and back down at my brother. "Yeah, things are gonna be okay now! I promise!" I tried to reassure myself with every comment taking flight from my lips. "We're gonna be okay." I gently squeezed his hand as his eyelids started to close.

The other nurse removed a tissue from the box and handed it to Sarah. After wiping her eyes, Sarah looked at me and smiled. I felt the warmth of her soft hand on my forearm. I battled an invasion of emotions screaming to escape from my trembling body. I clenched my teeth and squeezed my eyes shut. *I can't lose it right now,* I thought. I took several deep breaths, hoping they would relax me. Ironically, a short time before Michael regained consciousness, I prayed for him to open his eyes, but at that moment, I wanted him to close them again just so he wouldn't be besieged by confusion and panic. I wanted to see him resting peacefully once more. It was with a great sense of relief that his grip on my hand loosened even more, and his eyelids fully succumbed to the medication injected earlier.

Sarah moved around to my side of the bed and placed her hand on my shoulder. Something inside of me—something I'd barely remembered—was rekindled when she touched me. The familiar feelings of Grandma Gladie's embraces drifted back into my conscience. "He's only sedated, so he will sleep now," she whispered. "We can't have him struggling with the ventilator. It will likely come out soon, Phillip. Lori will call the doctor with the update."

Before the other nurse left the room, she patted me on the back and smiled. "You know, Sarah is right. I can easily see that you are an amazing brother to Michael. He's so blessed to have you."

I beamed with pride in knowing someone—even a stranger—somehow saw through my inadequacies.

Once Sarah and I were alone in the room, I broke down and sobbed. She rubbed my back to soothe me. "Phillip," she reassured, "the important thing is that he'll be okay. When we talked to the doctor from the emergency room, he didn't think Michael consumed the full amount of the drugs we suspect someone had slipped into his drink at the party. When you told the emergency room staff that he was struggling to breathe, that's when they checked and decided to intubate him. The doctor said for us to keep him comfortable. He surprised even us by waking up."

As Sarah rubbed my back, I reached over and grasped my brother's hand. Out of the corner of my eye, I could see that Samuel was now standing by the door, watching. Seconds later, he leaned forward and rested his forehead against the doorframe and wept.

While holding Michael's hand, I thought about the risk I'd taken when I decided to drive him to the hospital. Had I not done so, I would have lost him forever. I shivered after recalling the terrible act I was prepared to do to myself if my brother didn't make it through the night. Samuel arrived and changed everything. Now the puzzle of my life had some newer pieces to add, but where would they fit?

CHAPTER FOURTEEN

A veil of fear lifted after I noticed Michael's chest settling back into a steady rhythm. "Are you sure he's gonna be fine, Sarah?" I asked.

Sarah put her arm around me and replied, "I think after tonight, Phillip, we're *all* going to be fine."

I wasn't sure what she meant, but I was trying my best to trust her—a difficult task for someone like me. I was so used to adults betraying me time and time again.

As she turned to leave the room, she said, "I'll be back soon. You sit tight."

I sat in the chair, still numb from the agony of uncertainty. I wanted to scream, but I thought about the man standing just outside the doorway. After all, he at least cared enough to show up, even if it was nearly sixteen years late. When I leaned back in the chair, I looked out into the hallway and saw Samuel wiping his eyes before leaning toward his wife and placing his head on her shoulder. She slid her hand up to the back of his head and stroked his hair. They swayed from side to side. *Why can't they be my parents?* I thought.

An irresistible bitterness came over me when I thought about the fact that Dad already had Michael living under his roof for years, and he did nothing to build the kind of relationship Samuel could only dream of having with the possible son he'd left behind. I was haunted by the harsh reality that there was nothing Samuel and Michael could do to get back that lost time. They were gone—destroyed forever—replaced with nothing but the stifling emptiness of regret. That was Samuel's personal punishment—a kind of unyielding sorrow I assumed he couldn't escape.

My conscience made me realize that I was faced with an excruciating decision: Could I dare let Samuel leave without giving him a chance to see Michael? I shivered from contemplating whether I should walk over to them, or remain seated and wait for them to come to me.

But would they?

I gazed at my brother before looking again at Samuel and Sarah in the hallway. Hesitating no longer, I stood, leaned over, and whispered, "I'll be right back, Michael."

Filled with trepidation—my nerves set ablaze—I cautiously approached Samuel and Sarah as I cleared my throat to gain their attention. Samuel looked up at me from Sarah's shoulder. I felt awkward interrupting them.

What in the world are you doing, Phillip?

As they gazed at me, likely pondering my next move, I took my hand and rubbed it up and down my arm. I did that a lot when I was really nervous about making a decision I wasn't sure was the right thing to do. I knew the consequences could be dire—devastating, in fact. I took a deep breath, exhaled, and asked, "Samuel . . . umm . . . ." I nearly choked on what felt like a boulder-sized ball of saliva rolling down the back of my throat. "I was just . . . well . . . I was wondering if you wanted to . . . you know . . . would you like to see Michael?"

"Oh boy," Sarah mumbled.

Awaiting his reply, Samuel extended his hand in the gesture of a handshake. I had provoked the first physical contact from him. He looked into my eyes, and with a cracked voice, he whispered, "Thank you, Phillip! Thank you so much! You don't know what this means to me!"

His countenance changed when he glanced at Sarah. She nodded her head, indicating she wanted him to say something further—something important. He dabbed his eyes with a tissue and cleared his throat. "Phillip, Sarah and I have already talked about this, and as much as I would give anything to—" He pressed his hands together and held them to his mouth and nose as if he was about to pray. He fought to hold back more tears. He soon lowered his hands. "As much as I want to see him—" His lips quivered. "Phillip, I just want to hold him—" He ceased before raising the tissue to his eyes. "Oh God . . . Sarah . . ." He took several deep breaths. "Phillip, I can't right now. I think it will be too much on him if he knows I'm there in the room." He spun around and rested his back against the wall, gasping for air. Once again, Sarah embraced him. "Sarah, I don't know if I can really pass up this opportunity. This is so hard, baby! I don't think I can miss this." His head lowered toward the floor.

"It's to protect both of you, Sam. You have to believe that for now!" Sarah insisted.

"Oh, I see," I replied. My words were dripping with disappointment.

Samuel looked at me. "Phillip," he insisted, "I want to see Michael more than you know, but right now, I just can't. Sarah's right. Besides, what if he's not—" Samuel rested the back of his head against the wall. "I don't think Michael can handle it right now."

My chest collapsed like a house built upon sand.

Sarah reached over and lifted my chin with her finger. "Phillip, Sam will see Michael, but right now isn't the time. It's too risky. Michael is still fragile, so we can't do anything to jeopardize this, no matter how much my husband wants to see him. We have to wait for Michael to make that move, and we believe he will when he's ready. Besides, it took courage for you to even come out here and ask Samuel. I'm proud of you for being so brave. I really mean that, Phillip! We are both very proud of you."

My chest began to swell again.

I turned and walked back into the room and sat in the chair next to Michael's bed. A solitary tear raced down my cheek and rolled over my lips. I wiped it away and looked upward. "Did I do the right thing, God?"

Out in the hallway, there was a sudden explosion of excitement. I rushed to the doorway. Lori, the nurse, slammed the phone down. "The emergency room just informed me that a woman named Ellen Williams is down there pitching a fit," she said. "She's coming up here!"

My night was about to get a whole lot longer. At least now there wasn't any reason for the police to go to my home . . .

Home was coming to me.

CHAPTER FIFTEEN

After kissing Sarah, Samuel turned and headed for the stairwell. I ran after him. I didn't care that I looked like a little kid chasing after the ice cream truck. He entered the stairs and I followed. When he turned and smiled at me, I saw tears in his eyes, which made me wonder if he could even see me.

"Are you really going to meet Michael soon?"

"Yes, Phillip, I am. I promise. I just don't want to cause any harm to him."

As I was thinking about the amount of harm I knew was coming my brother's way, Samuel reached out to shake my hand, and I did the same. His hand was cold and clammy. "Thank you for coming tonight," I said.

"Well, thank you for talking to me, Phillip."

"I'm just glad you decided to be here with us," I replied.

After we released our hands, he said, "Well, your mom should be up here any second, so I better go. I'll be in touch soon."

Samuel turned and started down the stairs. As he descended to the next level, I leaned against the metal railing. I was alone again, and one horrible question remained: *Would Samuel really come back?* I turned and gripped the doorknob and opened the door several inches before closing it again. I listened to the thumping sounds of Samuel's footsteps getting farther away. I leaned my head against the door and whispered, "Please God, please let him come back soon. We need him!"

I took several breaths and opened the heavy metal door and stepped into the lobby just as the elevator door opened.

Mom stepped out and saw me. "I want to know why you didn't tell me Michael was so bad," she roared.

"I did, Mom, but you wouldn't listen to me, so I brought him here by myself. I really thought he was gonna die!" I insisted. "Even one of the nurses said that he would have died in his bed at home had I done what you guys told me to do."

With her teeth clenched, she protested, "Don't you dare blame any of this on me, young man!" She pointed her trembling finger in my face, barely touching the tip of my nose. "You have no idea the kinds of problems you've caused me over this stunt you pulled. I could just strangle you right now for doing such an idiotic thing!"

"I'm sorry, Mom" I pleaded. "Besides, I already have an idea what Dad's gonna do to me when I get home."

"Sorry isn't going to cut it this time, Phillip! Your dad is fuming mad right now. It took every ounce of my strength to keep him from coming after you, especially when he saw that you'd taken his car without him knowing it. I have no idea what he's going to do to both of us when we get back home." Mom's clothes and breath reeked of cigarettes, pot, and alcohol, but she appeared sober enough to put up a front that she was at least functional. "What did you tell them in the emergency room?"

"I told them that you guys were out of town."

"Oh my God, Phillip, we are so screwed," she said. "Everyone probably knows that we were home tonight. It's not like we didn't have a ton of cars in our driveway! Now we'll have to come up with some other story," she whispered.

"Mom, I think they believed the one I told them, so you don't have to worry." I noticed her bloodshot eyes, causing me to wonder whether they were filled with anger, or the effects of alcohol. "Mom, just *please* try and act like you weren't drinking, so they don't question us."

Mom stepped back and rolled her eyes. "You know, you need to get off my back about that issue. I'm fine! Now take me back to see Michael."

"Is Dad still thinking about coming here?" I asked. I pressed my fingers into my stomach to help ease some of the pain and nausea suddenly brought on by the reoccurring thought of having to confront him. "Besides, how did you find out we were at the hospital?"

"That stuck up little manipulator you call a friend happened to call the house and ask for you. When you didn't answer me, I went looking, and that's when your dad noticed his car was missing. I had to have Gloria drive me here because my car wouldn't start again."

"Gwen called the house?" I panicked at the thought of them speaking to each other. "Look, I'm really sorry, Mom, but Michael was pretty bad off tonight."

"Yeah, I know, because *Gwen* said he passed out after throwing up several times. Didn't I tell you that he was just drunk?" Mom insisted. "Gloria's the one who suggested that you might have taken him to the hospital. We called here and the lady said that some young man had brought in a teenager matching Michael's description, but she wouldn't give us your names. We had to drive all the way over here just to find out." Mom shook her head. "I could just strangle you right now! I looked like a horrible mother in front of them down there in the emergency room."

"Look, I knew I would be in trouble, but if you could have seen him, Mom, you would've brought him here yourself."

"That's beside the point, Phillip." Her reddened face burned with indignation toward me. I made her look bad, but Sarah was the only one who helped me realize that I did the right thing in spite of the permanent damage I caused my whole family. Mom grabbed my arm and squeezed. Her fingernails were swords piercing my flesh. "Now take me back to Michael's room!"

Mom stopped outside of the door long enough to glance toward the nurses' station where Sarah was working. She whispered to me, "Is that his nurse?"

"Just one of them, Mom."

"How do I look?" she asked.

"Fine." I rolled my eyes when she wasn't looking. I was somewhat certain that Mom knew Sarah, but she would have never admitted it to anyone.

We walked in, and Mom suddenly grabbed my shoulder. "Oh—my—God, Phillip!" Her hand rushed to her open mouth, but her words seemed to force her hand away when she bellowed, "I didn't know they had him on a ventilator!" Mom rushed over to my brother. Her face was soon soaked with tears. Seeing Michael in such a desperate condition must have resurrected some of her maternal compassion she'd abandoned years ago. "Honey, I'm here. Are you okay?"

"We are certain he'll be fine, Mrs. Williams." The familiar, friendly voice caused both of us to turn around. "Hello, I'm Sarah. I'm one of the nurses taking care of your son."

"I got here as fast as I could," Mom said. "My husband and I have been so concerned. I guess we picked a bad night to head out of town." My brief bout of sympathy for Mom had transformed into rage. "My husband said he will be here in a little bit. He wasn't feeling well this evening after we got back into town, and we really didn't know how serious Michael was until I got here." She grabbed my brother's hand. "Phillip didn't quite relay the message clearly enough to us on the answering machine."

Mom's searing glare, teeming with resentment, shot straight into my eyes. I looked away.

"Well," Sarah replied, "when Phillip brought him into the emergency room, I guess they were very concerned about Michael's breathing. He was alert a little while ago, but we had to sedate him just so he wouldn't fight us over the ventilator. The good news is that none of the tests are showing any serious injuries. The doctor doesn't believe he consumed the full amount of the drugs we suspect he ingested at the party earlier tonight. The interactions of the narcotics and alcohol are likely what suppressed his breathing, causing him to become unconscious."

"What do you mean my son was doing drugs?"

"We believe," Sarah replied, "that they were slipped into his drink without his knowledge."

"So," Mom asked, "will he be okay?"

"Yes, the respiratory therapist said that her reports indicated his blood gasses are pretty good, so when the doctor makes his rounds here in a few hours, he will likely have us remove the ventilator." Sarah looked at me and smiled. "Mrs. Williams, I just want you to know how much I have admired Phillip's bravery throughout this whole incident. He has been by Michael's side all night, and our entire staff believes he is a hero for saving Michael's life. You and your husband have obviously raised a very smart young man."

"Yeah," Mom said, in a curt response.

"If you have any further questions, please let me know. I have a few patients to check on. Just ring the buzzer and I will be in shortly."

Sarah patted me on the shoulder and winked.

Mom grabbed my arm after Sarah left the room. "Don't think for one minute that your dad is going to think you are some kind of hero for what you did."

I yanked my arm away and walked over and rested my back against the wall. A part of me wanted to laugh, knowing Sarah was the wife of the man Mom had slept with years ago, and I also knew I would be in trouble if Mom knew how close Sarah and I had become that evening. Mom would have also been inconsolable had she'd known I'd talked to Samuel.

Lori, the other nurse, brought another chair into the room for me. Mom and I sat next to Michael, one of us on each side of his bed. We glared at each other for several minutes before I leaned my head against the back of the chair, hoping for some relief from the unwelcomed headache that had begun to pound behind my eyes.

Several hours later, I was startled by a booming, baritone voice in the room. My heart climbed into my throat. When my eyes adjusted, I saw Sarah standing beside a man in a white lab coat. A shorter, blonde-haired lady was standing on the opposite side of the bed. I was able to infer from their conversations that she must have been the respiratory therapist. I cleared my throat and sat up in the chair. "I agree," the doctor said, "but I still want to check a few things."

I looked at Michael, and he was awake! The ventilator had been removed, but when Michael tried to clear his throat, it caused him to gag. Sarah comforted him, and he soon settled down. Although his voice was raspy, he was able to ask, "What happened to me?"

Mom started to talk, as Michael massaged his throat, but I interrupted her when I stood and stepped over toward Michael's bed. "We think you got drugged at the party last night," I said. I noticed Mom glaring at me. "Yeah, Mom and Dad weren't home, so I brought you to the hospital when Gwen called to tell me that you were really sick."

Struggling to speak, Michael said, "I don't remember passing out."

The staff seemed quite interested in hearing more of the tale. I hesitated at first, because I was uncertain whether or not I might say something that could get me into even more trouble. "Yeah, you must have hit your face on something when you passed out at the party because your cheek was really red." That comment was nothing more than my cover up excuse for Dad, who had hit Michael earlier that Friday afternoon in our yard. "You couldn't really breathe, so that's why they put that machine on you."

Sarah stepped forward and interjected, "Yes, Michael, your brother saved your life." She gazed at Mom and smiled.

Mom grinned, but as soon as Sarah looked away, disgust filled every square inch of her face. "Yes, he is quite the hero, I'm sure!" Mom sneered at me.

My nerves were tingling from the rage surging through my body.

By midmorning, that Saturday, rumors of Michael's demise had spread throughout the community of Westview like a massive wildfire. Cover ups, finger-pointing, and the deeply sought after fifteen minutes of fame were soon out of control and the police were intent on sorting it all out. All morning long, I pondered one other important question: When would the police return to the hospital for a further investigation? Sadly, Sarah had already left, but she was scheduled to return that night, so if the police did visit us at the hospital, I was hoping she would be there with me. She was the shield I needed in the battle against my parents. I was also hoping to convince my parents that Michael wanted me to stay with him again that night, but when Dad arrived around noon, I knew I was on borrowed time, and staying with Michael again was no longer an option.

When Dad first arrived, he walked over to Michael and hugged him. Then he sauntered over to me and pulled me against his chest. To the staff, his affection looked like nothing more than a sincere embrace, but no one knew what he whispered into my ear. I cringed when he said, "You're dead as soon as we get home." He started to pull away, but then he thrust the side of my head once more to his mouth. "Oh, and I ain't gonna forget about you taking my car. Jeff had to bring me here today." My ear was moist from his warm, alcohol-saturated breath.

Dad spent most of the afternoon in the lobby and outside smoking cigarettes; however, he was in the room when the police arrived to ask more questions about the party. The sight of policemen entering the room caused a sudden spasm in my gut, and I almost had to excuse myself to the bathroom. Dad stood and greeted the officers before moving over and sitting on the bed with Michael. He was making sure he controlled everything my brother might have said.

After the investigation, my parents and I went to the cafeteria, but I wasn't in the mood to eat after Dad threatened me several more times over the visit from the police. I counted and prioritized the list of threats Dad said to me since his arrival earlier that day. All that I knew for sure was that he was going to tear me into pieces pretty soon. I glanced out the window and saw the amber sky stretching across the horizon, ushering in the evening, so I knew I had very little time left.

As I sat at the table, pushing food around my plate with a fork, I recounted the investigation. When the officers started to question Dad's whereabouts that Friday evening, I knew my version of the story was going to have to withstand the officers' scrutiny. Dad's reddened, annoyed expressions indicated the depth of trouble I was going to be in later that night. When the officers questioned Michael, he said he couldn't remember much at all. I was also questioned, but I was truthful in stating that I didn't go to the party until someone called and told me that Michael was sick. I had to confess that it was Gwen who told me. I then explained how I decided to stay home by myself while my parents were out that evening. Dad's nostrils flared, and his lips seemed to tighten against his yellow teeth the longer I'd talked.

Throughout the investigation, Dad remained beside Michael, occasionally rubbing my brother's arm. He even said, "Me and my wife are just so glad Michael's okay now, 'cause I don't know what I'd do without him in my life."

I wanted to beat Dad to death. I hated him more than at any other time in my life. I wanted to scream to the police officers and tell them that he was just acting, and that he hated my brother, and likely hoped that Michael would have died that night.

I think Mom was sensing a little bit of scrutiny from the officers when one of them asked, "And what time was it that you arrived to see your son, Mrs. Williams?"

"We would have come sooner," she said, "but Phillip didn't inform us about his exact whereabouts, or how serious Michael's condition really was. We thought they were just out for a joyride last night."

Knowing that I had to redirect the suspicion away from my parents, I said to one of the officers, "Yeah, I guess I should have been more honest with them about his condition. Mom's right, she probably thought we were out running around with our friends." I suddenly felt trapped in my own lies. "Honestly, sir, I was afraid they'd be mad at me for not watching out for my brother, especially since he was at the party in the first place." I turned to Mom and Dad and pleaded, "I'm sorry for not being honest with you guys about everything. I just didn't know how to tell you that Michael was at the party you said he couldn't go to."

The perplexed looks on my parents and the officers' faces only added to the anxiety suffocating me.

"It looks like you only made things worse, young man," an officer stated.

"Yes, sir, I'm pretty sure I have." Dad's contemptible stare caused me to swallow what last bit of saliva I had left in my mouth. After a few moments, Michael seemed to be getting agitated. My brother must have figured out that I was hiding the truth about my parents and their illegal activities from the night before. Thankfully, Michael spoke up and said that he wasn't feeling well, so the officers stopped their questioning.

As tears welled up in my eyes, which I wiped away, Dad escorted the officers from the room and shook their hands. "I wanna thank you gentlemen for your concern. We'll take good care of Michael when we get him back home." My knees buckled and I collapsed into one of the chairs. After they left, Dad walked over and nonchalantly retrieved a tissue. As he handed it to me, he smirked and leaned down, leaving just inches between my face and his. With his teeth clamped, he whispered, "I am so gonna tear you up when I getcha home!"

Unhindered, my tears cascaded down my cheeks. "But Dad, Michael really wants me to stay here with him," I replied.

"That ain't gonna happen, boy!"

"Dad," I pleaded, "I promise I won't do something like this ever again. Please, don't make me leave Michael tonight. He wants me to stay with him."

He grabbed a handful of my hair. "Oh, I'm pretty sure you ain't gonna do something like this ever again." He slammed my head against the back of the chair and walked away. I grabbed several more tissues and wiped my sweaty, tear-stained face. As for my fear, nothing could wipe it away.

Later that evening, after we'd returned from the cafeteria, Mom suggested that Michael should get some rest. She leaned over and kissed him and walked to the door. Dad followed her for some reason. Like a toddler clinging to a parent for protection, I desperately held onto the metal railing attached to Michael's bed. I wanted to stay with my brother! I had so much to tell him, especially about Samuel, but I knew Dad wanted me home, and I knew why. As I leaned over to hug Michael, he noticed my eyes were brimming with a deluge of tears ready to burst like a dam.

"What's wrong?" he whispered.

"Nothing. I'm fine." I turned away. I noticed Mom and Dad were over near the door talking.

"Yes there is!" Michael whispered.

My head drooped to my chest as one of my tears dripped onto the back of my brother's hand. I quickly wiped it away before closing my eyes and taking a deep breath. I nodded my head and whispered, "Yeah . . . I'm scared."

Michael sat up, grabbed my wrist, and said, "Mom, please let Phillip stay with me again tonight? I don't really wanna be alone."

Mom looked over and said, "I don't think so, Michael, because Phillip needs to get some rest. Besides, he hasn't showered since yesterday morning."

"He'll be fine, Mom. I really want him to stay!"

Dad walked over and sat on the bed. His eyes narrowed, and he had a sadistic grin spreading across his mouth. He jerked his head, indicating he wanted me to walk away. Michael had no choice but to release my arm. Defeated, I meandered over to the door and stood beside Mom. Dad brushed Michael's hair away from his eyes, causing Michael to twitch. "I'll stay with you tonight, Mikey." Dad turned and said to us, "Now, how 'bout you two idiots let me have a moment with *my* son." The fear he invoked was hindering my ability to move my feet, similar to the way I felt the day before in our yard when Dad dragged Michael into the garage.

"That wasn't no suggestion, you two. Get into the hallway so I can talk to Michael alone for a second."

I waved to my brother and said, "I'll see you tomorrow, Michael."

"I love you, Phillip," he replied.

Dad had a contemptible sneer on his face.

Mom and I headed out the door and down the hallway toward the elevator. As we passed the nurse's station, I held my thumb and pinky finger up to the side of my head. Sarah smiled and nodded.

The thought of leaving my brother alone with Dad made my stomach heave from uncontrolled spasms. My muscles weakened with each step I trekked away from Michael's room. "Mom, please let me stay. I don't wanna leave Michael alone. *Please!*"

"You heard your dad! Besides, you're better off just doing what he says."

"Do you know what he's gonna do to me when we get home?"

"Stop being so dramatic, Phillip. After all, you caused all of this."

In the parking lot, Dad ripped the keys from my hand. During the ride home, he was silent, like the seconds that pass right before a verdict is read in a courtroom. I could tell he was up to something because of the demented, evil grin he couldn't seem to erase from his wicked face. I even considered leaping from the car when he stopped at one of the traffic lights in town. Dad loved giving us the silent treatment when we were in trouble. He knew the excruciating fear it caused us. I was almost paralyzed from the hopeless despair I felt when we pulled into the driveway. After Dad turned off the ignition, he twisted his body around and glared at me. Every word he said after that was dripping with fury and resentment. "Get out of the car, and get to your room, boy. I'll be up to deal with you soon enough." Mom stared straight ahead, leaving me defenseless.

CHAPTER SIXTEEN

I paced the floor in my room, envisioning every possible way Dad could destroy me. Every noise caused my chest to swell from the rush of air I sucked in, only to have it slowly retreat like the tide when I realized Dad wasn't coming. It was nearly an hour before I saw his shadow creeping in from under the door. The creaking noise of the door's hinges pierced my eardrums as Dad entered and stood, blocking my easiest escape. "So, whacha think I got behind my back, Phillip?" he smugly asked.

My words got tangled up in my tongue. "I . . .umm . . ."

Dad grinned.

I licked my lips and swallowed. He tapped his foot and raised an eyebrow, awaiting my response. My voice rattled with fear as I answered, "Probably a belt."

"Why, Phillip, you seem a bit nervous," he taunted.

"Look, I'm really sorry, Dad. I know I made you guys look bad, and I should have spoken up sooner to the cops about why I took Michael to the hospital."

Dad's stare melted away the rest of my dignity.

"Please Dad, I'm really, really sorry." Tears were about to breach the sockets of my eyes. "Honest, Dad, I didn't want them to find out that you guys were—"

"Find out what, Phillip?" The scorn on his face caused my body to wilt like a thirsty flower.

"Well . . ." I attempted to reason with him. "Umm . . . you guys were drinking and . . . and I thought I should . . ." My throat strained. "Dad, I was just trying to protect you guys! I had to take Michael to the hospital because I knew you guys were partying. I didn't want the police to come to the house."

"Awww, that sure was nice of you, Phillip, but I ain't buying it." He grinned again, taking one step toward me. I could feel the sharp corner of my dresser jabbing me in the back as I stepped backward. "Oh, and yeah, you should've said something quicker to those pigs." He smiled again. "So what do you think I got for you behind my back?"

I stood motionless, too terrified to answer at first. Finally, I exhaled the air trapped inside of my lungs, and more hollow words stumbled over my dry, trembling lips. "I told you it's probably a belt."

I wasn't sure, but that was often his weapon of choice. A wave of nausea intensified in my stomach as I contemplated the humiliation I was about to face—just to satisfy Dad's gross sense of pleasure.

Dad told me to turn around. I didn't comply with his demand right away, so he said again, "Boy, you better do what I say *right now*!"

I remembered how cowardly it was to attack someone from behind, but Dad was fully capable of such an act of aggression. My breaths were becoming more strenuous the longer I resisted his command. A tear escaped and raced down my cheek, which I wiped away. "Please, Dad, come on! I'm almost eighteen years old for God's sake. I'm too old for this!"

He glared at me.

"Can't you just ground me for a month or something?"

He continued to stare, as I tried to catch my breath.

"Come on, Dad . . . I get it! I screwed up, okay!" I swallowed. "I know I should have told you that I took Michael to the hospital."

Dad slammed his hand down on my other dresser and demanded that I turn around.

I jerked from the sudden noise.

"Boy, if I have to come over there, you ain't gonna like it!"

"Dad," I implored, "just try and understand why I did what I needed to. I had to save Michael!"

Ignoring my logic, Dad cleared his throat. "Turn around!"

"Why?" I inquired. "Dad, this is embarrassing. I'm too old for this!"

The unsympathetic look on his face left me no choice but to obey his cruel command. I knew what he usually did to Michael when it came to a beating with a belt. Many nights I would hear the ear-piercing screams from my brother, especially when he was younger. When Michael reached his teen years, he resisted crying out—at least when he could.

With his lips taut, Dad demanded, "I won't tell you again, boy!"

"Please Dad, don't do this!" I begged.

Dad continued to glare at me in silence. The sudden smirk on his face meant he was certainly enjoying my suffering. I actually thought about taking a swing at him. I was seventeen years old, getting pretty muscular, and I knew if I wanted to, I could probably hit him hard and run. Sadly, though, I had no place to escape to. I also knew I couldn't leave Mom and Michael alone with him if I did run away.

Dad pushed everything off the dresser, which crashed against the wall and cascaded to the floor, scattering like debris from a bomb.

I raised my arms to protect my face. I had no choice—I *had* to obey him. "Alright, Dad, I'll do it! Just get it over with!"

With no compassion visible on Dad's face, I knew I couldn't win, especially when he took one threatening step toward me. I turned around and leaned over my bed. As I envisioned how the stinging sensation of the leather strap would feel, I could faintly hear the creaking of the floor behind me. I squeezed my eyes shut.

At least five seconds had passed and nothing happened. I was afraid to turn around and witness Dad's forceful swing. I was certain that my breathing ceased while I waited another five seconds or so.

"Come on, Dad! Just get it over with, will you!" I gripped the sheet on my bed with my sweaty hands and held on tightly. I knew it would burn like the fires of hell.

Finally, with my eyes barely open, I turned my head and saw that no one was in the room behind me. Dad had already slipped out the door. He got exactly what he wanted! Dad had beaten me that night without once laying a hand on my body. It was just one more victory for him.

I collapsed onto my bed—angry that I had allowed myself to fall victim to his sadistic game.

CHAPTER SEVENTEEN

I had been victimized in some kind of perverted way. I was drenched in sweat, so I sat up, removed my shirt, and wiped my face and chest with it. After standing, I staggered over to one of my dressers, dodging the obstacle course of debris scattered across the floor. I sifted through the dresser, looking for some clothes before heading to the bathroom to wash off the humiliation that Dad seemed to have smeared all over me.

On my way down the hallway, Dad emerged from his bedroom. "Come over here, son. I'd like to talk to you," he demanded, even motioning with his finger.

My heart danced in my chest, but knowing I had no choice but to do as he said, I wandered over to him, making sure I didn't make any eye contact. When I stopped in front of him, he took his fingers and turned my head toward his face. His grin was menacing—threatening in some evil kind of way. He slid his hand along my jaw and soon started to massage the back of my neck, causing goose bumps to rise all over me. He pulled me closer. Just being that close to Dad was repulsive—a violation of my soul. Suddenly, he slammed me against the wall, thrusting his forearm into my throat. I dropped my clothes and grimaced.

"Dad . . . *please* . . ." I reached up and seized his arm.

"Get your hands off of me before I break your scrawny little neck."

Intermittent black spots blocked some of my vision, and I dropped my hands.

He moved his nose just inches from my face. As he spoke, the polluted odor of his breath caused me to wince. "I ain't done with either of you two. You shoulda thrown that worthless bastard in his bed like I told you." Veins popped up on my forearms as Dad looked down and saw my hands tightening into fists. He snickered. "So, you thinkin' about hittin' your old man?"

My nostrils flared as hatred swelled in my chest. I realized Dad wanted me to hit him.

"Hey, boy, you're thinkin' about hittin' me, aintcha?"

My hands eased and I managed to choke out the words, "No, sir . . ."

"Yeah, I didn't think you were that stupid." He released me, but not before slamming my head against the wall. "Now, go get your shower. You stink!"

He strolled toward the stairs and descended, displaying his arrogance in a sickening kind of stride.

I picked up my clothes and rushed to the bathroom, massaging my throat along the way. As I got undressed, I happened to look into the mirror. I became fixated on my distraught face. "You're pathetic!" I mumbled to myself.

After showering, I returned to my room, and picked up the phone and dialed the number to the hospital I had written down that afternoon on a piece of napkin. My hands shook as I pressed the numbers into the phone. My voice quavered as I told the operator, "Yes, I would like to speak with a nurse named Sarah Roberts, please."

Moments later, a woman answered the phone.

"Sarah?" I quickly responded.

"I'm sorry," the woman said, "but Sarah's on another call at the moment. May I help you?"

"Ummm . . . this is Phillip Williams . . . Michael's brother."

"Oh, it's good to hear from you, Phillip. This is Lori, the other nurse. What can I do for you?"

"Hi," I replied. "I kinda need to talk to Sarah if you don't mind."

"I'll let her know it's you, so please give me a moment to get her attention."

I paced the floor, eager to chat with Sarah. I even put my ear up to the bedroom door to make sure I didn't hear anyone outside in the hallway. It was quiet.

Finally, I heard that familiar, comforting voice on the other end of the phone. "Hello, Phillip. This is Sarah."

"Hey, you gotta minute?" I whispered.

"Phillip, are you okay?" she inquired. "Why are you whispering?"

The whole thing almost felt like some strange spy game. In a sense, it was.

"Oh, I . . . ahhhh . . . I don't wanna wake anyone up at my house."

"I see," she replied.

"Sarah, does Michael know anything about Samuel yet?" I paused and sucked in air like it was my last breath before plunging under water.

"I don't think so, Phillip, because he hasn't mentioned anything." I exhaled. "Didn't you mention anything to him today?" she asked.

"No ma'am. I was too afraid that he might freak out about it in front of my parents." I reached up and rubbed my hand through my damp hair. "God, Sarah, I don't know what to do!"

"Phillip," she said, "I know I don't know you and Michael that well, but my husband is a wonderful man, and he can't stop talking about either of you boys."

I sniffled and said, "Sarah, Michael needs someone like Samuel right now—we both do. He really needs to know the truth about last night, but I'm afraid."

"Would you like to speak with Michael?" She paused, awaiting my response. "I can connect you to his room if you'd like." My mind searched for the words I wanted to say. "Phillip?" she uttered.

"Yeah, I'd like that," I whispered.

The phone rang a few times while I nervously tapped my foot on the floor. I heard a faint, "Hello."

"Hey, it's Phillip. Can we talk a sec?" My voice was drenched with terror.

"Hey, did Dad do anything to you when you got home?" Michael asked.

"Not really," I answered, "but I'll tell you later." I was still obsessed with watching my bedroom door. "What did Dad do to you when he told us to leave your room?"

"The usual. He told me he couldn't wait to get me home, and then the evil jerk slid his finger across my throat like he had a knife. But I'm okay now," my brother replied.

"God, I hate him!" I said.

"Yeah," he replied, "so do I."

As I tried to figure out a way to tell my brother that I met Samuel, I looked to see if there were any shadows at the bottom of my bedroom door. I saw nothing. "Look, I didn't really get to tell you this earlier today, but . . . I met . . ." My heart launched into my throat. "I met Samuel—the guy from the letter."

"What? Where, Phillip?" Michael excitedly asked.

"In the lobby last night. He heard about you, and so he wanted to make sure you were okay."

Michael gasped. "Why didn't you tell me, Phillip? I wanna meet him too!"

I was relieved to hear him say that. "He came to the doorway and looked in on you last night, but you were asleep again."

"That might have been the only chance I had to see him!" he said. "Why didn't you tell me earlier?"

"I didn't want you to freak out in front of Mom and Dad. Besides, there might be another chance for you to meet him," I said.

I knew Michael was probably rubbing his hand through his hair like he always did when he was nervous or upset. "I wanna see him, Phillip!"

I got up and walked over to my bedroom door again. This time, however, I opened it slowly and peeked out into the hallway. No one was there. I closed the door and stepped back over to my bed and sat. "You know the nurse with the blonde hair that's been taking care of you?"

"Yeah," he said. "What about her?"

"Well, she's married to Samuel."

"What?" he bellowed. "She has to know who I am then, right?"

"Yeah, I wanted to tell you all day, but I wasn't sure how you'd take it."

"Do you think she'd let me talk to him?" Michael asked. "Maybe I could call him?"

I smiled and replied, "Well, I know he wants to meet you."

His breaths roared into the phone. "Do you think he could before I get released from here?"

"Maybe, but they're afraid to let you guys see each other right now."

"Why, Phillip?"

"They think you might be too weak to handle it."

"Handle it? I feel fine!" he insisted.

"Call Sarah into your room and see what she has to say," I replied. "I'm not sure how this all works, but Samuel probably isn't allowed to see you without you asking for him. It's not like Mom and Dad will give him permission."

"Oh my God!" Michael said.

"What? Are you okay?" I asked.

"That nurse saw me with no clothes on, man!" His face had to have been the shade of my Crimson Tide sweatshirt we always shared.

I burst out laughing, but I quickly covered my mouth, hoping I hadn't been too loud.

"It's not funny, Phillip!" he retorted.

"Yeah, little brother," I whispered, "she's seen more of you than Mom has in years." Although the laughter was a welcomed relief, I had to become serious again. "Michael, I have to tell you, though, I'm scared outta my freakin' mind right now. What if Mom and Dad find out what we're doing? I don't want them to take it out on you when you get home. And I don't want Dad going after Samuel and Sarah. You know he will."

"I don't really care about Mom and Dad. I wanna meet this guy! Do you think you could sneak back down here to the hospital? I don't have a clue what to do or say if he comes to see me, or even if I just get to talk to him on the phone."

"I don't know how I can get there without Mom and Dad knowing." I paced the floor again, contemplating the consequences of being caught sneaking out in order to go to the hospital. Suddenly, I heard someone in the hallway. "Hey, I gotta go. Someone's coming! Listen, I'll see what I can do to get there if Samuel comes to see you." Before hanging up, though, I demanded, "Get Sarah in there and see what she can do." Before saying goodbye, I whispered, "Hey, I love you, Michael. You know that, right?"

"Yeah, same here," he replied. "Call me back soon so I can tell you if he's coming to see me."

"Okay, I'll try," I said.

I hung up the phone and jumped into my bed. It was Mom putting something in the hallway linen closet near my room. I rested on my back for the next few moments—panting. In spite of the consequences, I had started something I knew I couldn't stop. Maybe this was my restitution to Michael for the years I neglected to stop Dad. Maybe it was my revenge on my parents. Maybe it was both. I couldn't tell.

About fifteen minutes later, I lifted the receiver from the base of the phone and listened to see if Mom was talking to anyone. The welcomed dial tone buzzed in my ear. Moments later, I was speaking again to Sarah. "Is Samuel coming to see Michael?" I asked.

"Yes, Phillip, but Michael insists that he wants you here as well. Is that possible?"

"I'll try my best," I said. "Maybe I can find someone to get me there."

"I understand," Sarah replied. "Do your best, though, because Michael's really frightened, and if I know Sam, he'll be scared out of his mind also."

I hung up the phone. Wearing yet another path in the carpet for several minutes, my mind begged for a solution on how to get to Michael's hospital room without either of my parents knowing. I couldn't walk out any door downstairs, so the only way out was through my bedroom window. I envisioned Samuel walking into Michael's room and me not being there. I also shuddered at the thought of one of my parents discovering that I wasn't in my bedroom either. I sat on my bed, and suddenly, the solution struck me. "A cab!" I whispered. "I can call a cab!"

My next dilemma was finding enough money to pay for the trip both to and from the hospital. I had to find the number for the cab company as well. Mom kept a phone book in the stand beside her bed, so I tiptoed over to my door, opened it, and peaked into the hallway. No one was there, so I sneaked down the hallway and stopped at the top of the stairs. I heard Mom downstairs. I also knew that Dad was out in the garage, because I heard him revving the engine of one of the cars just minutes before I'd spoken with Sarah again. When I popped into my parents' room, I practically slithered over to the phone book and retrieved the number. After retreating back to my room, I pressed the numbers into the phone. When asked where I wanted to be picked up, I told the dispatcher that I would be at the end of my road. They said they would be there within fifteen minutes. I also knew that Michael had a few dollars in his room, so I sneaked over and found it shoved down into one of his black Chuck Taylors in his closet. I hurried back to my room and called Sarah to inform her that I was coming to the hospital. She told me to go to the emergency room entrance and someone would be there to meet me. After hiding my pillows under my blanket, making it appear as though I was sleeping soundly in my bed, I hurried to the window, slid it open without a sound, and climbed out.

CHAPTER EIGHTEEN

Nausea held my stomach hostage all the way to the hospital, and a few times I thought I might have to ask the cab driver to pull over. Every nightmarish consequence about the visit with Samuel and my brother possessed my thoughts. If he *was* Michael's father, would he end up taking my brother away from me? And how would I deal with Michael's disappointment if it turned out that Samuel wasn't really who we thought he was? Exhausted from my own crushing thoughts, I eased my head against the door of the cab and closed my eyes.

"Ya got someone sick down there at the hospital?" the driver asked.

I opened my eyes. "Yeah," I said.

"It's kinda late, though. Ya sure the hospital will letcha visit?"

"They sorta know I'm coming," I replied.

"Oh, that's good. Hope everyone's okay. I'll have ya there shortly, man," the driver promised.

"Thank you, sir," I said.

About ten minutes later, we pulled up to the emergency room entrance. I paid the fare, and thanked the driver.

"Ya gonna need a ride back?" he asked.

"Probably, sir, but I'm not sure when, so I guess I'll call later if I need a ride."

"Okay," he said. "Good luck, buddy."

I closed the door and stepped back. The exhaust from the muffler filled my nostrils as the cab pulled away, causing my eyes to water. I turned and entered the emergency room. Waiting for me was Samuel, and he looked just as terrified as me.

After stepping off the elevator into the lobby on Michael's floor, Samuel grabbed my arm, forcing me to stop. "Phillip, am I doing the right thing? Sarah and I aren't sure about any of this right now, and besides, I don't want to jeopardize anything with Michael."

"Samuel, no offense," I said, "but you've waited almost sixteen years for this. Look, I know that my brother really wants to meet you."

I stepped toward the hallway, but Samuel wasn't coming with me. "Yes, Phillip, I know I've waited a long time, but I don't think I can handle it if Michael tells me to—" He locked his fingers behind his head and sighed. "To be honest, Phillip, I'm really struggling not to lose it right now."

I turned toward him. "Samuel, I know my brother, and he's not gonna tell you to leave. He just wants to know who you really are. Please come with me. Michael deserves to know the man who might be his real dad."

I took one step backward, coaxing him to follow me. He stepped forward and we headed toward Michael's room.

When we arrived at the door, Samuel stopped again and leaned his back against the wall. "Oh God . . . I can't believe this is happening!"

The nursing supervisor walked over and said, "Samuel, that boy has been waiting to meet you."

"I know, Dottie, but I—"

"No *buts*, Samuel. Now, get in there, and let that boy know that you're going to be there for him. He deserves some great folks like you and Sarah in his life."

I almost chuckled from the way she was bossing him around.

"Okay," he sighed. "I hear you."

She grabbed one of Samuel's arms and opened the door. After we entered, she winked at me and said, "I'll leave you folks alone. If you need anything, please let me know."

"Thanks, Dottie," Sarah said.

My muscles stiffened, and my throat strained as I attempted to swallow. Michael's widening eyes seemed to scream for my help. I was certain that he needed me to offer him something—anything that he might say to the nervous stranger staring back at him from across the room. Sarah walked over and hugged me before gripping Samuel's hand. As she guided him closer to the bed, she said, "Michael, this is my husband. His name is Samuel Roberts, and he has waited a *very* long time to meet you."

I walked over to Michael's bed and smiled. I let Sarah take control of the formal introductions. After clearing his throat, Samuel continued to stare at Michael, observing the face of the possible son he was officially meeting for the first time. He said, "It's a real pleasure to meet you, Mike—I mean—Michael."

I was surprised that Samuel didn't shake my brother's hand. It was as though something was holding him back—some kind of resisting force determined not to breech a forbidden territory. Tears glistened in Samuel's eyes. Perhaps he realized that he had spoken his first words to the boy he had dreamed of meeting for the past sixteen years.

"I'm glad you came to see me, sir," Michael said.

"I'm truly honored you invited me," Samuel replied.

I caught myself gazing back and forth between Samuel and Michael, almost as if I was watching a tennis match. Their resemblance was undeniable.

"Sir," Michael blurted out, "may I ask you something?"

Samuel's eyes widened, and his breaths seemed rapid and shallow.

"When I read the letter that you wrote to my mom, it sounded like you might be my real dad."

Samuel looked at Sarah, and then back at Michael.

"Are you?"

I couldn't believe Michael's boldness.

Sarah gripped Samuel's arm.

"Well, Michael, I . . . umm . . ." Samuel licked his lips. "I think it's quite possible that I might be." Samuel's body was shaking as he politely asked, "Michael, may I sit down please?"

My brother nodded.

"Phillip told me that you came in to see me last night, but I was sleeping," Michael said.

"Yes," Samuel replied, "I did see you briefly from the doorway, but I didn't get to stay too long. Your mother was coming in to see you, so I left. I didn't want to interfere."

"Oh, I understand," Michael said.

Samuel opened his mouth to speak, but nothing escaped. He seemed agitated—like he wanted to avoid the topic. Samuel's eyes began to rapidly scan the room, almost as if he was in search of some kind of Divine guidance. He glanced at the television where ESPN was broadcasting a game. Samuel's head jerked toward Michael, and he asked, "Besides soccer, what are your other favorite sports, Michael?"

Shock erupted across Michael's face. "Well . . . I . . . ahh . . . really like baseball a lot, and since I'm an outdoors kinda person, it's always nice when I get to play soccer, but my dad won't—"

My eyes sprung wide open, and I shook my head as inconspicuously as possible at Michael, while moving closer to the bottom of his bed. Michael's eyes began to tear up, and his shoulders and head slouched as if his chest was imploding with grief.

Samuel's hand lifted, almost as if he was reaching out toward Michael, but instead, he subtly withdrew and forced both hands onto his legs. Silence filled the room like a thick, blinding fog.

Sarah ended the stillness when she said, "You know, Samuel, I was telling Michael, while we were waiting for you two, how much his looks reminded me of yours. It is so uncanny, don't you think? Just look at those eyes!"

Samuel squinted. "Yeah, I see what you mean. In fact, Phillip said my eyes are what made him think I might have some connection to you, Michael. Right, Phillip?"

"Yes, sir," I replied.

Michael leaned forward and looked into Samuel's eyes. "Yeah, I see what you mean," he replied.

I chuckled at how familiar his response was to Samuel's just moments before.

Michael leaned back and said, "You know, I actually look a lot more like you than my dad at home."

Samuel and I smiled at each other.

"Sir," Michael continued, "can I ask you a question that's been bothering me and Phillip?"

Samuel's cheeks puffed outward and retracted. Hesitantly, he replied, "Sure, Michael, I'll do my best to answer."

"Why did you write my mom that letter?"

I was relieved that Michael brought it up.

Samuel seemed to mull over his thoughts before speaking. "Well, Michael, I . . ." One of his legs started to bounce. ". . . I met your mom when she worked at your grandfather's store." He noticed his jittery leg, and pressed his hand down onto it, stopping the motion. "Sometimes, we would write little notes to each other and hide them in a stack of invoices we passed back and forth. We didn't want anyone to know that we had fallen for each other." Samuel shifted in his chair. "Well, after some occasional . . . meetings . . . after work, I walked in one day and she slipped a card into the invoices, but I didn't notice it right away until I got back to work. That's when I learned about her expecting another child."

"But, didn't you know that she was married?" Michael asked.

Samuel shifted again, like some terrified person on the witness stand in a trial. His face turned red. "Well, yes, but I'd heard things weren't very good between your mom and dad, so I thought maybe she might leave him."

Michael rolled his eyes. "Yeah, I wish she would have."

"Anyway," Samuel continued, "I returned the next day, wanting to talk to her, but your grandfather was there, and they were pretty busy, so I quickly shoved my letter into some other work orders, assuming she'd see it. I wrote it just in case we couldn't talk then. Since your mom never responded back, I figured she hated my guts after reading it. I won't deny that I was petrified over what she might do, so I simply avoided going to your grandfather's store until I'd heard she'd quit."

"I guess I can understand that," Michael said.

"I know this might be a lame excuse," he stated, "but I was so scared over everything, and I surely wasn't ready to be a father, especially when the baby's mother was married to someone else. Truthfully, it was easier to just think that she hated me, and never wanted to see me again. I figured if you were mine, she'd get in touch with me."

"I never knew any of this," Michael said.

"No Michael, I didn't suspect that you would." He smiled. "For months, I panicked every time I went to the mailbox," Samuel said. "I was always expecting a letter from an attorney or something. Since I never heard from her, I kind of wondered if you were really my child after all." He cleared his throat. "Well, Michael, since I assumed everything was over between us, I figured I had to move on with my life, and that's when I found Sarah." He glanced up at her, and she smiled. "We got married about a year after your mother and I parted company."

Michael looked up at Sarah. "Did you ever know about me?"

"Yes, Michael," Sarah replied. "Sam told me everything after our daughter was born."

"Believe it or not, Sarah never held it against me," Samuel explained. "She's actually the one who kept persuading me to reach out to you and your mother, but as you can tell, I was too afraid."

Sarah rubbed Samuel's shoulder.

"Boys, Sarah's a remarkable woman, and I hope you guys really get to know her someday outside of this hospital." He reached up and gripped her hand.

"I'd really like that," I said.

"Me, too," Michael responded.

"Michael, even though your mom never got back in touch with me, I guess I sometimes did feel strongly that you were my boy. There were nights I couldn't sleep just because I kept wondering what you were doing, and if you were okay. Every October 23rd, I can hardly function. Just knowing another birthday has gone by—another year I wasn't there for you. It absolutely kills me." His tears returned.

"How did you know that was my birthday, sir?"

"I actually cut your birth announcement out of the paper."

"Oh," Michael said, "so you must have thought I was your kid. But am I, sir?" Michael inquired—his eyes wide with anticipation of the answer he'd hoped to hear.

Sarah glanced at Samuel.

"Well," Samuel's voice trembled, "as I said before, I really don't know the answer to that, Michael. I truly wish I did."

"Well, I guess I'm just being stupid asking it in the first place." Michael replied—his tone doused with disappointment. Sarah glanced at Samuel, her eyes bursting with compassion. "So, why did you come to see me last night?" Michael asked.

Samuel rested his head against the back of the chair and sighed. "Michael, I . . ." He tapped his foot on the floor again. "Michael, I thought I should come and see if you were okay. Sarah was concerned about your condition, and she thought that I should maybe come and—well—look in on you."

"You thought I was gonna die, didn't you?" Michael asked.

I was saddened by the thought that Samuel may never have tried to contact Michael had the incident at the party never happened.

"Oh, God, Michael, I—" Samuel gripped the handles of the chair. "Michael, I—" He thrust his fingers through his hair before looking down at the floor. Samuel whispered, "Yes, Michael, I thought you might . . ." Hesitantly, he looked up. He rubbed his neck and upper chest, acting as if he was trying to force more words from his mouth. Samuel cleared his throat. "Michael, when . . . when I heard that you were really sick, I just . . . well, I thought I should come in to see you." A deluge of tears were on the brink of surging down Samuel's face like an avalanche of snow.

Samuel quickly glanced up at Sarah, who folded her hands and quickly raised them to her mouth, appearing almost as if she was about to pray. Tears streamed down her rosy cheeks. Samuel looked up at the ceiling before squeezing his eyes closed. Tears raced down his pale face as well. He opened his eyes, and his quivering lips could no longer block his silence.

"Michael," he cried out, "I've always wanted to see you—and just—hold you, but I was always too afraid of what you might do, or say to me." Samuel lowered his head and gazed at the floor. "I suspect I might be your dad, but I don't know for sure, Michael." He looked up at my brother. "And we can't count on anything unless we know for sure. I should've fought harder for you long before tonight." His head lowered once more. "I wasn't there for you, and I know I'm such a disappointment to you right now."

Sarah placed her hand on his shoulder and rubbed his back. Their affection toward each other was so genuine.

"Sir . . ." Michael looked up at me before saying, "my dad . . . well . . . you know . . . that letter . . . it caused a lot of—" My brother glanced away.

I was afraid Michael was about to share everything. My survival instinct took control, and I said, "Yeah, but Dad settled down eventually."

Sarah reached over and rested her hand on Michael's arm. "Boys, I'm sure your father wasn't very happy when he found the letter. I think I can understand how he might have felt. It must have been a horrible strain on your parents' relationship."

Michael's head pressed deeper into his pillow, and I saw him roll his eyes. "Well, yeah, I guess you could say that," he said. He looked at me, appearing as if he was upset that Sarah seemed to have sympathy for Dad. Michael's eyes shimmered, and his fingers rushed to them to block tears from escaping. Michael whispered, "You guys have no idea what he—" His hands quickly covered his whole face, and his body shook violently.

Samuel's shoulders sank. Instinctively, he had to have known that Michael must have endured a hellish life at the hands of a bitter, resentful man who had been betrayed by his wife. *How could Samuel possibly be ready to face the horrible, violent truth about my brother's life, and all that he had endured?* I thought.

Samuel started to sob uncontrollably. "I'm so sorry my letter caused all your pain, Michael. I hope you can forgive me! I never meant for anyone to get hurt, especially you." He glanced up at me. "And I'm so sorry, Phillip! I honestly don't know what I can do to make it up to you boys!"

With that agonizing admission, he leaned forward, rested his forehead on the mattress beside Michael's leg, and cried even harder. Michael glanced up at Sarah and watched as she stood over Samuel and stroked the back of his head. She was weeping softly.

After a few minutes, Samuel was able to subdue some of his emotions. He said, "Michael, I know I made a horrible mistake by not immediately going back to your mother when I read the card she gave to me, but I was such a stupid young man at the time, and I was too afraid to own up to my responsibilities. Please, Michael, *please* forgive me for what I did to you."

My eyelashes were soaked, and I wiped them with the sleeve of my shirt.

Before I could say anything, Michael said, "I understand, sir. I guess we all make mistakes we later regret."

To me, it was an unexpected response.

Samuel leaned forward and clasped his hands in front of him. "Now that it's all out in the open, I will do anything I can, and everything I can, to help you and be here for you, Michael. And that includes you, too, Phillip. You have my word, boys. I truly mean that."

Sarah excused herself and stepped out into the hallway, saying she needed to check on something. She was wiping her face with several tissues as she bolted for the door. "Is she okay?" Michael asked Samuel.

Samuel sat up and nodded. "Yes, Michael," he said. "I just think it's been hard to deal with everything happening so fast and all."

"Yeah, I guess so," Michael replied. "Sir," he said, "I hope this doesn't—" He closed his eyes and lowered his chin. "I'm sorry I've kinda made things bad for you and your family right now."

Samuel's hand rested on the mattress, just inches from Michael's forearm. "Oh, God, Michael, please don't think that! We're glad we finally got to meet you. This is just so—well, unexpected." Samuel's hand slipped farther away, and he placed it back onto his own knee. "Michael, I've dreamed more times than you know about having this opportunity, and now that I'm here with you, I'm kind of ashamed that I don't really know what else to say to you. I simply don't know where to begin."

Michael rested his head on the pillow and asked, "Does anyone else in your family know that I might be your son?"

"Well, yes and no, Michael," Samuel replied in a cracked voice. "Please don't take this the wrong way, but we've never told our two kids about you, because we weren't sure if you and I were really related. It would be so confusing for them."

"I guess that makes sense," Michael said.

"Yeah, Samuel," I interrupted. "You can see how well *we're* all handling this whole thing." I smiled at him.

"Thank you for your understanding, boys," Samuel said. "Sarah's father does know about the situation, and he encouraged Sarah to help set up this meeting between us. He's a very understanding man. I think you boys would really like him."

The situation, I thought. *Is that what my brother is to them?*

When Sarah reentered the room, she apologized for her sudden retreat. "I'm so sorry, but I had to check on a few things." Her face was flushed, and I could tell she wanted to avoid returning to the previous conversation, because she asked, "So Michael, do you plan on going to college in the future?"

Michael acted as though he found it refreshing to talk a little about his personal goals. Mom and Dad never cared about our future. "I like math a lot, and Phillip thinks that I should do something like engineering, but I'm not really sure. I have trouble in school sometimes."

"Engineering is a great field to get into, Michael," Samuel affirmed. He stood and moved closer to Sarah. "That's actually one of my degrees from college. My other is in business."

"Sir," Michael inquired, "what exactly do you do for a living? I already know what Sarah does." My brother grinned at her.

"Yes," Sarah responded, "I guess you learned that rather quickly when you woke up and saw me staring at you."

I remembered laughing at Michael over how much Sarah really did know my brother—up close and personal.

"Well, it's a long story," Samuel said, "and I really don't want to bore you with too many details."

Michael and I were intrigued to learn that Samuel had owned his own company for many years. We also learned that Samuel and Sarah met at her father's church after the affair with Mom, but when Michael asked them about their kids, Samuel mentioned very few details. All that we knew was that their names were Megan and Paul.

"So, Michael," Sarah said, "tell me how you came to love soccer so much . . ."

As Sarah and Michael continued to talk, I noticed Samuel staring at Michael again, appearing captivated by the boy resting before him. Michael was the very essence of Samuel's features—almost a carbon copy. Somehow, I'd also felt that there was an emotional connection between them—a real sense that they belonged to each other, but without fully understanding why. Then suddenly, the crimson mark on Michael's cheek caused me to see something different—something I didn't want to remember from the horrible events of the day before. Behind the engaging, handsome looks was the barren shell of a young man desperate to get connected with anyone or anything besides the hatred Dad brought into our lives. Could it be that Michael just needed Samuel's unconditional acceptance? I also noticed again that Samuel's gaze was still fixated on Michael, and maybe his guilt forced him to think that he had no choice but to accept Michael as the possible son he'd left behind from a forbidden love.

". . . Did you hear that, Sam?" Sarah asked.

"Hear what?" Samuel shook his head, returning once more to the conversation. "I'm sorry, I must have gotten distracted. What did you say to me, honey?"

"Michael was telling me that his grandmother was Gladys Williams. She and my mother grew up in the same neighborhood."

"Oh, that's really neat. I guess it is a small world after all," Samuel said.

There was a slight tap at the door. Dottie stepped in to inform Sarah that they were getting several admissions from the emergency room. "The ER supervisor has asked me to assist her. I'm so sorry, but we are going to need your help out here, Sarah."

Sarah suggested that Michael needed to get some rest anyway. Samuel appeared to resist the directive to leave, which was the opposite of his feelings in the lobby earlier that evening. Still a bit hesitant, he stepped closer to Michael and extended his hand. Michael paused, gazing at the trembling hand that was just a few inches away from his chest. My brother raised his hand and grasped Samuel's for the first time. A physical connection had been forged.

Sarah placed her hand on Michael's shoulder and smiled. "Michael," she said, "I'm so sorry that we have to cut this short, but I better get out to the nurses' station. If you need anything, you know I'm close by."

As she turned to leave, Michael continued to grip Samuel's hand, refusing to let go.

"Sarah," Samuel said, "just give us a few more minutes!"

She smiled and replied, "Okay, but my patient needs some rest, so don't be too long." She winked at Michael and walked over and hugged me again. "Thank you for coming here tonight, Phillip," she whispered. "It meant the world to us."

"No problem," I said. "I'm glad I came."

Once she exited, Michael gazed up at Samuel, and then at their joined hands. "Sir . . ."

"Michael, please feel free to call me Samuel . . . if that doesn't make you too uncomfortable."

Michael took a deep breath and said, "Samuel, I was just wondering if I would really get to see you again." Michael released his grip, but not before a tear rolled down his cheek.

"Michael, I would be more than happy to talk with you and Phillip whenever you'd like."

"We can't let our parents know that we met you," Michael said. "They'll be really upset."

"I understand, Michael. I'm fine with this being our little secret. You boys can trust us. I really mean that!"

Michael wiped away a tear. "Yeah, I believe you, but I'm not sure why. I don't trust adults that much."

"Thanks, Samuel," I said, "that really means a lot to us."

Samuel placed his hand on Michael's shoulder. "Michael, I want you to know how much this meant to me tonight. I've waited so long to meet you." He looked over at me. "And, Phillip, I can't thank you enough for being here with us. You are a remarkable young man, and Michael's so fortunate to have you as his brother. I'm honored to get to know you."

"I'm glad we were able to do this too," I said.

My mind sucked me back to the problem I'd left behind at home. *Had my parents discovered I wasn't there?* I wondered.

"Samuel, I know you said you weren't sure if I was your son, but do you feel like I am?" Michael asked.

Samuel seemed to hold his breath. In my heart, I believed that Samuel was convinced that he had just shaken the hand of his firstborn son—instinct had to have revealed it to him. He moved the chair closer and sat beside my brother. "Michael, it's possible that I am your real father, but there are a lot of things we have to go through to see for sure, and I really don't know how to move forward at this moment. There's definitely a way, but it's going to take some time."

"Can't we do a test to find out?" Michael inquired.

"So you do know about such things!" Samuel responded. Michael nodded. "Well," Samuel replied, "I will check for sure, but I think your mom would have to agree to that. Do you think she will?"

Michael's head leaned back onto his pillow. "I doubt it."

"Michael, if this is really what you want, I will get some answers for us."

"Yes, I really wanna know if you're my real dad." Michael gazed at Samuel, whose eyes were nearly bursting with tears again. "Samuel, do you have to leave tonight?"

Samuel reluctantly replied, "Yes, I do have to go, Michael, but I will somehow be in touch with you and Phillip again. Just try to be patient with me while I look into things."

"It's kinda hard to be patient when you live with—"

I wished my brother could have recaptured his words before they reached Samuel's ears. A full confession about the abuse was too dangerous to reveal, even to someone Michael felt he might be able to trust.

"Michael, does your dad make it kind of tough around the house for you boys?" Michael closed his eyes and nodded.

Samuel looked at me, waiting for my response, which I hesitantly offered. "Yeah, Dad can be complicated at times."

Samuel heaved a long sigh. "Just give me time, boys. I'll figure something out." Samuel reached down and grabbed the sheet and pulled it up to Michael's chest. "You get some rest, and I'll be in touch soon. I promise." He placed his hand on Michael's shoulder.

"Thanks. I'll try," Michael replied.

"Are you leaving as well, Phillip?" Samuel asked.

"Yes, sir, I better get back before Dad—" I stopped myself. Samuel had to have known I was hiding something, but he didn't pry.

Samuel shook my brother's hand once more. "Michael, you have no idea how much this has meant to me. I'll never forget this moment as long as I live."

"I won't either," Michael replied, releasing Samuel's hand.

As Samuel and I walked toward the door, he stopped and turned around. I did as well. After a brief chuckle, he said, "Hey, Michael, I guess I just tucked you into bed for the first time."

My brother and I smiled. "Yeah, I guess you did," Michael replied.

"Goodnight, Michael. It sure was a pleasure finally meeting you," Samuel responded.

"Yeah, I'm glad you came to see me."

"Remember, I'll be in touch, Michael. I promise," Samuel insisted, before turning and exiting the room.

As we stepped onto the elevator, and the door closed, Samuel asked, "Phillip, are you going to be in trouble because you came here tonight?"

I leaned against the wall. "Not if my parents don't know that I left."

"I understand," Samuel replied. "I'm going to take you home, but is there some place I can drop you off close to your house?"

"Yeah," I said, "the end of my road would be fine."

Samuel sighed and shook his head. "Phillip, I really am so sorry over all of this mess I've created."

"It's okay, sir. It is what it is."

Samuel reached out and grabbed my arm. "Look, Phillip, I promise that I will do everything I can to get things moving toward getting a paternity test. I want to do everything I can to help you two out."

I extended my hand.

Once he gripped my hand in return, he asked, "Do you think you boys can hold out just a little longer?"

"Yes," I said, "we've managed to get through things this long."

The doors rumbled open. "Phillip, are you seriously going to be safe returning home tonight?"

"I think so."

On the way back to my road, I wanted to tell Samuel everything about the horrible existence we suffered, especially Michael, but I knew the consequences for betraying Dad. I couldn't risk anything at that point. Samuel had to remain a secret. I had to give him the time he needed to get things in order.

Fifteen minutes later, I managed to quietly enter through the kitchen door and retreat to my room. In my mind, I imagined Dad standing outside my bedroom door, waiting on me. I was relieved to see that he wasn't there. After crawling into my bed, I pulled the sheet up to my neck and hoped that my parents had never checked in on me while I was gone.

CHAPTER NINETEEN

As expected, Michael was released from the hospital on Sunday morning. Mom and I went to pick him up. He wasn't supposed to go to school right away; however, avoiding Dad was impossible, so Michael decided to return to school on the Tuesday following his release. Although it was an abnormally peaceful week, it changed when we arrived home that Friday afternoon, and we were met with an interesting comment from Dad after we stepped off of the bus. He was standing in the doorway of the garage and waved for both of us to come over to him. I knew we were being summoned to his version of the Inquisition. Michael and I looked at each other, and I knew we had no choice but to do as Dad wanted.

By the time we approached him, my stomach had done a dozen somersaults. The interrogation started with the comment: "I'd like to thank you two for cleaning out the garage a while back," he smugly said. His sarcasm pierced my chest like a sword.

"You mean when we cleaned it out last Friday?" I questioned.

"No—no—no. I'm talking about a few weeks ago, or at least I guess it was then," he replied.

I wanted to punch the smirk off his face. I looked toward Michael and his throat was pulsating as rapidly as my own heartbeat. "What do you mean?" I asked, looking back at Dad.

From behind his back, he pulled out *the letter*. There was no way to hide the sudden trepidation in both my voice and trembling hands. "I . . . umm . . . I don't understand," I stuttered, before swallowing hard.

"Yeah, I think you do, Phillip. How 'bout you both come into the garage with me so we can take care of a few things." Dad's threats were dripping with rage. "Come on, both of you. This will only take a few minutes." He tapped his Harley-Davidson belt buckle several times.

I glanced over at Michael, soon realizing that neither one of us could move.

"What's the matter, Mikey? Is something bothering you?"

My brother said nothing.

"Why, you sure do seem a little nervous. You're not gonna pee your pants like you used to, are ya?"

"I'm just not feeling too good right now," Michael replied, as tears began to fill his eyes.

"Dad, I don't know what you're talking about," I said, while trying to hide a guilty tone.

"I think you two know exactly what I'm talking about."

"Well, I kinda remember sweeping under the workbench, but I don't remember seeing a letter or anything." I tried to swallow, but my mouth was an arid desert. "Honest, Dad!"

"Oh, so you two *were* snooping around my garage, 'cause I didn't say nothin' about no letter being under the workbench now, did I?"

I glared at Dad. "Umm . . . well, no sir," I replied, as a bead of sweat rolled down from my temple. I licked my lips and wiped the moisture from my brow with my shirtsleeve, knowing I'd screwed up. "We really don't know what you're talking about." I turned toward Michael and asked, "Do we, Michael?"

Dad could always get my brother to confess to anything, because he knew Michael was always terrified over the retribution, especially if he was caught lying. "I had this attached carefully under my workbench, but I found it hanging down towards the floor. You two oughta know by now how I like to keep an eye on my personal things every now and then." Dad clenched his teeth and asked, "Now, are you sure you don't know nothing about this letter being messed with, Mikey?" Dad glared at my brother—a malevolent blackness filled his eyes, exposing his sheer disgust for the boy he likely considered to be the symbol of his dismal failure as a husband, apparently unable to satisfy the desires of his wife.

"Dad, I—"

"Shut up, Phillip!" He stepped closer to Michael. "So, Mikey, how's it feel to know you probably ain't my kid? I guess you might belong to some worthless bum out there who never wanted you in the first place."

My mouth opened slightly because of the cruel, spiteful words spewing from Dad's vile lips.

"I guess you really know you're nothing but a worthless bastard 'cause you ain't sure who your real daddy is. Maybe you're that Samuel's kid . . . and maybe you ain't."

Michael's neck strained from swallowing. He couldn't, or he refused to speak. My words were too timid to leave my mouth. A tear rolled down my brother's cheek as his hands clenched into tight fists. My brother's chest swelled, likely from anger.

"Well, well, well," Dad responded, "you sure look like you're a little upset, boy." Dad looked my direction and said, "You know what, Phillip, how 'bout you leave me and this little bastard alone for a while. I'd like him to understand how disappointed I am in him findin' out about maybe having some other daddy."

He grabbed Michael by the shirt and started to push him into the garage. As the huge garage door lowered, I noticed a large shadow descending down the back wall of the garage. It soon overshadowed about six partially crushed beer cans sitting on the workbench. The deadly cocktail of anger, hatred, and alcohol likely possessed Dad's body like a demonic spirit. He came to the side door. "Get outta here, Phillip!" he demanded. "I'll deal with you soon enough."

He slammed the side door and disappeared into the fading darkness.

"No!" I whispered to myself. "Not this time!" I stepped toward the side door, and with an unstoppable determination emanating from somewhere in my gut, I turned the handle of the door and thrust it open and stepped into the garage. With my fists clenched tightly, I thrust my chest forward and yelled, "No, Dad! You get away from him!"

"*No*?" Dad replied.

His raised eyebrows, and reddened face, seemed to absorb the defiance that was exploding from my lips.

"You heard me, Dad! I'm *not* gonna let you beat him for something he didn't do! It was *my* idea to search for your stupid letter! If you wanna beat someone, why don't you hit me instead!"

I didn't know whether to pat myself on the back, throw up, or run out the door.

"Boy, you're gonna be taken outta here in a body bag if you don't leave right now!"

Dad started to unbuckle his belt.

Once I gazed at Michael's terror-stricken face, I knew I had to stand my ground. With the fury still in my voice, I yelled, "So what are you gonna do, Dad? Are you gonna make him pay for Mom screwing around with some other guy behind your back?"

Dad's nostril flared like a fire breathing dragon ready to scorch everything in sight.

"What kinda sick animal would beat his kid over something he didn't do?" At that point, I was looking for *any* insult I knew would tear Dad's chest wide open. I wanted him to pay. Without hesitating, I yelled, "What's the matter, Dad? Are you upset 'cause Mom decided to go out and spend the night with a decent guy for a change? Maybe she was just tired of a sadistic pig like you!"

Dad pushed Michael away and stormed across the garage. It only took a split second to feel the throbbing pain caused by Dad's closed fist across my mouth. I fell backward about three feet and somehow grabbed on to one of the ladder hooks attached to the side wall. Blood squirted from my lip.

"Don't you hit him!" Michael screamed. "Leave him alone!"

Before my brother could yell another word, Dad punched the side of his head, and Michael dropped to the cement floor like a rock. I quickly regained my balance. He began beating Michael uncontrollably. I tried to stop him, but he threw me backward, and I fell to the floor—hard. Dad was strong when he was in a rage, and he continued his assault on Michael without mercy. *He's going to kill Michael!* I thought. Swing after swing, Michael begged him to stop.

I looked around the garage for something I could use to get Dad to stop his attack. Moments later, I spotted it.

The ax!

It was hanging on the wall next to me. Dad's assault had worsened, so I grabbed the weapon. By then, Dad was in a frenzied rhythm of brutal lashes with his belt.

I had no choice but to end it.

Michael could hardly lift his arms to fight back against the force of Dad's blows. He even kicked Michael in the legs a few times as he continued to swing his thick leather belt, striking Michael any place he knew would cause my brother to scream out in agony. I thought I saw a few kicks to my brother's stomach and chest as well. I had to do something fast. No matter what, I had to stop Dad *forever!* I was willing to sacrifice my freedom to save my brother's life.

I lifted the ax as far as I could over my head. Its sharp, metal blade glistened from the beaming light above the workbench, causing a brilliant glow, like an aura, on the back wall of the garage. A surge of intense fury was discharged throughout my body, like a shockwave rippling out from an explosion. Surprisingly, one unexpected image of someone appeared in my mind as I thrust the ax downward with a violent and fatal swing. I couldn't resist the power I felt.

The sound of the ax striking its target, along with the clanging echo of the belt buckle falling onto the concrete floor, allowed me to know that the brutal attack had ceased. I had spared my brother from certain death. I had stopped my dad from killing him.

The handle of the ax was still firmly gripped by my quaking hands, and I could see veins protruding from my forearms. My breaths echoed throughout the garage as Michael remained curled into a ball, still trying to protect himself from the attack Dad had unleashed on him.

Dad was silent.

In amazement, I stood motionless while observing a portion of the shiny blade of the ax sticking into the top of Dad's workbench. The blade penetrated the surface several inches. It was enough to cause Dad to back away. The unexpected sight of Samuel's image in my head, at the last second, was just enough for me to turn the blade away from Dad's back. As much as I hated Dad, I had to let him live—to possibly see Michael in the embrace of Samuel and Sarah someday soon. It would be far worse than the sentence of death I was about to execute upon him. In an odd sense, Samuel had saved Dad's life.

Even though I had a little trouble removing the ax, I pulled it out and pointed it at Dad. "I told you to stop beating him, and I mean it! Don't you *ever* lay your dirty hands on him again!"

Dad did nothing but grin. He soon released a slight laugh and said, "Phillip, is this the way I raised you to treat your old man? Now you're threatening me with an ax?" He stepped toward me and said, "I think I'm gonna have to teach you a lesson!"

When he started to advance toward me, I raised the ax once more. "Get out of here, or I swear to God you won't have any arms left to hit anybody ever again! I mean it! Get outta here, Dad!"

I raised the ax even higher. The hatred radiating from my eyes must have convinced Dad that I was prepared to do whatever was necessary to protect Michael. For once, I had become an unpredictable pawn in Dad's game of control. Just the uncertainty of my actions was enough to persuade him to leave. He may have been a barbarian, but he wasn't *that* stupid.

"Boy, I ain't gonna forget this!" he warned. "I mean it!" As he started to walk away, he threatened, "You're gonna be mine *real* soon, boy!" I could sense the fury building in his voice.

He opened the side door and exited.

CHAPTER TWENTY

The ax made a revolting, clattering noise on the cement when I dropped it. I helped Michael to his feet. He leaned over on the workbench, barely able to stand. Blood was spewing from his mouth and nose. I practically dragged him out the side door and to the car parked in the driveway. I eased Michael into the front seat. He grimaced and cried out several times when I touched any part of his chest and back.

"He kept . . . ahhhh . . . kicking me," he cried out.

"I'm sorry, Michael, but we have to get outta here before he comes after us!"

Dad always kept a spare set of keys somewhere near his workbench, so I rushed into the garage to find them. My heart raced. I was frantic to find the right set. Several times I glanced over at the door, expecting Dad to ambush me. My hands shook so hard that I could barely hold onto the keys once I'd found them. I dropped them twice while rushing to the car.

"Phillip, I—" Michael clutched his chest. "I'm having trouble breathing, man!" The front of his shirt was soaked with blood. Once the engine roared to life, I peeled out of the driveway—hurling gravel like debris from an erupting volcano.

As I sped down the road, I didn't have any clue where I was going, but I knew it had to be away from Dad. Frustrated, I hollered, "*Where to now?*"

Michael gagged several times. I pulled him over to my shoulder and wrapped my arm around him to secure his body against mine. "Take me to Samuel," he faintly murmured, "I wanna go see Sa—" Michael coughed, and seconds later—nothing.

"You gotta hold on, Michael!" I pleaded. I tried desperately to keep my eyes on both my brother and the road. "God, I don't know what to do!"

I didn't even know exactly where Samuel lived, but I realized I had no choice but to get my brother to the hospital once again. There was no turning back.

Several miles down the road, flashing red lights appeared in my rearview mirror. I knew I had been swerving from lane to lane, struggling to hold onto Michael. I pulled the car over as best I could. As he cautiously approached my car, the officer ordered me to turn off the motor and toss the keys onto the road.

"I can't," I hollered back. "I need help! My name is Phillip Williams, and my brother is injured! *Please help us!*"

One of the two officers recognized my name for some reason. He rushed to the car, and once he saw my brother's condition, he called for an ambulance. The other officer quickly opened the passenger side door and held onto Michael.

"Phillip," the other officer ordered, "I still need you to toss the keys out of the vehicle and step out." I did as he commanded. "Please come with me to the back of the vehicle and stay there."

He soon joined the other officer attending to Michael.

Beads of sweat clung to my forehead, and my stomach was ready to eject whatever I'd had for lunch. I couldn't believe I was about to invite the police into another investigation involving my family. I waited for several minutes before one of the officers approached me and introduced himself.

Even though I'd recognized him, Officer Bailey said, "Phillip, why don't you tell me what happened to your brother."

My lips quivered, and several tears tumbled down my flushed cheeks. "Sir, my brother—well, he got into a fight." My head drooped toward the ground.

"With you?" he questioned.

"No, sir, he . . ." I struggled to force the words from my mouth.

"Who beat him up, Phillip?"

Unable to glance up at the officer, I whispered, "Our dad, sir." They were condemning words that had taken flight—never to return to my mouth.

"Tell me what happened, Phillip."

I looked through the back window at Michael. "Sir, is the ambulance coming? I really need to get Michael to the hospital!"

I tried to distract Officer Bailey from the truth, but he was determined to find out what had happened to us.

"The ambulance is coming, Phillip, but I need to know how your brother was injured. What happened?" he insisted.

I sighed before rolling my head upward and glancing at the dimming afternoon sky. "Sir, my dad . . . he was upset over something, and he . . ." I leaned forward and rested my elbows on the trunk of the car. My head collapsed into my hands. "I shouldn't be doing this," I whispered.

Officer Bailey placed his hand on my shoulder. "Doing what, Phillip?"

"Telling you this. It's gonna cause me and Michael a whole lot of problems."

I could hear the faint sound of a siren in the distance.

"Look, Phillip, you stay right here. I need to get your car keys."

Officer Wallace, who was attending to Michael, continued to help my brother until the ambulance pulled up beside us. Michael was conscious when the paramedics pulled him from the car and placed him onto a gurney. His wails of pain were gut-wrenching.

As the ambulance pulled away, Officer Bailey assisted me into the backseat of the police car. "We need to follow the ambulance to the hospital, Phillip," he said.

His partner locked up our car before getting into the front seat of the police cruiser. Officer Bailey tried to make small talk, but *anything you say, can, and will be used against you* was drumming its familiar mantra into my conscience.

"Hey, Phillip, you go to Westview High School, right?"

I was almost too afraid to answer. "Yes, sir."

"My daughter goes there. I'm pretty sure you know her."

"Yes, sir, you're Brooke's dad, right?"

"Yes, Phillip, I am. Didn't you and your friend stop at my house this past summer?"

"Yeah, she was going out with one of my friends."

"I thought so. When you yelled your name back there, that's when I thought it might be you, but I wasn't sure right away."

"Yeah, I thought I recognized you. You've been at my house a couple times," I said.

"Yes, I know, Phillip, but can you tell me what happened to your brother? It will help if the hospital knows how he was injured."

I saw Officer Bailey staring at me in the rear view mirror. Hesitating at first, I thought about Michael curled into a ball, trying to protect himself from Dad's ferocious attack. I knew it was time to garner the support I needed to get my brother away from Dad forever. I knew I couldn't do it alone.

"Officer Bailey," I nervously answered, "I really thought my dad was gonna kill my brother today!" With my head bowed, I admitted, "I grabbed an ax and threatened my dad because—" My fingers rushed to my eyes, frantically trying to stop my tears. "I just knew he wasn't gonna stop beating Michael." I lifted my shirt and wiped my eyes. "Sir, it was really bad. I've never seen Dad beat my brother like that before." I began to cry from the overwhelming fear of being arrested for what I would consider attempted murder. "Sir, I couldn't let him take my brother away from me! I just couldn't! Michael's all I have in this rotten world."

"Son," Officer Bailey said, "right now I need to know what he did to Michael. We'll sort out the facts about why it happened when we get to the hospital, but it sounds to me like you were protecting your brother in self-defense. Just tell me what he did to your brother."

I explained the incident in detail, terrified still that I was in trouble for having gone after Dad with a weapon. For several agonizing seconds, we rode in silence before I asked, "Sir, could you let a guy named Samuel Roberts know that we are going to the hospital again?"

"Are you talking about the guy who owns that factory on the edge of town?"

"Yes, sir. That's him."

"Well, I know Sam. How do you know him?"

"Well, it was this whole big secret my mom kept from us for years," I answered. "She had an affair with him a long time ago, and we think Michael might be Samuel's son instead of my dad's. We found this letter about a month ago, and Dad found out we read it. That's what the fight was all about today. Dad's pretty sure Michael knows the truth about Samuel now."

Somehow, now that I had started talking, I couldn't stop. All of the family secrets I'd been keeping inside for so long were spilling from my lips like I'd been given a truth serum.

"Well, I'll be. I didn't know Sam had another son."

"It's a big secret, sir. Please don't tell anyone! It could get Samuel and us into a lot of trouble! My dad's an animal, and I don't want him going after Samuel, especially if he finds out that Michael got to meet him in the hospital last weekend."

"Yeah, Phillip," Officer Bailey replied, "I've been in on the investigation about the overdose. You nearly lost your brother last week according to what I've learned."

"I know, sir."

"I understand your concern, son," Officer Bailey said, before he pressed the talk button on his radio. "Hey, Marsha, could you somehow get Sam Roberts on the phone and give him a message for me?"

"You mean the one who owns Roberts Industries?" the dispatcher asked.

"Yeah, that's him," he replied. "Tell him to come to the hospital emergency room to meet me. We're taking in a Michael Williams right now, and I know he knows him. I have his brother, Phillip, in the car with me."

By the time we pulled into the parking lot, the dispatcher had informed us that Samuel and Sarah were on their way to meet us. The feeling of security bathed me with a sense of real peace for the first time that day. I needed them just as badly as Michael.

We saw my brother being removed from the ambulance. Minutes later, he was rolled into a small area sectioned off with a curtain in the emergency department. I could barely stay in the room with him as he shrieked when the nurse pressed on certain sensitive areas. My whole body shook, and I was getting nauseated from the sight of my brother's blood. Before I retreated into the hallway, Michael threw up all over the front of his clothing and onto the bed.

After pacing the floor in the hallway for about ten minutes, I heard the comforting voices of Samuel and Sarah coming through the double doors. My strength was resurrected. Officer Bailey was still there to greet them. Both Samuel and Sarah embraced me and asked what had happened. As I described the attack, we heard screams coming from behind the curtain where Michael was being treated. We dashed over. Sarah grabbed my hand.

Moved by her compassion, I sobbed. I leaned onto her shoulder and cried out, "Can't you do something to help him, Sarah?"

"Phillip, I know the staff, and they will do everything for him. He looks worse than he probably is. He's a tough boy."

Samuel walked over and said, "Phillip, you need to calm down now, because Michael needs to see you being strong for him."

"I understand, sir. I'll try." I wiped my face with a tissue he had handed to me. When I looked up again, I saw that I had ruined Sarah's shirt with the blood that was all over me from Michael. "Oh God, I'm really sorry," I said.

She smiled, and hugged me.

CHAPTER TWENTY-ONE

Officer Bailey stayed as long as he could in order to follow up on what had happened to Dad. He also seemed particularly interested in speaking with Mom. I could only guess the kind of lies she was planning to say in Dad's defense. Dad's attack on us, along with his belligerent behavior after the police arrived to investigate, forced him into a weekend retreat in the county jail. Without Samuel and Sarah being there with me, there would have been no way I could have spent another night alone, wondering whether Michael would be okay. Mom wasn't making a frenzied rush to come to the hospital, and according to Officer Bailey, she was almost arrested for interfering with Dad's arrest.

Sarah was sitting next to me when the doctor stepped into the hallway and informed us that Michael was going to stay the night for further observations and tests. The doctor asked me why my mom wasn't there, but I honestly didn't know what to say to her. Samuel left again to check on Michael after the doctor went to another room to see a different patient. After a few moments of silence, I noticed that Sarah's demeanor was somewhat distant, which was strange for her. I wondered if she was having second thoughts about getting involved. Perhaps she was concerned about her own children? After all, she didn't know me that well, and already, my brother and I had upset the delicate balance of her secure life.

I lowered my forehead onto the palms of both of my hands and sighed. "Man, my head is really pounding," I whispered. "I can't go through this anymore, Sarah." *Would she take the bait and open up to me again?*

Sarah gazed up at the ceiling and forced a puff of air from her mouth. Her eyes closed, as if asking for Divine intervention. She reached over and patted my back. "It's okay, Phillip. It's been a difficult day."

I was relieved she'd responded.

She placed her arm around my shoulders and pulled me over to her side. My head soon found sanctuary on her shoulder. She lowered her cheek onto the top of my head and whispered, "I know what you're thinking, Phillip, and no, Sam and I aren't going anywhere."

I sniffled. "Thank you, 'cause I don't know what else to do. We don't have anybody."

As Sarah was rubbing my upper arm, Mom arrived and saw us. I pulled away from Sarah when I saw Mom's glare. I'm not sure how she got there, but she looked as though she had just rolled out of bed and threw on whatever was crumpled on the bedroom floor.

"Oh man," I mumbled.

Samuel walked into the hallway and stopped like he'd run into a wall. His eyes protruded from their sockets, as did Mom's. She stormed over and grabbed my arm. Her fingernails were like spikes, digging into my flesh as she pulled me down the hallway. I was forced into a small room where there were vending machines.

Mom thrust her finger into my face and screamed, "What is *he* doing here? And isn't that lady the same nurse from last week? Tell me why she had her scrawny arm around you, Phillip?"

I managed to yank my arm away from her. "Mom, Michael just wanted Samuel to be here, and his wife came with him." The sting from her slap caused my head to jerk to one side. "What was that for?"

"You told him what happened, didn't you?"

While massaging my cheek, I bellowed, "Come on, Mom, we needed *someone* here with us. It's not like Michael would want that drunken bast—"

She slapped me again. "How dare you do this kind of thing to me, Phillip! Now I'm sure he knows all about us!" She thrust her hand to her forehead. "You pathetic backstabber!"

"Look, Mom," I yelled, "where were you last week when we thought

Michael was dying? You were at home getting high and drunk with those worthless idiots you guys call friends!"

Mom jammed her hands onto her hips.

"And what about today? You hid in the house while Dad was killing Michael in the garage! And now you have the nerve to be ticked at me for having a decent man like Samuel come here to be with us?"

My knuckles instantly throbbed from the pain I felt after hitting the solid wall beside me. "Seriously, Mom, what is *wrong* with you? You're supposed to be the one protecting us!"

Mom pushed me against one of the vending machines and pounded on my chest with her fists. "I never wanted to see that jerk ever again! How could you do this to me, Phillip?"

I grabbed her wrists. "Do what to you?"

She struggled to free her hands. "Mom, this doesn't have anything to do with you! You haven't even gone in to see Michael yet! You're more concerned about some guy you haven't seen in years! Why are you like this?"

She jerked her arms away from me and bolted out of the small room. Samuel told me later that Mom ignored him when she rushed by him and Sarah before calling out my brother's name. A nurse pointed her to the correct area where Michael was recovering. She darted straight over to Michael and tried to give him a hug. "Oh, honey, are you okay?" she asked.

I walked back into the hallway and up to Sarah, who grabbed my arm and whispered, "Phillip, your face is really red. Did she hit you because we're here?"

I nodded.

She ran her hand along the side of my face. "I'm so sorry, Phillip."

I walked into the small room and heard Michael say, "Not now, Mom! Just leave me alone!"

I wasn't sure if he didn't want her touching him due to the pain, or if he was too angry to deal with her. Either way, it worked because Mom stepped back and held her hand to her mouth—shocked by his words.

The doctor walked in behind me and patted my shoulder. She glanced at Mom and asked, "Are you Mrs. Williams?"

"Yeah, I'm his mother!" Mom's eyes shot me a look of disgust.

"I understand that it was his father who inflicted the injuries on him this afternoon," the doctor stated.

"Well, I wasn't there in the garage with them, so I don't know how he got hurt."

The doctor glared at Mom. "Are you suggesting that your son inflicted these injuries on himself?"

Mom was silent.

"Mrs. Williams, it would help us even more if I knew exactly what happened so that I can have a better idea about other possible injuries, especially to his head." The doctor glanced over at me. "Can you provide us with more information, young man?"

I looked at Mom, and then at the doctor. "Yes ma'am. My dad kicked him in the stomach, chest, legs, and he beat him pretty badly with a belt all over his body. He hit my brother in the head, too, and he fell on the cement floor pretty hard."

I was expecting flames to shoot from Mom's nostrils. She folded her arms and shifted her weight. "Does that sound accurate, Mrs. Williams?" the doctor asked.

"I told you I wasn't out there, but I guess that might have happened. I don't know! My sons wrestle and play around all the time, so Phillip could have injured him for all I know."

"Are you kidding me, Mom? *Really?* You're so pathetic!" I turned to the doctor and replied, "Yes, it's accurate. My dad almost beat my brother to death today. He's abused Michael for years!"

Mom pointed at me. "You lying son of a—"

The doctor raised her eyebrows.

"I am so done with this!" Mom stormed out of the room.

Several times throughout the evening, Michael whimpered when anyone pressed too hard on one of his injuries. After moving Michael to a room, I noticed that Samuel's fists would clench, his lips would press together, and his sighs would grow louder as Mom pouted in the corner.

Michael kept gagging from the sight of his own blood coming from the packing they kept pulling from his nose and replacing with new. Dad didn't break his nose, but the source of the blood was still a concern for me. Michael reached out for my hand as the nurse started repacking some gauze into one of his nostrils.

"I can't go through this anymore, man!" He started to cry. "Somebody's gotta get me away from that sick pig."

"Michael, I know people are taking care of that here, but you have to let them do their job," Samuel reassured.

Mom sprang up in her chair. "What is that supposed to mean?"

As her abrasive words ricocheted around the room like a stray bullet, Michael wailed when the nurse pressed too hard on his nose. Tears streamed down his face and dripped onto his gown.

His pleading eyes turned my direction, and I whispered, "I'm sorry it hurts, man. Just hang in there."

As Michael squeezed my hand, I thought how much I wanted Dad to die.

Mom bolted from the room and slammed the door.

Minutes later, Sarah quietly entered. She walked over and grasped Samuel's hand and looked at us. "Hi, boys. Your mom took off down the hallway, so I thought I would come in and check on you guys."

"Mom's just ticked off that everyone's ignoring her, and I don't think she really liked it when the officer talked to her earlier," I said. "She wouldn't tell me what he asked her."

Sarah stepped over to me and took my hand. "How about you and I head down to the gift shop and grab a few new shirts."

Like a contagious disease, the blood on my shirt had also spread to Samuel's as well. I apologized again.

Sarah smiled and said, "It's not like I haven't had this type of thing happen before. Will you come with me, Phillip?"

"Sure, I guess I could use the fresh air," I replied. As we walked toward the door, I suddenly stopped and said, "Sarah, I don't have any money on me again."

"Oh, and neither do I," she chuckled. She walked over to Samuel and held out her hand.

He grinned and handed her his wallet.

"I will buy all of us matching shirts." She grinned. "That way, everyone will know that we belong to the same gang."

Samuel smiled at her.

"I'm going to buy one for you too, Michael."

"Thanks," Michael said. As we turned to leave, surprisingly, my brother snickered and said, "Hey, make sure you buy Phillip an extra small shirt; everything else will be too big on him."

We laughed, and Sarah and I left the room, leaving Michael and Samuel alone.

CHAPTER TWENTY-TWO

A social worker arrived to speak with us concerning our fight with Dad. Mom's demeanor had deteriorated when she stepped back into the room and saw someone new. Obnoxious sighs, the abrupt folding of her arms, and the slamming of her foot to the floor when crossing her legs were just a few of Mom's ways of making sure we knew that she was there. Samuel and Sarah had planned to step out when the social worker walked in, but Michael insisted that they stay. "This is none of *their* business, and I want them to leave!" Mom bellowed at one point.

The tone for the meeting had been set.

In the past I wouldn't want to make a scene, but anger was clawing its way up my throat from somewhere deep in my gut. "Yeah, Mom, even when it was *your business*, you never seemed to care!"

"Don't you dare speak to me like that, Phillip!"

Sarah stepped out into the hallway, while Samuel stayed, lowering his head in shame.

Mom glared at me, as her hands clenched shut.

We were in the presence of the social worker, so I knew Mom would do her best to be somewhat restrained. At least her upbringing, from what I'd heard, had taught her that.

She looked at the social worker and argued, "I just don't understand why *he* gets to stay in here while we discuss personal family business. After all, my husband isn't here to defend himself against you guys. And besides, who knows what my sons have already said about him before I came back into the room?"

Michael yelled, "Who do you think beat me up, Mom? Do you think I did this to myself?" He turned toward me and demanded, "Phillip, get her outta here! I'm done with her!"

"Why should I have to leave?" she protested. You're *my* son!" She pointed at Samuel and insisted, "*He's* the one who should get out!" She threw her arms into the air. "After all, I'm not the one who abandoned you all those years ago, Michael!"

Michael struggled to sit up. He pointed directly at Mom. "Ever since Dad found out I might not be his kid, he's beaten me every chance he got! You never try to stop him! You *always* leave me, Mom!" Michael began to cry. "You have no idea what he did to me every time you turned your back and walked away! Didn't you hear me yelling for you all those nights?" Michael's whole body trembled. "You *never* came for me, Mom! Not even the night he showed you that letter and dragged me all over the house before he threw me in my room!" Michael gripped the sheet. "*Why?* Why didn't you come for me?" Michael sat straight up in his bed. "He hurt me all the time, Mom! Didn't you see the blood on my clothes after he beat me sometimes?" He crumpled the sheet in his fists. "*I hate you!*"

Michael fell back against the mattress and sobbed. I reached over and placed my hand on his shoulder as Samuel buried his face in his quaking hands. Michael had finally started to purge his troubled soul.

Mom started to walk toward my brother, but Michael moved back and screamed, "*Don't touch me!* Just leave me alone! I mean it!" He looked at me and demanded, "Get her away from me, Phillip!"

Mom thrust her hand to her mouth before turning and running from the room. The social worker followed her. Michael tugged on my arm and pulled me closer to the bed. I sat on the mattress next to him.

I handed him a few tissues. "You were just telling the truth, Michael. Mom needed to hear it."

I glanced over at Samuel—his face was still entombed in his hands. His guilt had to be crushing him.

CHAPTER TWENTY-THREE

The embittered expression on the social worker's face, when she returned to the room, meant that she had likely grown weary of Mom's usual inability to take responsibility for anything concerning Michael's abuse. She told us that Mom was still sitting in the lobby, and she had refused to come with her after they'd talked. I was glad Mom wasn't with her.

Sarah had also entered the room with the social worker and stood beside Samuel.

He reached over and squeezed Sarah's hand. Samuel also reached out and placed his hand on the top of Michael's forearm. I was concerned that my brother would pull away, but he didn't. "Michael, this is all my fault!"

Sarah gently rubbed the back of Samuel's head, running her fingers through his hair.

"Regardless of whether you're my son or not, Michael, I caused an innocent boy to suffer for my mistakes." He wiped his eyes. "I can't believe I abandoned you to that sadistic—" He stopped and squeezed Michael's hand. "Michael, I don't know how I'm going to live with this! It kills me to see what he did to you today—all because of that letter!"

Sarah knelt beside Samuel and said, "Honey, God works in mysterious ways; you know that!"

Samuel leaned back, releasing Michael's hand. He glared at Sarah. "God didn't cause the abuse; *I did!* Michael paid for *my* mistakes! He paid for all of them while I just walked away, like a pathetic coward!"

Sarah placed her hand on Samuel's knee. "I know what you're trying to say, Samuel, but no one would have ever guessed that an almost fatal overdose would have brought you two together for the first time. God used the bad things in Michael's life to guide him to us in a way we never expected. We can't change the past; we can only embrace what could be."

Michael glanced up at me and said, "Nana Gladie used to say something like that."

Sarah smiled at us as she stood. "Michael, you might not believe this right now, but I know that no matter what, Sam will be an exceptional friend to both of you."

"Yeah, we could use one," I said.

Sarah leaned over. "Michael, we are going to be here for you no matter what."

I knew it had to be a terrifying risk for Sarah to say that.

"Sarah, my parents aren't gonna make it easy," I said.

Samuel leaned forward and placed his hand on Michael's forearm again. "We know, guys," he said, "but God will work it out somehow."

I was concerned over where we would go when Michael was released, so I asked. The social worker informed us that my brother could only be released into the custody of a legal guardian, such as a close relative—if one could be located. The other option was a foster home. We had no one to turn to except Grandma and Grandpa Stewart, but Michael and I didn't even know them. Aunt Sylvia, Mom's sister, was definitely not an option, because we knew Mom wouldn't leave us alone if Michael was with her.

"God, Phillip," Michael said, "I don't wanna go to some strange foster home."

"What about our grandparents?" I reluctantly asked.

Michael's head fell back onto his pillow, and his head rolled in my direction. "We don't even know them, Phillip."

"I know, but they might be better than a foster home," I said. I turned to the social worker. "Their names are Jack and Madeline Stewart. They own Stewarts Home Improvement Center." I chuckled, as I glanced at Michael and said, "How ironic! It's not like they ever helped improve *our* home."

Michael moved, causing him to clench his teeth and grab his side.

Samuel flinched, as if he was hurting right along with Michael.

After telling us that she needed to speak again to our mom before contacting our grandparents, the social worker left the room. Samuel and Sarah stayed with Michael while I went to see Mom as well.

In the lobby, I stood several feet away from Mom while the social worker sat next to her and said, "Mrs. Williams, I know you're upset over everything taking place tonight, but I really need some information from you regarding your son."

"Are you sure he still wants me as his mother?" Mom grumbled.

"Mrs. Williams," the social worker said while placing her hand on Mom's knee, "I am here to help you as well, and I really need you to help me do the best job I can for you and your sons."

"Having my son at home is the best thing you can do for me!" Mom insisted.

"Mrs. Williams, please feel free to call me Beth."

Mom asked, "Do you think Michael still loves me?"

"Mrs. Williams, you are Michael's mother no matter what, but can you try and understand his feelings right now? He's confused, angry, scared, and hurting all at the same time. He needs every adult around him to be loving and supportive no matter what."

"Yeah, I suppose," Mom replied. "I'm sure you think I'm nothing but a piece of garbage right about now."

"It is not my job to judge anyone," Beth replied. "We all have choices, and for some reason, perhaps you thought you had none."

"I guess," Mom said. Her next words were little more than a whisper. "You have no idea what he's like behind closed doors."

Beth grasped Mom's hand, causing her to flinch. "Mrs. Williams, let's focus on what's best for Michael right now, and we can certainly get you some help as well." The social worker glanced up at me. "The boys said they have grandparents that Michael might be able to stay with for a while."

"He's *definitely* not staying with them!" Mom protested. "And there's no way I will ever let my son stay with Sam and that woman he's married to! I shook my head and resisted the urge to yell at the soulless woman I had been glaring at since I entered the lobby.

"Mrs. Williams, because of so much uncertainty, Michael can't go home until we know that he is safe. Emotionally, I don't think he can return there right now anyway. Just the sight of the garage will be very traumatic for him, especially since we suspect that he may already be suffering from some form of PTSD. Please understand that I can only release Michael into the custody of either a relative, like a grandparent, or I'll simply have to look into a foster home until we can get a final decision, which could take some time. I believe his grandparents would be the best alternative for right now."

"Michael doesn't even know them, so I don't think he should go there," Mom argued. "Besides, my father can be mean, too. Maybe a foster home would be best for now."

My heart slammed into my ribs. "Seriously, Mom?" I threw my hands into the air and stormed away.

Beth spoke in a firm tone that settled the matter. "I'm going to contact his grandparents first."

While we waited for our grandparents to arrive, Sarah decided to return home. Michael was adamant about Samuel staying with him, especially since he was about to meet our grandparents for the first time. Mom also returned to Michael's room once she knew that our grandparents were coming. Samuel was growing weary of Mom's obnoxious stares, but he still chose to stay for a while longer. Beth continued to step in and out of the room, waiting on our grandparents to arrive.

About forty-five minutes later, I heard chatter in the hallway, and when I looked, our grandparents were standing in the doorway. Our grandfather grasped Grandmother's hand. Their feet seemed to be glued to the floor. Samuel walked over and greeted them with a handshake. Grandpa's chest seemed to collapse from relief, as Grandma and he walked toward us. Grandma Madeline shook while she hugged me, and her kiss was moist against my tender cheek. Grandpa's hand was clammy when he shook mine. When he turned away, I wiped my hand on my jeans, trying to look inconspicuous. Their greeting was warm and inviting, even though I felt numb inside—like I wasn't there but was watching the scene from overhead, wondering how it would all work out. I couldn't return the affection like I'd wanted, but I still greeted them with a smile.

Grandpa turned and stepped over to Michael and asked, "So, how are you feeling there, Mike?"

Michael glanced at me before saying, "I guess, okay, sir."

Grandma walked over and kissed my brother. "I'm Grandma Madeline, Michael, and I'm so happy to finally meet you."

I stared at Michael, waiting for him to respond. Michael smiled. I happened to see Mom rolling her eyes just as I glanced over at her.

Grandma reached into her pocket and pulled out a tissue, which she used to wipe her swollen, wet eyes. Several times, she glanced at Michael and me before saying, "My . . . my . . . you boys are so handsome, and so grown up." She turned away.

My grandparents never acknowledged Mom, who was still sitting off by herself—sulking. I'm not certain whether it was deliberate or whether they didn't know what to say to her. I could see Mom fidgeting in her chair, causing it to move slightly from the force.

Beth said that the visiting hours were nearly over, but she also insisted that it was important for us to spend time with our grandparents.

"I'm not leaving my son alone with strangers!" Mom insisted.

Samuel interrupted the impending tantrum. "Michael, I do have to be going, and I know you're in good hands here."

Michael's eyes flooded with tears. "Please, can't you stay a little longer, Samuel?"

Mom mumbled, "What am I?" under her breath.

No one reacted to her self-pity.

She abruptly folded her arms and slammed her back against the chair, causing it to scoot backward into the wall with a thud.

Samuel gently placed his hand on my brother's arm and said, "As much as I would like to stay, Michael, Beth is right, and you need some alone time with your family."

They shook hands as Samuel winked and smiled.

Grandpa Jack said, "Sam, you know that you're welcome to stop by the house any time."

Mom's reddened face was priceless.

I wanted to walk out into the hallway with Samuel; however, I didn't dare leave Michael alone with Mom and my grandparents. Samuel and I waved and said good-bye as he disappeared around the corner. I suppressed the fear that he was growing weary of the drama unfolding in what I assumed was his comfortable, normal life.

Once more, Beth reassured Mom that Michael was going to be fine, but he did need some time to visit with our grandparents.

"Well, I don't like this whole thing, but since *my son* obviously doesn't want me around anymore, I guess I should go."

"Come on, Mom, did you have to say that?" I barked.

"Whatever," she grumbled.

Grandma grabbed the railing on the bed, and I noticed her labored breathing.

"I just hope that no one turns *my* son against me over this ridiculous bull—" Mom stopped talking.

Showing greater restraint than I had expected, our grandparents remained silent.

"Mrs. Williams," Beth said, "please try your best to keep calm. It is important that Michael and Phillip get to know their grandparents better, especially given the circumstances."

Mom glared at the social worker. "Well, I just think this whole thing has been blown out of proportion. It's two against one in my opinion. Tony even said that Phillip swung an ax at him!"

Grandma gasped, and her hand covered her gaping mouth.

"For God's sake, Mom!" My hands clamped shut. "I did it to get that sick animal off of Michael before he killed him!"

The social worker grabbed my arm. "Phillip, you need to settle down, or I'm going to have to ask you and your mother to leave. We can't disturb the other patients."

Mom stormed toward the door. "That's fine with me! It's obvious that you boys don't love me anymore," she yelled. "I'm going to go wait in the lobby!" As she walked away, she said, "Don't keep me waiting too long, Phillip." Seconds later, Mom vanished.

I released my grip and leaned my back against the wall. I raised the palms of my hands and pressed them against my temples, trying to relieve some of the pain.

Grandma walked over and placed her hand on my shoulder. "Honey, I'm so sorry that you boys have had to put up with so much."

My arms tumbled to my sides. "I'm sorry ma'am, but it was pretty bad this afternoon."

"Phil," Grandpa interrupted, "we're not about to let that ever happen again." He turned to Beth and asked, "Ma'am, is Phil old enough to decide where he wants to go, because he is more than welcome to come with us tonight."

"If Phillip would like, I see no reason why he shouldn't stay with you folks. That is up to him, though," Beth confirmed. "I will have to let his mother know what he decides."

My heart fluttered, and I glanced at Michael. He nodded and said, "Forget about Mom, Phillip, you should go with them!"

"I don't know," I said, while looking at my grandparents. "Please don't take this the wrong way, but . . ." I was trapped again between a sense of duty to Mom, and not wanting to hurt my grandparents. I spent years wanting to leave my house, but I suddenly found myself too afraid to go somewhere else.

"Phil," Grandpa said, "if you don't feel right leaving your mom this evening, I completely understand. You can always settle things at home and come to our house whenever you're ready. We would love to have you stay."

"Maybe you're right, sir. Besides, I don't have any clean clothes with me," I said. "Maybe it would be best to just go with her tonight and then come over when Michael gets released from the hospital."

I didn't think I could have stayed with my grandparents unless Michael was there with me.

"No problem, Phil," Grandpa said. When he turned back to Michael, he asked, "So, Mike, how long do they think you'll be in here?"

"I hope I get out tomorrow, sir." Michael grunted when he shifted in the bed. "I'm still hurtin' pretty bad."

"Yeah," I said, "Dad really worked him over this afternoon, but—" I stopped. I didn't really want to talk about the fight again in front of them.

"Michael, I'm so sorry it took something like this to bring us together," Grandma said. "It's our fault for not getting involved in your life years ago!"

"Our dad probably wouldn't have allowed it," Michael replied.

Grandma grasped my brother's hand and said, "I'm so glad you'll be coming to our place soon. We have a lot of catching up to do."

Michael smiled. "Yeah, I guess we do."

After one of the most awkward thirty minutes of my life, Mom came to the doorway and demanded that it was time for us to go.

Grandma cleared her throat and said, "Yes, Jack, it is probably time for us to go as well. Michael looks very tired."

She grabbed her purse and leaned over to give Michael a kiss.

Mom must have felt she should do the same, so she brushed by Grandma and leaned over the bed to kiss Michael as well. He turned his head and her lips ended up making contact with his ear. Her exasperation was announced by a long sigh.

Grandma headed for the door. "Jack, are you coming?"

"Just give me a minute, Madeline. Meet me down in the lobby."

Grandma waved at us and left.

"Phillip," Mom demanded, "I really want to leave *right now*!" She started for the door. "I'll be in the car."

"Hey, Ellen," Grandpa said, never making eye contact with her.

Mom stopped.

"It was good seeing you," he said.

Mom said nothing and walked out the door.

Grandpa Jack stepped closer to Michael's bed. I moved to the other side. He reached for the handkerchief in his back pocket. "Boys, I know you probably think I'm some kind of cantankerous old geezer, but I . . ." He paused and grinned. "Well, I guess maybe I am." He wiped his nose and declared, "But I want you to know I really am looking forward to getting to know you two. I've waited too long, and I hope someday you'll be able to forgive me." He wiped a tear from his cheek.

"I appreciate you taking us in, sir. I really don't wanna go back home," Michael replied.

Grandpa Jack extended his arm toward Michael and they shook hands. "Well," Grandpa said, "I guess now it's a deal then."

"What is?" Michael asked.

I, too, was perplexed by his statement.

"That we are all officially partners in crime." Grandpa chuckled.

Michael's bewildered expression caused Grandpa Jack to smile.

"I don't understand, sir," my brother said.

"Well, now I have someone else at the house who can help me drive your grandmother crazy. We have a lot of planning to do, boys. Your grandmother and I only had girls, so she's going to get a taste of what it's like having a couple boys around."

Michael grinned. "Oh, I see what you mean."

"Sure," Grandpa replied. "I know that we're all going to get along just fine." He smiled at me, so I returned the gesture.

Grandpa Jack put his hand on Michael's shoulder. "Yeah, after what you boys told us about your life at home, you two can't be split up. Besides, we wouldn't have it any other way." Grandpa patted my brother on the shoulder and said, "Look, you seem pretty worn out, so I better let you get some rest. Your grandmother will be all over me for keeping you up. We'll see you first thing in the morning." He reached over and shook my hand. "Phil," he said,

"I'm glad that social worker called and asked if we could take you two in. We should have done this a long time ago."

"Yeah, me and Phillip have missed out on a lot, sir," Michael said.

"You know, boys, you can call me Grandpa Jack—if you're comfortable with that. I know I haven't earned your respect enough for you to be so polite in calling me 'sir.'"

Michael beamed as he replied, "Sure, Grandpa Jack."

After patting Michael's knee, Grandpa took several steps away from the bed and paused. He suddenly turned and stepped back to Michael. He bent down and gave my brother a hug. He stood straight up and said, "You know, Mike, I really am terribly sorry for not being there for you, and I'm going to make it up to you boys somehow. I promise."

"It's okay. I'm just looking forward to getting to know you and Grandma." Michael said.

"Me, too, Grandpa," I responded. "It's been a while since we've had any grandparents around."

"I know, Phil. Listen, I'll see you boys in the morning." He winked at Michael and said, "You better get some rest, Mike."

"I'll try."

Once Grandpa had gone, I looked at Michael and said, "I better get to the car. You know how Mom gets when she's upset."

"Yeah, but I still wish you were going home with our grandparents instead."

"I know, but it just wouldn't be right without you there." I said. "Well, I'll see you first thing in the morning." We bumped our knuckles together and I headed toward the door.

"Phillip," Michael said."

I turned and gazed at him.

"I'm really scared."

"About what?" I asked.

"Everything."

I snickered and said, "Yeah, I understand, but like Sarah said, maybe God is gonna work something out in some mysterious way."

Michael rested his head on his pillow. "Yeah, I never expected so many adults asking me for forgiveness. There's definitely some mysterious things going on."

I smiled. "I hear you!" I took a couple steps toward the door. "I'll see you tomorrow."

"Hey, Phillip!" Michael said. I turned again. "Thanks for stopping Dad today." In a nerdy tone, he said. "You're my hero!"

I laughed. "Yeah, that's twice in one week, so you owe me big time!"

Michael smiled.

"Hey," I said, "just try and get some sleep."

"I will," he said.

As I stepped into the hallway and headed to the elevator, my mind was once again consumed with what I would have to face on the way home.

CHAPTER TWENTY-FOUR

My ride home was a lot like driving into a blinding snowstorm. I didn't have a clue where I was headed, and I wasn't prepared to deal with the emotional train wreck driving the car. I gazed out the side window, watching flashes of light bouncing off the reflectors on the guardrails. I couldn't stop thinking about how heartless my mom's behavior was that entire evening. She knew Samuel was out there, and he might have been willing to rescue my brother from Dad, but she did nothing to reach out to him. It was unbelievable and cruel to think that she denied my brother the life he could have had—the one he deserved—because she likely couldn't face her own regrets from her choices. Mom robbed Michael of the chance for a real father. How could she do such a vindictive thing?

After pulling into the driveway, Mom put the car into park, but she didn't get out. As I reached for the door handle, I heard, "Phillip, I think I've lost Michael forever, and I'm not sure how I can ever forgive myself for that."

Mom leaned down toward the steering wheel and cried. Something tugged at me, compelling me to ease her suffering with encouraging words, but I chose to ignore the sensation, insisting my compassion would somehow betray Michael. She deserved to shed some tears for what she had done.

"Phillip, Michael's right about me. I didn't do enough to protect you boys from your father." She turned toward me. "Your father is so mean to me at times, and I'm afraid if I protect you two, he will make things even worse."

"Worse than they already are, Mom?" I stared at her. "Mom, Dad's evil and rotten for what he's done to Michael all these years. He only did it because he thinks Michael might not be his son. What kind of man does that to a kid?"

She leaned back, placing her head on the headrest. "Phillip, your father is just a complicated man." She hesitated for a few moments. "I don't know what to do to make things better."

"I do," I said. "I think you should leave him and find a better life for us!" I leaned my head against the window, exhausted from the vacillating emotions of anger, sorrow, and guilt fighting for my full attention. "Mom, maybe if you help Michael now, especially where Samuel is concerned, things will get better for him. Even if Samuel isn't his dad, Michael deserves someone like him in his life. I think they should get a paternity test done so we will all know for sure."

Her hands dropped into her lap, as if weakness had stolen her energy. "I can't believe I'm going to tell you this, Phillip, but I really did love Sam at one time, and I just don't know how I really feel about him possibly being a part of Michael's life after all these years. I can't deal with that right now."

"Come on, Mom, this isn't about you; it's about Michael! Look, I really think Samuel is a good guy, and Michael really seems to like him."

I glanced out the windshield and felt my pulse racing as I looked at the garage. I saw Dad waving the letter in Michael's face earlier that day. His threats were so merciless. He actually enjoyed it! I squeezed my eyes shut, hoping the vision would disappear. When I opened them again, the image was gone. I looked over and said, "Mom, do *you* think Samuel could really be Michael's dad?"

She sighed, causing a layer of condensation to form on the window in front of her. "I honestly don't know, Phillip!"

"Then why not let Michael get tested to see for sure?" I pleaded.

"Well . . . I'll have to think about it."

I rolled my eyes over her blatant hesitation. "Oh, and besides, I want to know how that backstabber knew Michael was even in the hospital, Phillip."

I took pleasure in telling her how it all played out. She slammed her elbow onto the door panel and thrust her head into her hand.

"Mom, are you afraid to face up to the fact that Samuel might be Michael's real dad?"

Her head turned toward her window. More condensation formed, and she lifted her hand and wiped the moisture away. Moments later, she mumbled, "Who knows?"

"Can I ask you something else, Mom?"

"I guess," she said with a long sigh.

"What's the *real* reason you didn't stop Dad from beating Michael all the time?"

She looked at me. "I already told you that I'm afraid of him, Phillip. I never know what he is capable of doing to me. Besides, I have nowhere to go."

"Why didn't you ask Grandma and Grandpa Stewart for help? After all, they don't seem like the jerks you always said they were."

Mom folded her arms, almost as if she was about to pout. "Gee, thanks for bringing up even more mistakes I've made in my life," she replied.

"What mistakes, Mom?"

"Years ago, your grandma and grandpa offered to help me—"

"Like with that job at his company?" I interrupted.

"Yeah, they knew I was having a tough time with your father, so your grandmother called and offered to let you and me stay with them if we needed to. I told her to shove it because she wouldn't include helping your father out, too, and that's when I quit working for my dad. I slammed the phone down on her and never returned to work."

"Oh, so that's what happened," I said. "I thought it was because you got pregnant."

"Well, that's part of it, but I also heard through my sister that Mom and Dad told her that I was on my own from now on. Ever since then, I have been. It will be a cold day in hell before I ever ask for their help."

"But Grandpa actually spoke to you tonight," I said. "You ignored him."

"He was just showing off."

A spark of animosity struck me when I considered how selfish her decision was to not seek their help. How much did she even care about us back then? "Mom," I said, "people have affairs all the time, and sometimes women end up pregnant, so why did this have to be such a dirty secret for so many years? I just don't get why Michael's the one who ended up paying for it."

"Well," she replied, "I know it happens all the time, but your dad would have done everything he could to take revenge on Sam if he knew about the affair back then. He also threatened to turn me in for neglect, drugs, and God knows what else, if I ever tried to call the police on him for what he was doing to us. The courts would have taken both of you away from me. I couldn't protect you then." She slammed her hand on the steering wheel, and yelled, "That letter ruined *everything*!"

"No offense, Mom, but I think the letter is the key piece to the puzzle. It at least let us know about Samuel. I don't think you would have ever said anything about him to us."

She glared at me. "Thanks, Phillip! That sure makes me feel better," she replied.

Ignoring her sarcasm, I argued, "Mom, I just don't understand any of this."

"I guess I don't understand it either, Phillip. Your father was always like an addiction to me. I couldn't walk away. It's sick, I know, because we aren't good for each other; we never were. After all, your dad is part of the reason I started some of my—well—habits. In the beginning, I thought I could save him from his addictions, but I ended up just like him, I guess."

"Mom," I pleaded, "you have a chance to do the right thing now. Please let Michael get tested to see if Samuel is his real dad!"

"Phillip, I told you I would think about it! Besides, I don't think your father would allow it."

"Come on, Mom," I yelled. "You still don't have the guts to make things right even now!"

Her pathetic excuse pierced me in the heart, and my stomach twisted from the revolting thoughts ravaging my mind. I knew I couldn't listen to another word, so I opened the car door and stepped out.

"I'm getting a shower and going to bed."

I slammed the door, leaving Mom in the car alone. I was too exhausted to argue with her.

CHAPTER TWENTY-FIVE

"I'm not going, Phillip! Since your worthless grandparents decided to take my own son away from me, why should I bother seeing him? Besides, Michael told me he hates me." Mom took a puff of her cigarette and blew the smoke into the air. She looked as though she hadn't slept the entire night, and the closer I got to her, the more I was able to smell alcohol spewing from her mouth, like a lethal gas.

"Mom, I really want to go to the hospital! We don't have time for this! Let's just get in the car!"

"Oh, you mean your dad's car that you left abandoned along the side of the road yesterday? The one Gloria and her husband had to bring back here?"

Exasperated, I sat down at the table on the opposite end from her. "Please, Mom," I pleaded. "Michael's expecting me to get there as soon as possible." She took another drag from her cigarette and blew the smoke in my direction. The stench caused my nostrils to burn. "Okay, then, I'll just take your car," I threatened.

"That is *not* going to happen," Mom insisted. "Besides, I'm not the one who messed with your dad's stuff in the garage. You brought this on yourself!"

I slammed my hand on the table and stood. The chair fell backward onto the floor. "I don't get you, Mom! What happened since last night?"

Her smug look punched me in the gut.

I pointed my finger at her like it was a dagger and yelled, "Why are you being so heartless? Yeah, I messed with Dad's stuff because we wanted to find out about the letter. It's not like you would ever fess up to what was in it. After all, Michael's the one who got tortured all these years because of your sleazy affair."

Mom sprang to her feet. "Don't you dare judge me!" she screamed. "If you don't like it around here, Phillip, why don't you go live with your stuck-up grandparents, too! You don't have to pretend to love me, you know!"

"Fine!" I hollered. I bolted up the stairs and started tossing a few clothes into a backpack. I also reached under one of my dressers and retrieved Michael's kindergarten photo I had hidden there the night Dad kicked it down the hallway. After stuffing in other personal items, and digging for any spare change I could find laying around my room, I stormed down the stairs and headed for the front door.

Mom grabbed my arm as I passed by her in the dining room. "Where do you think you're going?" she bellowed.

"Away from you, you drunk bit—" The sting of her hand across my face caused my head to jerk to one side. I reached up and rubbed my cheek. "Yeah, I get it now, Mom, you really don't care about anybody but yourself. Why don't you go back to your worthless cocaine and booze, and just leave me alone." I opened the door. "That's the last time you'll ever lay a hand on me!"

"Fine, I don't want you back in this house either, Phillip! Just go and suck up to your grandparents, and we'll see just how long they'll put up with you two!"

I slammed the front door shut, and headed down the road. I had no idea how I would get to the hospital, but I just knew I was done with both of my parents. As I walked, still massaging my sore cheek, I started wondering where I would stay that night if Michael didn't get released that day. *Maybe I had no choice but to go to my grandparents without him*, I thought. Regardless, I knew Michael would be safe, but panic struck me like lightning when I realized I had abandoned my own home—the only place where I had a guaranteed roof over my head. With no money, except for some spare coins jingling in my pocket, I realized the pangs of hunger were already starting to pester me. I was empty of every resource I needed to survive, except for the drive and determination to make it to my brother's bedside as quickly as I could.

As I was passing the convenience store on Grant Road, I saw a payphone near the entrance. I ran up to it and dropped in one of the five quarters I had and dialed my best friend's home. After a few rings, I heard a familiar voice. "Hi, Mrs. Dawson, this is Phillip. Is Andrew home?"

"Phillip, are you okay? You sound out of breath," she inquired.

"Yes, ma'am, I'm fine. I just need to talk to Andrew for a minute."

"Sure, let me wake him up. Give me a minute."

Moments later, Andrew got on the phone and I asked if he could come and get me so I could get to the hospital to see Michael.

"Hey, man, why do you need to go to the hospital? What happened to your brother?"

"My worthless parents . . ." I blurted out. "Look, man, I just have to get to the hospital." I leaned my head on the cool metal casing around the phone. "Can you pick me up?"

"Hold on," he said. Moments later, he came back to the phone and said, "My mom and I are on our way to get you."

"Andrew, I don't want your mom knowing about this."

"Just stay there and we'll be there shortly. Where are you?" he asked.

"At the store on Grant Road."

"Okay, give us ten minutes."

I hung up the phone and walked into the store, looking for anything I could purchase that wouldn't cost more than $1.57. I located a small package of powdered sugar donuts. With only 27 cents remaining, I didn't have enough for a drink, so I walked back outside and decided to eat only half of the package. I thought it might be best for me to save some for later. As I was putting the remaining donuts into my backpack, Andrew's mom pulled up and I got into the car. The brief interrogation was a bit unnerving, but I managed to conceal most of the details. Andrew's mom did ask why my mom wasn't taking me, but I told her it was a long story, not worth repeating.

When we arrived at the front entrance of Westview Memorial, I stepped out of the car and thanked them for the ride. They insisted on going in with me, but I told them I was leaving right away to go to my grandparents' home—*I'd hoped*—so there wouldn't be enough time for anyone to visit. Andrew's mom sighed several times, but she decided not to meddle, and they soon pulled away. I saw Andrew gazing back at me with a bewildered look. I felt guilty for the many times I wanted to tell him what my life was *really* like, but I knew I couldn't. Michael's safety always depended on my silence—a trade-off that haunted my conscience every day.

My grandparents were already in the room when I arrived.

Compared to my tattered jeans and stained sweatshirt, Grandma was well-dressed, bedecked in a gray suit jacket with a matching skirt and white blouse. Her pearl necklace and earrings shouted wealth and elegance. Grandma walked over to give me a hug. When she got closer, she gasped. "Good heavens, Phillip! What happened to your cheek, honey? It's all red!"

I gazed over at Michael. My lips started trembling, and tears were soon clinging to my eyelashes. I squeezed my eyes shut and lowered my head.

"What happened, Phillip?" Michael asked. "Where's Mom?"

I sighed before opening my eyes. I looked up at the white paneled ceiling as an avalanche of tears cascaded down my cheeks. "Nothing, Michael. I just had an argument with Mom, that's all. She's at home."

Grandma grasped my hand. "Honey, are you sure you're okay, because you sure don't look it?"

I turned my head away from her before taking a deep, piercing breath. "No, Grandma, I'm not okay."

She pulled me close to her chest and hugged me.

Grandpa Jack moved over to me and placed his hand on my shoulder. "Phil, please tell us what happened," he said in a gentle tone.

"Mom threw me out," I said, without lifting my head from Grandma's shoulder, "I definitely can't go back there now."

Grandpa Jack squeezed my shoulder. "Phil, we told you last night that we're planning on both of you staying with us, so don't worry."

I stood up straight and looked back at him. Grandpa pulled me toward him and wrapped his arms around me.

"Thank you, sir. That means everything to me right now."

While my grandparents hugged me, the social worker arrived and apologized for being late. She explained she'd had a traumatic situation to deal with that morning.

"It's that little six-year-old boy who got beat up by his drunk dad, isn't it?" Michael asked.

Beth stepped closer to Michael and placed her hand on the bed railing. "Well, I can't really say, but did you overhear someone talking about the situation?"

"Well, Samuel told me this morning when he called to check on me," Michael said. "He told me that the little boy's grandma works in the office at his company. That's how he knew about it." Michael looked over at me before returning his gaze back to Beth. "Besides, I kinda heard some people sorta upset in the hallway last night. It woke me up, so I figured it had to be something really bad. Samuel said the little boy was in a coma, and they didn't think he was gonna make it."

Michael's mouth sagged, and his head lowered toward his chest. The boy was around six years old—the same age as Michael when Dad found the letter.

"I see," Beth replied. After adjusting her cross necklace, she said, "Well, let's talk about you for now, Michael."

Some chatter in the hallway prompted her to walk over and close the door. After returning, she readjusted her necklace again and flipped her dark, curly hair over her shirt collar and asked, "In spite of the commotion, did you sleep well last night, Michael?"

"Yeah, I actually did," he replied.

"That's good, Michael. You do look like you are feeling a little better already this morning."

"I'm still sore in a few places, but the doctor said I'll live," he jested. "Nothing is broken, I guess."

"Well, the staff said they don't really have any reason to keep you any longer than they have to. Did you have breakfast?"

With a disgruntled look on his face, Michael replied, "Yeah, if that's what you call it."

We all smiled.

"Mr. and Mrs. Stewart," Beth said, "the nurse said she will be in shortly with the release papers. You'll just need to sign them, and then you'll be free to leave after that. I will be in touch with you soon in order to fill you in on the details of the investigation."

Michael looked over at Beth. "What investigation?"

Grandpa placed his hand on Michael's knee and said, "I'll explain later, Mike. It's all fine, so don't worry about it."

"And the nurse said something about the doctor requesting that Michael stay home from school at least for a few days this coming week," Beth said. "I agree that that might be for the best. Phillip can make his own choice as to whether he is ready to return. Hopefully there won't be too many questions from his peers."

"I understand," Grandpa replied.

I helped Michael get dressed while our grandparents waited in the hallway. We chuckled over the shirt from the gift shop he'd put on. "I have one just like it," I snickered.

Like children excited about getting ready for a vacation, Michael and I uttered sentences almost too rapidly to understand. I also shared about the events that had occurred between Mom and me that morning. No matter how sore Michael was, he did his best to ignore the sharp pains still jabbing his sides. He slipped on the crumpled jeans I had stuffed into my backpack earlier that morning. A new life was waiting for us outside of the hospital, and he was anxious to explore unfamiliar surroundings where Dad wouldn't be lurking in the shadows.

As he and I stepped out into the hallway, he looked toward the opposite direction we needed to go. "Hey guys," he said, "can you just meet me down by the elevator. There's something I need to do before I leave."

"Like what?" I asked.

"Just give me a minute, Phillip. It's personal," he replied.

I shrugged my shoulders and headed down to the elevator with my grandparents. I thought he might be searching for one of the nurses who had cared for him that morning.

After waiting for about ten minutes, Michael met us at the elevator. I could see that he had a tissue in his hand. I asked once more where he went, but Michael said he just needed to talk to someone. I left it alone at that point. His curt responses indicated he didn't feel comfortable sharing his whereabouts, even with me.

We were soon in the car and heading to our new destination—*Freedom!*

CHAPTER TWENTY-SIX

The late morning sunlight smothered the vast, pristine estate, leaving me speechless. Given the crude existence Michael and I had languished in for years, I felt uncomfortable even considering that such an immense property was going to be our new home for a while.

There was an iron gate at the entrance, requiring a code for entry, and huge oak trees seemed to greet us like soldiers standing at attention along the entire length of the paved driveway. Just beyond the majestic trees, I was able to see the large white pillars supporting the low-pitched gabled roof on the front of the house. We had arrived at our grandparent's home.

Once Grandpa parked the car, I helped Michael from the backseat. As we meandered up the walkway, I kept staring at the absurdity of the excessive landscaping. Each of the small flower gardens were manicured and sectioned off so that one plant didn't overpower the brilliance of the next. The blending of each color seemed to flow in a continuous cascade of luster, almost as if the hand of God had planted each one. From the ornamental bronze chandelier hanging over the front porch, to the fancy lace drapery suspended in each window, I knew our upscale surroundings were a huge transformation from what we'd inhabited with Mom and Dad. A brief moment of anger struck me when I realized what we'd been deprived of for so many years. My grandparents lived in luxury; we lived in hell.

Grandma Gladie had said I had an uncanny ability to notice details, but even I was having trouble trying to sort it all out in my mind. Hardwood floors, marble table tops, hand-woven rugs full of ornate designs that I had never seen before, all combined to give me the feeling that I didn't belong there. While Grandpa showed Michael to his room, Grandma grasped my hand and led me into the parlor. Seizing the opportunity, I asked Grandma Madeline why Mom ever abandoned such a life for someone like Dad. She walked over and opened a roll top desk and picked up a photo she had in a frame. It was a picture of Grandpa Jack and Mom when she was about four or five years old. In the photo, Mom was sitting on Grandpa's lap while he was reading her a book.

"They looked very happy, Grandma," I said. "What happened?"

Grandma Madeline sat next to me. "I don't know, Phillip, but when your mom started high school, we often fought over her selection of friends. She seemed different when she was around them, so your grandfather and I threatened to move her to a private school out of the area. Your mother certainly didn't like that idea."

I looked around the room. "Why would Mom want to ruin what she had here?"

"Honey," she said, "your mother was as strong-willed as your grandfather, and she couldn't resist the chance to argue with him. Your grandfather wouldn't tolerate it, so your mom started hanging out at the homes of different friends. We wouldn't see her for days. Your Aunt Sylvia couldn't stand the chaos either, so she wanted out of the house as well."

"It's a shame that Mom couldn't realize what she was leaving behind."

"Yes, you're right, Phillip. And Tony Williams was all too willing to take her away from us. It was the bad boy thing, I guess. It was so hard losing her to someone like—" Her eyes widened. "I hope I'm not offending you, honey."

"Trust me," I said, "you're not."

"Speaking of your mother, do you think you should call her?"

"Yeah," I said, "but right now, I'm kinda happy, and I don't wanna ruin the feeling."

Grandma smiled and nodded.

After lunch, Grandpa received a call from a gentleman named Mr. Busby. He had something to do with the prosecutor's office, which was going to handle the case against Dad. I guess he also wanted to collect more information from us about the fight, along with some of our past abuse. Mr. Busby said he would come to the house that afternoon. I wasn't sure how Michael and I would handle telling him our secrets, but it didn't seem like we had any choice in the matter. After all, he was making a special trip to the house on a weekend.

After Mr. Busby left later that day, my brother's mood around the house was as oppressive as the dew on a humid summer night. Michael flinched almost every time he heard the slightest noise. I asked, "What's the matter, Michael?"

"I feel like Dad's gonna come after me for telling that Mr. Busby guy some of our business," he replied.

"Dad's in jail for the weekend," I reminded him.

My words didn't help, because he insisted that Dad wouldn't be there forever.

Dinner seemed to break the awkward silence we had been trying to ignore. I was embarrassed by the speed at which Michael consumed his meal. I did notice him massaging his jaw several times, but that didn't prevent him from eating the heaps of roast beef, mashed potatoes, and green beans Grandma kept piling onto his plate. Michael asked, "Grandpa, do you think we could ask Samuel to come over? You said he was always welcomed here."

Grandpa glanced at Grandma, and his chest heaved as if capturing his last breath before death. "I guess we could give him a call," Grandpa replied.

"Michael," Grandma said, "we don't mind him coming over, but please don't be disappointed if he can't."

Michael started to lift a fork full of mashed potatoes to his mouth. He stopped. "Well, can we still try?"

Grandpa got up from the table and walked into the kitchen. Michael shoved the food into his mouth as Grandma reached for the bowl and attempted to put another scoop of potatoes on his plate. Michael raised his hand to stop her.

"Phillip, did you call your mother like we discussed earlier today?" she asked.

"Yes, ma'am. She handled me staying here pretty much like I thought she would."

"That's to be expected." Grandma stood and headed for the kitchen. "I hope you two saved room for dessert."

Michael looked at me as he grasped his stomach. "Man," he said, "I don't know if I can eat another bite."

I chuckled.

Samuel arrived right after we'd finished helping Grandma with the dishes. Michael and I were anxious to learn more about his life. If we were ever going to fully piece together the puzzle involving Michael's *mysterious beginnings*, we needed answers. With the curiosity of a news reporter, Michael wanted specific details about Samuel's personal life. We learned that he was born in a small town just south of Decatur, but he'd moved to Westview because of the available space to expand his factory. He mentioned that he was told about the building by a friend who lived near our town. He mentioned a Mr. Hill, a realtor, and my grandpa said he knew who he was. I had always longed for the kinds of connections that Samuel and Grandpa seemed to have with others.

Samuel started doing a lot of business with Grandpa's store, which is how he'd met Mom. Samuel loved her, I believed, but the mix up with the letter is what guided them down different paths in life. Unfortunately, both of them believed the other was no longer interested once Mom became pregnant. When it came to Michael, Samuel kept his distance until the night of the overdose, but he still kept a watchful eye over my brother in inconspicuous ways, like at soccer games.

Samuel explained that since things with Mom never worked out, he chose a new direction in his life. He told us again about attending church with his friend, and that is where he'd met Sarah. They began dating, which eventually led to their engagement and marriage. It wasn't until his daughter Megan was born that Samuel confessed to Sarah the details of the affair with Mom. Sarah was upset at first, but she eventually encouraged Samuel to make contact with Michael, but he was too afraid of the possible repercussions. From what I could understand, Samuel's greatest trepidation in pursuing a relationship with Michael was centered on the possible reaction from Dad. I guess I could understand that, but once Dad found the letter, the secret was out. Samuel's son, Paul, was born a few years after Megan. Samuel admitted that Paul was a constant reminder of Michael. Seeing Michael around town, and the fact that Paul and Michael looked so much alike, probably made it even harder on Samuel.

In the distance, we heard the enormous, antique clock in the hallway chime ten times. As much as I wanted the night to last forever, I knew Samuel was planning on leaving when I saw him glance at his watch a couple times. My grandparents decided to give Michael and Samuel some private time to themselves.

As Grandma fussed over clearing the tables on the porch, I heard Grandpa say to Samuel, "Mike may or may not be your son, but it looks like you have another one anyway. I'm telling you, Sam, that boy really likes you. He was hanging on every word you said tonight."

"Yes, I noticed that too," Samuel said. Grandpa shook hands with him as Samuel got ready to leave.

When I did the same, Samuel held on to mine and asked, "Phillip, would you mind hanging out a bit longer as well?"

I gazed at Grandpa, who nodded and said, "That would be a great idea, Phil."

"Sure," I replied.

Michael was still sitting in the lounge chair when Samuel pulled a chair up beside him. I sat on the other side of my brother, not knowing what to expect. It had been the first time we were comfortably alone with Samuel without the threat of being caught. I was also hoping that I would never become the wedge between their new relationship, so I decided to remain silent and just listen to their intriguing conversation.

As we sat in the midst of the symphony of creation's sounds from the nearby woods, Samuel suddenly took his finger and placed it up to his own lips. He softly whispered, "Shhhh!" My brother seemed as puzzled as me over the abrupt gesture. Samuel whispered, "Do you boys hear that?"

We listened for a few moments.

My brother smiled. "Do you like listening to them too?" Michael asked.

"I've always loved listening to the tree frogs," Samuel whispered. "My Nana Helen used to sit on her porch with me and listen to them for hours." With tears building in his eyes, and his voice cracking from emotions, he said, "You have no idea, Michael, how many times I've dreamed about spending time with you. The fact that we are able to sit together and listen to the tree frogs just reminds me of all of the great memories with my nana."

"Me and Phillip always did the same thing with Nana Gladie. We still listen to them, don't we, Phillip?"

I nodded.

"That's funny," Samuel responded, as he wiped his eyes. "When I've had a bad day, I'll sit on my porch for hours and listen to them. I would spend countless hours thinking about you, Michael. I'd imagine what you were doing at that exact moment." He wiped more tears. "The peaceful sounds coming from the forest gave me a lot of comfort for some reason, especially as I tried to sort everything out in my mind about the mistakes of my past." He reached out for Michael's hand. "Michael, I never knew the torment you and Phillip suffered because of me." I could see Samuel's tears glistening because of the burning candles sitting on one of the tables. "I hate living with regrets," he said.

"Yeah, but that's all over with, I hope!" Michael replied. "Me and Phillip used to dream about running away and living with a new family that actually wanted us." Michael's teary eyes started to shimmer in the flickering light of the candles as well. "Samuel, I think you and Sarah are the family in our dreams."

"Maybe we are, Michael. It's just going to take some time to figure it all out," he said. "I know we all brag about the medical advances we have here in the nineties and all, but there's just some things we still can't control as fast as we'd like." He looked at his watch. "Boys, as much as I hate to go, I need to get home. I have to be up early for church in the morning."

Samuel helped my brother to his feet and gave him a gentle hug. I also received one from him. When Samuel started down the steps toward his car, I felt my heart start pumping faster. I didn't want him to go. He made my night purposeful, and when I saw him walking away from us, fear crept in like the overcast of a cloud blocking the sun. Perhaps it was because Michael and I would soon be alone in a place that had been forbidden to us for years.

"I'll see you boys sometime soon," he said. "Remember, everything will be okay, so don't worry."

"I know," Michael responded, "but I just want to get all of this crap behind us."

As Samuel opened his car door, he said, "Hey, I love—" He ceased talking for a moment, and I wasn't sure why. "I . . . umm . . . was just thinking about how much I loved being here tonight."

"I'm glad you came over, too," Michael replied.

"Yeah," I said, "I'm glad we got to spend time together."

"I'll be in touch soon, boys. I promise."

Samuel got into his car while Michael and I remained on the porch. We watched as Samuel drove down the long driveway. Even after the red tail lights faded in the distance, Michael stood there leaning against a pillar.

"Is everything okay, Michael?"

"Yeah," he replied, "I was just thinking about how funny it is that Samuel likes listening to tree frogs like us."

"It's pretty cool, actually. Maybe it runs in the family," I jested. It was comforting to hear him chuckle. "Hey," I said, "it's been a long day, so let's get some sleep."

I walked over and blew out the candles on the small table in front of the large picture window. I put my arm around my brother's shoulders and opened the screen door. With a smile on our faces, we walked inside and headed for our bedrooms.

Later that night, I was struggling to fall asleep. Perhaps it was my new surroundings or that I couldn't forget about Dad's court hearing scheduled for Monday. As I was lying on my side, staring at the kindergarten photo of Michael I'd placed on the nightstand before going to bed, there was a tap at my door. It was Michael. He popped his head into my room.

"Phillip, are you up?" he whispered.

"Yeah."

"Can I come in here and sleep?" he asked.

"Sure," I said. I was relieved he still needed me.

After he crawled into bed, he asked, "Hey, where'd you get that photo of me?"

"I found it, so I thought I'd bring it here."

"Wow," Michael said, "I thought Dad got rid of that thing years ago."

"No, I guess he didn't," I said. I couldn't tell him that Dad had kicked it down the hallway the night he brought the letter home.

After a brief pause, Michael asked, "Phillip, do you think Samuel is my real dad?"

"I think you look like him a lot," I replied. "He even said Paul looks like you."

"If he is my dad, would you be mad if I changed my last name?" Michael asked.

"Why should I be angry?" I responded without hesitation, but deep down I couldn't distinguish whether the sensations I felt were good feelings or bad ones. What would a name change mean to us?

"I just didn't know if you'd be angry or not. I want to make sure everyone knows we're brothers, even though our last names might be different."

With a smile on my face, I rolled over toward him and said, "Everyone will always know that we're brothers! Hey, if I have to, I'll even chisel it into stone!"

I rolled back over, and Michael whispered, "Thanks, man."

"For what?" I asked.

"For not leaving me alone in the garage with—well, you know . . ."

"I will never leave you again," I said.

After a few minutes of silence, I could only hear him breathing soundly. My brother had drifted off to sleep.

I started to wonder why Michael wanted to come into my room that night. Even though it was a comfort to me, since I wasn't used to sleeping alone in such a large and strange room, I was afraid Michael was concerned that he might have one of his nightmares. That would have really upset our grandparents. Regardless of his personal reasons, I was thankful that my brother was safe, and for the first time in years, he had hope wrapped around him like a warm security blanket. Best of all, the window was slightly ajar in my bedroom. I was eventually serenaded to sleep by familiar tunes coming from the nearby trees.

CHAPTER TWENTY-SEVEN

I rolled over in the morning and discovered that Michael was gone. I placed my hand on his side of the bed and felt the familiar dampness of his sheets. Michael had had another nightmare, but apparently it wasn't bad enough to disrupt my sleep this time. Sometimes his dreams caused him horrible night sweats, and I was used to him coming into my room when he would have a cluster of nightmares after something traumatic had happened at home. I could usually get him settled down before Dad heard him.

I got up and put on my shirt and headed for the bathroom. After looking in the mirror, I realized that I was in dire need of a haircut and some new underwear. After putting on my jeans I'd had on from the day before, I headed down the stairs toward the chatter in the kitchen. It was early, but the house seemed busy. The robust aroma of fried bacon awakened my senses. My stomach had been growling ever since I got up, so after greeting everyone, I sat down and grabbed a bagel and some cream cheese. There was even a glass of freshly squeezed orange juice handed to me by Grandma, who greeted me with a kiss on the top of my head. Although unexpected, I welcomed the affection.

"Are you okay?" I whispered to Michael. He nodded, and went back to eating a bowl of grits with a heaping side of bacon.

"Hey boys," Grandpa said, "I could use a little help this morning."

"Sure," I said, "but don't you go to church?"

"Well, usually, but we wanted you two to sleep in this morning, so maybe we'll head there next week."

"Oh, okay. So what did you need help with?" I asked.

"For weeks, your grandmother has been nagging me to trim up some of the hedges at the front gate. Do you mind helping out with that?"

I was surprised he didn't have someone hired for that job.

"Sure," Michael mumbled, as he gulped down the glass of milk Grandma had just refilled for him.

After finishing breakfast, I started to clear the table. "Phillip," Grandma said, "I've been after that old goat to get those hedges done for a long time. You better go and help him while he's in the mood. I'll take care of this."

"Okay, Grandma. I'm sure we'll have it all done by lunch. It was nice having a real breakfast for once."

After she hugged me, she said, "And, I need to take you and Michael to the store this afternoon. We need to get some new clothes for you two."

After lunch, Michael went to his room to wash up and rest, so I decided to walk around the yard and see what else my grandparents had on their property. I'd seen a large barn when we arrived the day before, so I thought it might be an exciting new place to explore sometime soon with Michael. I walked by a red aluminum sided shed, which housed two large Farmall tractors. To me, I imagined them as antique machines that had roamed countless miles across fertile fields, tearing up the soil in order to cultivate the produce that had likely fed many Westview residents over the years. I also spotted a small, shimmering pond off in the distance. I was hoping it was full of fish. There was also an army of towering pines assembled on a bluff, sheltering the endless fields that seem to plunge into the horizon. I thought about *The Legend of Sleepy Hollow* that I had read in junior high. My grandfather's estate reminded me so much of the Van Tassel farm I'd imagined in my mind when I read the book in class.

The road that my grandparents lived on was named after Grandpa Jack. Stewart Road was once a dirt lane, barely wide enough for two vehicles, and my grandfather's house was the only one on the road for many years. When people started building homes along the road, after my grandfather had sold off some of his acreage, the county paved the road and named it after him.

With the gentle breezes dancing over the fields, the feeling of losing myself in the embrace of nature, and the knowledge that I could find solitude—simply because I wanted to—was such a relief to me. I couldn't wait to get to Michael's room and share what I'd experienced. An unfamiliar sense of comfort settled upon me, and I felt at home for the first time since we'd arrived.

CHAPTER TWENTY-EIGHT

I opened Michael's door and peered into his room, hoping not to disturb him. The sound of his deep breathing told me he was asleep. I decided to walk over and sit in a chair next to the fireplace. My intent was to rest there for a short time before waking him up before dinner, which I smelled baking in the oven as I passed through the kitchen on my way to his room. I leaned back in the chair and thought about the life we could have had—had we known our grandparents. I imagined us growing up and helping Grandpa with his farming, the business, and even Michael and I fishing in the pond I saw off in the distance during my self-guided tour of the estate. While daydreaming, I felt a bit lethargic, so I rested my head onto the soft, plush cushioning of the chair. The last thing I remembered was seeing Michael curled up on his bed with his arms tucked under his chest.

About an hour later, I was awakened by the sensation of something smooth brushing across my face. Upon opening my eyes, I saw Michael standing over me just moments before he was about to slide his dirty sock across my nose again. He had a joyous grin on his face I hadn't seen in a really long time. "You jerk!" I said, as I quickly rubbed my face before snatching the sock from his hand. "I thought there was a huge bug crawling on me."

Michael chuckled.

"How long was I asleep?" I asked.

"I don't know, but it's almost 3:30." As he retrieved his shirt from the back of another chair, he said, "Hey, don't get bent outta shape. I was just messing with you."

I stood and stretched.

"Where'd you go earlier?" he asked.

"I walked around the property. It's unbelievable," I replied. "There's even a pond!"

"We'll have to go check things out later," he said. "Hey, Grandma's dinner sure smells good."

"Yeah, she had something baking when I came in."

"I thought you said she was going to take us shopping for some clothes today," Michael said.

"Yeah, but maybe she knew we were sleeping and didn't want to bother us. Probably after dinner or something," I replied.

"I gotta take a shower," Michael said. "You know, I never realized how nice it was to have my own bathroom. No fighting for space!"

"It's pretty nice," I said. "I can pee whenever I want without you pounding on the door."

"Tell me about it," Michael agreed. "It's hard to tell what you were doing in our old bathroom when you were alone."

"Oh, real funny!" I said.

Once I heard the water running, I started for my own room. Michael yelled for me, so I slipped my head into the bathroom and asked what he wanted. "Can you wait for me to get done?" he asked.

For some reason, several years earlier, Michael started asking me to stay close to the bathroom when he showered, especially when Dad was home. Although it seemed awkward at first, it soon became a kind of ritual to us. He never told me why, even when I asked, but I always suspected that Dad had something to do with his discomfort.

"Sure," I told him, "but try and hurry. I have to get a shower, too."

"I will," he replied.

I sat in the chair closest to the bathroom door and picked up a magazine. I started thumbing through an article about different breeds of horses. Ten minutes later, Michael emerged from the bathroom with a towel wrapped around his waist. Almost as if they were screaming for my attention, his bruises reminded me of some obscene graffiti spray painted onto a billboard, and I found myself fixated on them.

"I know I look terrible," he said.

"Sorry," I replied. "It's just hard to avoid them. Man, I really hate Dad for what he did to you."

"They'll go away soon," he said. He stopped. "Oh, I forgot one thing."

Before I could fully react, he thrust his dirty underwear over my head.

"You jerk!" I yelled.

I chased him across the room and pushed him hard enough that he fell across the bed and crashed onto the floor on the other side. For a split second, I'd forgotten about his injuries.

His foot also hit a small nightstand. It crashed against the wall before toppling over. The echo of the collision caused both of our grandparents to rush into my brother's room. Michael was still on the floor when the door swung open.

"Good heavens! Is everyone okay?" Grandma shrieked.

Knowing I had to say something, I replied, "Ahhhh . . . yeah . . . we're okay."

Grandpa Jack let out a hearty roar of laughter.

"Oh dear!" was the only thing Grandma could say before thrusting her hand to her gaping mouth. I just stared at them, wondering what was so shocking and funny. When Grandpa pointed toward my head, I soon realized what had drawn his attention to me. I hurriedly removed the underwear and dropped it onto the floor beside me. My face was flushed.

"Where's your brother?" Grandpa asked.

"Well, he's . . . umm . . ." I pointed toward the other side of the room.

Just then, Michael's arm popped up over the bed. "I'm right here, Grandpa," he replied. "I'm really sorry about the nightstand. I hope you're not mad at me. My idiot brother pushed me across the bed."

He still had not revealed himself; however, I soon realized why. Hanging halfway off of the side of the bed closest to me was his towel.

Grandma started toward Michael. As she moved in that direction, she asked, "Are you okay, honey?"

Michael screamed, "No, Grandma! Don't come over! I don't have any clothes on!"

I could see the expression on her face as she got a quick flash of Michael's body, which he tried desperately to cover up, but it was too late. Her eyes bulged from their sockets, and her hand rushed to the side of her head as she tried to block the view.

"Good heavens!" she cried out. As she hurried out of the room—her face beaming a crimson shade—she passed Grandpa and said, "Now I know why God gave me girls instead of boys."

Grandpa Jack doubled over with laughter. I threw Michael his towel, and he got up and hurried across the room in order to throw on his pair of jeans that were hanging over the back of a chair. Grandpa moved over to the chair I'd been sleeping in earlier and completely collapsed into hysterics. He kept wiping his eyes with the sleeve of his shirt.

"I think that's the funniest thing I've seen in years. I should have had you two living here years ago. It would have kept me young!"

After we all settled down, we went downstairs and found Grandma in the kitchen finishing dinner preparations. She rushed about, looking busy. Michael walked over and threw his arm around her.

"Well, Grandma," he teased, "you said you should have seen more of me years ago, so I guess I've made up for that now."

"Oh, good heavens!" she said, as she waved her hand in the air, looking like she was swatting at a fly buzzing around her face.

"Well, Madeline," Grandpa snickered, "at least you have definite proof that you have a grandson."

Her look of disdain caused Grandpa to laugh even harder.

That night, we continued to laugh about the incident in our bedroom. It had been a long time since Michael and I had the opportunity to goof around with each other without the threat of being punished for making too much noise. Yet a few issues lingered in my heart. As if his previous injuries weren't bad enough, I felt bad that Michael was sore from the shove I gave him earlier that day. Also, there was still that nagging feeling about the following morning involving Dad's appearance in court. It helped that Samuel called that night, and Sarah also got on the phone and reassured Michael that everything would be fine, and not to worry. Still, no one knew how Dad would react to being in court.

Michael and I couldn't sleep that evening, so we sat on the porch for a while, talking about the possibility of Dad going to jail. I could tell my brother was nervous because of the way his words shot out of his mouth like bullets from a gun. Grandpa mentioned that Mr. Busby had discussed further charges regarding Dad's abuse of Michael, and I wondered if Mom would be next. I was also afraid that all of the focus on the abuse would trigger another violent nightmare for Michael that night.

When I stood and headed for the door, I asked, "Are you sleeping in your room tonight?"

"I don't know, Phillip. I'm scared about what *you know who* will do in court tomorrow."

Throughout the night, I felt the vibrations from my brother's tremors. They seemed to rattle my conscience, and the unwelcomed guilt had returned like the symptoms a chronic illness. Because of my cowardice, and not protecting him sooner, Michael's dreams were likely drenched with remembrances of the abuse Dad inflicted on him for years. I slept very little, hoping Michael wouldn't wake up screaming like he'd done so many times in the darkness of his own room at home.

CHAPTER TWENTY-NINE

The next morning, I awakened to the smell of sausage saturating the air, and my stomach seemed to do cartwheels as my mouth watered from the unrelenting sensation of hunger. I rolled over and saw that Michael was not in bed. I reached over and felt the sheets. They were cool and damp to the touch, just as I had predicted.

Within a few seconds, however, I remembered it was Dad's court appearance that day. He'd spent the weekend in jail, and now it was time for him to face the judge. I placed my hands behind my head and rested in the bed for a while longer—forcing my appetite to wait. It was nice having the quiet time before heading downstairs and facing what I knew was going to be a challenging day. A spark of anxiety was rekindled at the thought of the possible outcome of the hearing. The hatred Dad brought into our lives was so powerful, and I wasn't sure we could tolerate it ever again if we were forced to return home. Besides, Dad still had some unresolved business with me over my threats involving the ax.

As I rested, an odd feeling started to take root in my mind. I realized that my grandparents had nothing to do with us for years, and yet, they were suddenly there—in our lives—and doing everything to make things right. What was driving their ambitions to take both of us into their home without hesitation? I sat up in bed and swung my feet around and rested them on the hard, cool floor.

"I can't believe it," I whispered. *Could it be that easy for some people to love others they hardly know?*

I walked into the bathroom and stared at my reflection in the mirror. For once, I didn't see a hopeless, pathetic teen glaring back at me. I realized that Dad's hatred may not have won just yet. Maybe it never could. Perhaps there was some stronger force that kept me going all along—and it wasn't my hatred and revenge I harbored for Dad. How did I really miss it? Maybe I wasn't so observant after all!

After washing my face, I walked downstairs and into the kitchen. Grandma hurried over and hugged me and asked me how many hotcakes I wanted.

"A couple would be good," I replied.

Before I could thank her, the phone rang. The bustling movement ceased, and we all stared at the black phone jingling on the wall. We were reluctant to answer it, but Grandpa lifted the receiver and offered a friendly greeting. The instant smile on his face let us know it wasn't either of my parents. It was Samuel! He told Grandpa that he wanted to take Michael and me to lunch. We eagerly agreed, since neither of us planned on going to school that day. I knew for certain I didn't want to sit around all day and wait to see if our parents would come banging on the door, demanding to have us back. It was recommended by the social worker and Mr. Busby that neither of us needed to attend the hearing. Our grandparents agreed. Mr. Busby said he would contact us later that day with an update.

Once Samuel picked us up later that morning, we headed north for lunch. After about a thirty minute trip, we arrived at a small diner. Samuel seemed to know the owner quite well. He introduced us, but the owner seemed a bit confused. He kept staring at Michael and then at Samuel.

After a few minutes, he said, "You know, Sam, if I didn't know ya'll already, I'd swear these boys could be your sons, especially that one."

The gentleman pointed at Michael, of course, but I was so proud that he included me in that comparison. I, too, would have loved to have been Samuel's son.

Samuel just laughed. "Yeah, they are pretty handsome, just like me, right?"

Joe, the owner, kept shaking his head. "Yeah, they're handsome, but you sure ain't."

We all laughed.

"Seriously, are they kin or something?"

Samuel grinned, "Yeah, I guess you could say that."

Joe looked toward the counter and yelled, "Hey, Tabbie, come here a minute!"

After she walked over, Joe asked, "Don't these two look like Sam?"

She tapped her lips with her pen for a few seconds. "You know, Daddy, I think they do, especially that one." She also pointed at Michael. "Sam, he's got your nose and chin, and definitely those deep blue eyes," she commented. "How's come they ain't been in here with you before?"

Samuel snickered. "Well, they're new friends of mine, and I'm just taking them to one of the best restaurants around." He winked at us.

Joe patted Samuel's shoulder and said, "Now, that's the first nice thing I've heard you say about me in a long time. Maybe you're not such a jerk after all."

We all laughed.

"Tabbie, how about getting our new guests some of your ma's apple pie." Joe grinned at Samuel before gazing back at us. "Don't worry boys, the pie is free," Joe said. "I already know Sam's too cheap to buy you guys dessert."

Two large pieces of warm pie soon arrived with big scoops of vanilla ice cream dripping down the sides. We had a race to see who could scarf down the pie the quickest. Michael won, of course.

Samuel laughed. "That certainly didn't take long."

Michael and I grinned at each other.

"You oughta see Michael with pizza," I said.

"That's sounds like a great plan, boys," Samuel replied.

We also stopped at a store to buy some of Samuel's favorite homemade candies. This shop owner was really nice to us as well. As soon as Samuel introduced us, Miss Ruth came straight over and embraced both of us as if we were family. In less than two minutes, she'd complimented us more than our own parents had in years. I was amused by her candor. Regardless of her short stature, she seemed to dominate the tough businessman we were with. He was no match for her zealous interrogations, which seemed suited for her outgoing personality. She was relentless on Samuel for not telling her about us during his previous visits to her shop.

After insisting that we fill a bag full of any candy we wanted, she pulled Michael aside and examined his facial features. Although awkward at first, Michael seemed to accept her curiosity, knowing in his mind what she was likely thinking.

"You know, Sam," she said, "if I didn't know ya'll any better, I'd swear this handsome boy could be your son!"

Michael grinned.

She stepped over to me and grabbed my wrists and gazed intently at me. "Phillip, you sure do remind me of Sam, too." She released my arms and stepped back over to Michael. After nudging my brother closer to Samuel, she tapped her cheek a few times with her finger as she closely studied Michael's features. She took a couple steps back and pointed. "Yep, I'm telling ya'll, there's something about this boy that reminds me of you, Sam." Several moments later, her eyes widened, and she exclaimed, "My God!" she gasped, "It's those blue eyes!"

Samuel laughed. "Okay, I'm guilty!" He tossed his hands into the air and confessed, "Yep, I secretly had an affair, and these two were the result. Now, don't tell Sarah," he chuckled. She thrust her hands onto her hips and smiled. "No, seriously, Miss Ruth," Samuel said, "they are pretty special to me."

"Oh, I see," she replied. "Well, I could swear they were related to you somehow." Moments later, she stepped back over to Michael and gently touched his cheek. "Honey, did ya'll fall or something? I noticed earlier that you have a bruise on your cheek."

Samuel responded, "Yeah, he's quite the daredevil on his ATV."

He winked at Michael, and my brother smiled back.

"Well, I'm sorry to hear that, Michael. Ya'll be careful now and not bust up that handsome face of yours." She smiled at my brother. "Now, let's finish filling a bag of candy to take with you."

My favorite candy happened to be the pretzel sticks wrapped in caramel and dipped in chocolate. I ended up eating five of them before we had gotten several miles down the road. Miss Ruth gave Samuel a special heart-shaped box of candy for Sarah as well, and she even jokingly offered her shop assistants, Jessica and Angela, as possible brides to my brother and me.

Our grandparents were sitting on the porch when we returned to their home.

"Have you guys heard from anyone?" I asked, as I stepped onto the porch.

"Yes, Mr. Busby called. He said your dad was charged with a misdemeanor of the first degree. I guess it can carry up to a six-month prison sentence. And he also said that your dad didn't have the money for bail, so he's staying in jail until the official hearing, which he said would take a few days."

Michael, forgetting his manners, blurted out, "Really? I thought Dad would just get a slap on the wrist."

"Yeah," Grandpa said, "but I heard he angered the judge pretty badly with his cocky attitude, so he may end up with the full sentence after all. I also know the judge ordered him to have no contact with either of you boys. That's official also."

"So, Dad's still in jail then?" I asked.

"Yes," Grandpa said," and Mr. Busby said that they are investigating further into some child abuse charges. Your dad is in a heap of trouble."

"Thank God," I said.

"What about Mom?" Michael asked. "The social worker mentioned an investigation, so is she in trouble, too?"

Hesitant at first to mention anything, Grandpa cleared his throat and said, "Well, they are investigating her, too, boys. They can charge her with allowing the abuse to happen."

My heart lodged in my throat, blocking the air that was trying to enter my lungs. *Could Mom end up going to prison, too?* I wondered. Finally able to breathe, I asked, "Grandpa, do you think Mom will get charged if we don't want her to?"

"Phillip, you and Michael are minors, so it's not up to you. The police are involved. We'll just have to let them do their work."

"Let's hope they don't blow it off like I think they did with that stupid party I was at," Michael stated.

Grandpa placed his hand on my brother's shoulder. "Mike, I know the family that owns the house where you got drugged. He's a powerful man in town, and it isn't the first time his son mysteriously escaped getting into trouble."

Moments later, Samuel said he had to get home, so we shook his hand and thanked him for taking us with him that day. My grandparents went into the house, and I walked Samuel to his car with my brother.

"Samuel," Michael said, "I don't think my parents will sign any papers to have me tested."

"Yes, I suspect you're right about that, Michael, but a judge can order that without their consent. My attorney is working on it."

"I understand, but I just wish we could get it done," Michael said.

"Look, I really didn't want to ask this," Samuel said, "but maybe now is the time."

Michael cocked his head, appearing confused.

"Will you be okay if things don't work out with ... you know ... if things turn out differently than maybe you'd hoped they would with the testing?"

Michael leaned against the car. "You mean if we find out that I'm not your son?" His head lowered toward the ground.

Samuel leaned against the car as well, placing his elbow on the roof. "Yes, Michael. That's what I mean."

After sighing, Michael looked up and replied, "Well, can me and my brother still see you guys?"

With a huge smile on his face, Samuel declared, "Michael, I would be honored to have you and Phillip in our lives no matter what happens."

"Thank you, sir," I replied. "You've kinda grown on us a little," I snickered.

"The same with me," he said. My brother opened the door for Samuel. Right before he got into the car, Michael said, "Hey, thanks again for the really nice day. It helped a lot. You know some great people."

"Yes, there really are nice people still out there, Michael." He slid into the car. "Hey, boys, Sarah's been working a lot, but I know she wants to see you two real soon."

"That's great," Michael replied, with a proud grin. "We can't wait."

I headed for the house while Michael stood in the driveway and watched as Samuel headed toward Stewart Road. A tear must have rolled down his cheek, because I saw him brushing something away from his face once Samuel headed up the road.

Later that evening, Michael came into my room to talk. I fully expected him to mention the court hearing and investigations into the abuse, but all he wanted to discuss was our day with Samuel. Michael kept eating from the bag of chocolates like it had been the only meal he'd had available all day.

"You know," he said, "I'm actually in a really good mood tonight, so I think I'll stay in my own room for a change. That jerk's in jail, so I guess I don't have to worry."

"I understand, Michael," I said. "Besides, I'm tired of listening to you snore."

"Yeah," he laughed, "like you don't keep me up half the night doing the same thing."

After reliving most of the day's activities, Michael started to yawn. Before too long, he stood and walked to the door. "I'll see you in the morning," he said.

"Yeah, you too," I replied.

I got up and opened the window halfway. A medley of songs from the tree frogs filled the evening breeze with a harmony that made me wonder whether their symphony was something unique—perhaps a sonata composed just for me that night. I even imagined that their ancestors might have been the ones that sang us to sleep so many years ago at Grandma Gladie's house. Listening for distinct voices was the last thing I remembered that night.

CHAPTER THIRTY

Samuel flipped through the radio stations, looking for something he felt we might enjoy. "Love Takes Time" was playing on several stations. "I guess Mariah Carey seems to be the popular singer on the radio these days," Samuel commented.

Michael stared out the passenger side window, appearing preoccupied with something else on his mind.

"Yeah," Michael mumbled, "but I'm more into *Nirvana*, I guess."

"I still like it when the stations play hits from *Journey*," Samuel said. Sarah loves "Open Arms" and "Don't Stop Believin'." I suddenly noticed his head shaking as he chuckled, realizing, of course, what he'd said. I smiled when I thought about how much those two songs matched Sarah's personality. "Sarah also likes gospel music, but I don't think that's much like *Nirvana*, you guys."

I laughed. "No, I don't think so either."

"Exactly," Samuel replied.

"Come to think of it," I said, "Grandma Gladie always liked to sing a couple of her favorite gospel songs to us when we were little. If I remember right, they were called "He Touched Me," and "The Family of God."

Without looking our way, Michael sighed and said, "Yeah, that was them."

Samuel made eye contact with me when he glanced into the rearview mirror—sensing the same feelings as me. "Speaking of grandmothers," he said, "how have things been at your grandparents the last few weeks, Phillip? I assume you've adjusted to them quite well by now."

"It's good," I answered. "They really are great to us. We all seem a lot more relaxed these days, especially since Sarah's dad has been counseling us."

"I remember telling you a while back that you boys would really like Pastor George," Samuel said.

"Yeah, you were right. He's really helping us a lot," I said.

"That's great. You know, the Stewarts are great folks. I'm just sorry that you didn't get to know them until now. They sure seem crazy about you two. Your grandfather tells me that you guys sure keep them young at heart."

"Yeah, Grandma is still trying to get used to having two teen boys around," I said. "She still gets all embarrassed when we talk about the day she saw Michael in his birthday suit. Grandpa still teases her about it."

Samuel laughed.

"She also says we're bottomless pits when it comes to mealtime."

"I bet you are. Paul's starting to do the same with us," Samuel said.

"When do you think I'll get to meet your kids?" Michael asked without looking at Samuel.

Samuel cleared his throat. "Well, Sarah and I are dying to have you guys meet them, but—"

"You're afraid I might not be your son," Michael interrupted.

"Oh, God no, Michael, we would be honored to have them meet you guys, but we just . . . well . . . it's just difficult right now, Michael." Samuel looked over at my brother and then back at the road. "Okay, I owe you boys this," he said. "With all of the investigating going on with your parents over the abuse, and the uncertainty of the outcome of the paternity test, we just felt we shouldn't put any more stress on you. Getting to know my kids right now could be very difficult on all three of you. Legally, I'm stuck in limbo, and I hate it, Michael. I just want to get on with everything, but it will confuse my kids pretty badly if they get to know you and then your parents refuse to let us see you, especially if the test is negative. Your Mom could still deny me any contact with you until you turn eighteen years old."

"Yeah, Phillip is almost eighteen years old, so a custody battle wouldn't affect him," Michael said. "He can tell our parents where to go if he wants."

"I think I already have," I said.

I thought that might ease the tension I felt, but Michael was still serious. He sighed. "I could see my parents refusing to let me see you guys if it ends up I'm not your son."

"I still can't believe that Judge Betz pushed the paternity test order through so quickly," Samuel said. "I expected it might have taken a couple months, not a few weeks."

Michael lifted his head and replied, "Yeah, Grandpa Jack told Phillip that the judge probably did it because he was so angry at what my dad did to me in the garage that day."

"You know Michael, Sarah and I were preparing for a really long, ugly court battle with your mom over the right to have you tested. With your dad still serving out some time for a few more months, I didn't think we had a chance in getting your mom's signature. I'm just glad the judge moved forward with it in spite of them. I've been looking forward to getting this done."

"Samuel," Michael said, "Aunt Sylvia told me that my mom said you'd probably walk out on me again if I wasn't your kid, and she even said Sarah wouldn't want some other woman's *juvenile delinquent* invading your family."

Samuel's head jolted in the direction of Michael. "She said *what*?" I could see Michael pulling away from Samuel. "Why would your aunt even tell you something like that?"

"If I'm not your son, maybe Sarah wouldn't want me hanging around you guys." Michael glanced out the side window and took a deep breath. "I guess I can understand that."

Samuel found the next available parking lot and whipped the car into a parking spot. He jammed the car into park and unfastened his seatbelt. My muscles tightened with fear. Samuel turned toward Michael, whose shoulder was now pressed against the passenger side window.

"Guys, listen to me! I promise you that no matter what that test shows, we have really enjoyed getting to know both of you, and we would love to have you guys as a part of our lives, regardless of whether you turn out to officially be my son or not, Michael. I thought I'd told you that several times over the past few weeks! Boys, you have to believe me when I say that I'm not walking away!"

Michael looked over and wiped away his tears with his shirt. "Yes, sir."

"In my world, boys, we say what we mean, and we keep our promises! I know you're not used to that from adults, but I stand by my word!"

More tears rolled down Michael's reddened cheeks. *Was Samuel's tone actually a scolding?* I wondered. Regardless, Michael seemed embarrassed and afraid. "I'm sorry, Samuel. I didn't mean to make you mad, and I won't ever do it again! I promise!" Michael was horribly nervous; I could hear it in his rattled voice.

Michael flinched when Samuel suddenly turned even more in his seat. "Oh God, Michael—" Samuel suddenly stopped and thrust his hand to his forehead. "Michael, I didn't mean to sound like I was yelling at you guys. I'm not going to hurt you! Michael, please try and understand that I will never walk out on you ever again! Look, I don't have to take a test to prove I love someone. I would be honored to have you both in my life, no matter what!"

"I'm sorry," Michael pleaded, "it's just that my aunt really hurt me when she told me what my mom said. I wasn't sure if you'd want me around if I wasn't your son."

Samuel reached over and unlatched Michael's seatbelt. He pulled Michael close and hugged him. "I hate seeing you this way, Michael. God, I can't even imagine what your parents put you through. I'm so sorry, but I'm going to do everything I can to help you through all of this." Samuel looked directly into my brother's soggy eyes. "I promise you, Michael! Please believe me!"

Samuel turned and placed his hand on my knee. "Phillip, please understand that I'm doing everything I can. You are both very important to us." A tear rolled down my own cheek.

"Yes, sir, I know you're trying, but our dad really did some awful stuff to us, especially to Michael, and we both have trouble trusting people."

"I understand, Phillip, and I'll do everything in my power to prove to you boys that I'm a man of my word."

After we composed ourselves, Michael refastened his seatbelt as Samuel did the same.

"Samuel, do you think Megan and Paul will like me?" Michael asked.

"Absolutely, Michael! They are great kids, so I know they'll accept you both as either a brother or a friend when the time is right."

"I hope we know soon," Michael replied.

As Samuel continued driving, I started to think about the paternity test. Did they really need to know for sure? After all, it seemed as though Michael had already embedded himself deeply into Samuel's heart. I was certain that no test could change the way Samuel felt toward the young man he'd accepted as a part of his life.

"Michael," Samuel said, "I really meant that I don't need the paternity test to prove anything to me about you. I really mean it when I say that every single time I look at you, I see myself when I was sixteen. It's so overwhelming at times."

"Yeah, I kinda found out from Mom that—" Michael suddenly stopped. "Never mind," he mumbled.

I already knew what my brother wanted to say. Michael had shared with me—during one of our talks on the old fallen tree at home—that he felt Mom resented him because he looked so much like Samuel. After all, he was the man who had walked out on her as well.

Samuel cocked his head and asked, "What are you not telling me, Michael?"

Michael turned and looked out the window. There was nothing but silence as a response.

"Michael, you can tell me anything. I'll do my best to always understand."

Still staring out the window, Michael whispered, "Not this, Samuel. Well, at least not now."

Samuel was quiet for several moments. "Okay, Michael, I'll respect that, but I don't want you to ever feel you can't tell me something, okay?"

"Yes, sir." Michael rested his head against the glass again.

After a few more minutes, Samuel said, "Well, we aren't too far away from the clinic."

Michael thrust his head against the headrest. He took a deep breath, which was followed by a robust exhale of air.

"Have you told anyone about this yet?" Samuel asked. "I mean, have you told any of your friends at school?"

"Not really, just Brian. He's my best friend," Michael said. "I don't want anyone getting in the way, so I've kept it to myself." He sniffled and looked out the side window again.

"Yeah, Sam," I said, before confessing, "we have a couple great friends, but in order to protect ourselves, we never said much to them about the way Dad was with us."

My brother remained silent.

"Michael, are you okay?" Samuel asked.

Refusing to look at Samuel, Michael started to tear up again. "Samuel."

"Yes, Michael."

"I'm really scared that—that the test might come back and . . ." Michael lifted his shirt and wiped his face. "I promised myself I wasn't gonna do this."

Samuel reached over and placed his hand on Michael's shoulder. "It's going to be fine, Michael."

"Yeah, man, it's going to be fine," I repeated.

"You know, Michael," Samuel continued, "you didn't say anything when I mentioned I didn't need any test to prove what you mean to me. Do you feel that way, too?"

Michael paused. "Well, yeah, but I just think it'll drive me crazy if I don't find out for sure."

Samuel squeezed Michael's shoulder and said, "Okay then, let's get this done for all of us."

CHAPTER THIRTY-ONE

The Tuesday after the paternity testing, Mr. Busby called and asked if he could come over for a visit. When he arrived, he asked for all of us to have a seat around the table while he explained what the prosecutor's office was prepared to do after investigating the abuse. Dad was still in prison for the assault, and I knew Mom didn't look like she was going to escape the penalty for allowing the abuse to take place.

Mr. Busby pulled out several documents from his brown, leather briefcase. "Phillip and Michael," he began, "I'm here because the prosecutor, Mrs. Bowen, needed me to discuss the investigation into the years of abuse you two suffered at the hands of your father and mother. From what we have been able to gather from several reports, especially from the sheriff's office and hospital staff, your mother obviously permitted the abuse to take place for years."

"But, she never laid a hand on me that much," Michael insisted.

Mr. Busby shifted in his chair, adjusted his light blue tie, and cleared his throat. "You're correct, but she isn't being charged like your father. You see, there is a felony charge that can be filed if another parent stands by and does nothing to stop the abuse."

"Does that mean my mom could go to jail?" Michael asked.

"Well, Michael, I understand that you may not have been aware of such a law, but this is out of your hands, as well as your brother's, because you are both minors. The investigation started the night Officer Bailey discovered the fact that you and Phillip had both suffered some abuse, and your mother did nothing to stop it over the years."

"What did you tell that officer about Mom, Phillip?" Michael demanded to know.

I pulled my hand up to my forehead and closed my eyes for a moment. "I don't really remember," I said.

He slammed his hand on the table. "I know I made Mom furious when I yelled at her that night in the hospital, but I didn't think she'd go to jail for anything. Now she'll really hate me!" I was surprised Michael even cared about that, but his reaction to the investigation was starting to scare me.

"I'm sorry, Michael," I yelled, "but I was a little stressed out that day, so cut me some slack, will ya!"

Michael leaned back in his chair and gazed up at the ceiling.

"Besides, you were passed out and bleeding all over me in the car. And it's not like you didn't almost die the week before that. So, I freaked out, man! Maybe I said something to the officer, but I really don't care. Mom let Dad do all sorts of evil stuff to you for years, and I finally had enough guts to do something about it!"

Grandma stood and walked over to me. Her gentle touch on my shoulder tamed the anger tearing up the inside of my chest.

Grandpa reached out and placed his hand on Michael's forearm.

"Mike, you don't have to be afraid anymore. No one—not your dad or your mom—is going to do anything to you. I won't allow it."

Michael's face drained of its color. He looked up at Grandpa and said, "I never thought it would come to something like this!"

Grandma moved over and wrapped her arms around Michael from behind. "Sweetie, you don't have to be afraid. Grandpa and I won't let anything happen to you."

With tears flooding his eyes, Michael gazed at her and said, "But, Grandma, you were never involved in putting your own mom in jail."

Grandma signaled for me to move to her vacant seat, and she sat down next to Michael and grasped his hand. "Honey, Mr. Busby is here because he needs to ask and tell you some important things."

"Michael," Mr. Busby said, "because this is a felony case, the facts from the investigation will need to be presented to a grand jury first. They will determine whether the case goes further or not. All you need to do is tell the grand jury what happened to you. And besides, your parents won't be there, so you'll be okay."

Michael glared at me, and then back at Mr. Busby. "Do I have to?"

Mr. Busby placed his pen on the table and leaned forward. "Michael, you won't have to be alone. Mrs. Bowen will be in the room with you. This is not a testimony like you might see in a jury trial in a courtroom. You will simply tell your story. It's a standard procedure, Michael. You have nothing to worry about."

"Yes I do!" Michael yelled. "My life for one thing! You have no idea what he said he'd do to us if I ever said anything." Michael's hands erupted with tremors, and beads of sweat clung to his forehead. He looked over at me and cried out, "Phillip, you know what he's capable of doing! I'm dead if I tell people what he really did! You know it, too!" Michael clenched his hands before slamming them onto the table. "He'll really hurt me bad! I know he will!"

Mr. Busby sat motionless—likely surprised by the intense terror he was witnessing from Michael.

My brother pushed his chair back and bolted through the back door.

I started to run after him. As I forced the door open, I stopped and looked back at the stunned adults assembled around the table. "I think you get it now."

"Phillip, I have to be honest," Mr. Busby pleaded. "I need Michael's testimony. You guys are scheduled, and there isn't a choice in the matter. We can even film his testimony and play it for the grand jury."

I shook my head.

"Look, everything he's been through really angers me more than you know, Phillip. Your father and mother shouldn't get away with what they did to you guys, especially to your brother."

"I know," I said, finding it somewhat comforting just knowing someone acknowledged our need for vindication. "I will get through to him. You will hear his testimony somehow."

I found Michael standing by the pond, skipping rocks. I picked up a stone and ran my thumb across its smooth surface. "I see you've discovered the pond," I said. I spotted a patch of cattails on the other side of the pond and aimed for them. The rock jumped four times before sinking—missing the intended target completely.

"So, does everybody hate me?" Michael sheepishly asked.

"Not at all." I replied. "But Mr. Busby is afraid we won't be able to get you to testify to that jury. He wants to really nail Mom and Dad to the wall for what they did to you."

Michael walked over and sat on the grass. I meandered over and sat beside him. He stretched his legs out and crossed them as he leaned back onto his arms and rolled his neck around several times. "I can understand them going after Dad, but how can I help send my own mom to jail?" He shook his head. "I know I always say I hate her, but I really never meant it."

"Michael, we can't let either of them get away with everything they did. I know that Dad was mean to Mom, too, and I did try to protect her, but you see how good Grandma and Grandpa are to us, and I can't believe Mom never asked them for help, knowing it could have gotten all of us away from Dad." I sighed as I thrust my knees up against my chest, pleading for Michael to understand. "Look, man, you have no idea how selfish Mom really is. Remember, she even refused to sign the papers to have you tested with Samuel. Doesn't that prove that the only person she really cares about is herself? Trust me, Michael, I get it now."

The sunlight shimmered off of the pond, causing me to squint and turn away.

Michael shook his head. "I know, but I still don't want Mom to go to jail." He sighed. "I can't believe you actually want me to testify against her."

"I know," I said, "but Mom is just as guilty as Dad." I waited for Michael to respond, but he said nothing. "Do you think it might help if you talked to Samuel about this?" I suggested.

My brother lifted his arms and rested his back on the ground. "Dad's in jail, and the sadistic pig still scares me."

I decided to lie next to him.

"Phillip, I don't want to bother Samuel about this. I don't want to lose him over this kind of garbage." He pressed his fingers to his temples and rolled his head toward me. "Are you gonna testify?"

"Yes," I said, "I'm doing it for both of us. Besides, I don't think we have a choice."

Michael sat up. "We don't have a choice?" Michael sprang to his feet and forced a hand to his forehead. "I am so screwed, Phillip! We both are!"

I sat up. "I don't think we can back out from a grand jury, Michael."

My brother stomped his foot.

"Besides, what did Dad tell you he'd do to us?"

"I can't get into this right now!" he insisted.

"Look," I said, as I started to stand, "I always said you can tell me anything, so why won't you?"

"I just can't right now!" he screamed.

"Okay, whatever you say, but I'm sick and tired of everything in my whole life being nothing but some huge secret."

Michael picked up a stone and hurled it into the middle of the pond. The ringlets dispersed like the waves of anger rippling outward from my brother.

Afraid of what he might do next, I said, "We better head back. They're probably worried about you."

"Whatever," Michael replied.

As we walked away, silence whirled around us like a brisk, chilly wind, causing me to shiver.

That night, the violent crashing sound of glass hitting the hardwood floor caused me to leap from my bed. Shrieks emanated from Michael's room. I barged through the doorway, not knowing what had happened.

His bed was empty.

"Michael? Where are you?" I spotted the top of his head over in the far corner on the other side of his bed. I ran over just as my grandparents arrived. I hit the floor and latched onto my brother. Like a frightened child, he was curled up in the corner, shaking.

"What in the world happened?" Grandpa yelled. He charged to the side of the bed where Michael and I were huddled on the floor. Grandma followed.

"No!" Michael screamed out, while pressing his upper body even deeper into the corner. *"Don't touch me!"*

Michael tried forcing me away, but I grabbed his arms and started shaking him. "Michael! Wake up! It's just another dream!"

He blinked several times and gazed around the room. He was still pulling away from me in an attempt to free his arms from my grip. After a few moments, he started to settle down. Tears instantly filled his eyes as he grabbed me around my neck, pulling me forcefully into his chest. I could feel the ferocity of his heartbeat against my body.

Grandpa started to walk closer, but Grandma grabbed his arm and pulled him back. She shook her head and put her finger to her lips.

"What did you see, Michael?" I asked.

"Phillip, I—" He buried his head into my shoulder. His warm breaths coated my bare skin with moisture.

"Michael, you're scaring me. Please tell me what you saw in your dream. You're safe now!"

I pulled the sheet over and wiped his tear-stained face. "Dad was hitting you with the ax! There was blood everywhere!" Michael thrust his hands into my face, trying to show me his imagined blood-stained fingers. Michael slammed his head against the wall several times, causing our grandparents to flinch. "Why can't I get these dreams outta my head? *Why?*" He thrust his knees against his chest and sobbed.

"It was just a dream, Michael! I'm fine! See, there's no blood on me!" I insisted. "Michael, we're safe now. Dad's in prison, remember? He can't hurt us!" When I placed my hand on his back, I could still feel the booming pulse of his heartbeat. "Michael, I'm here with you, and I'm not gonna let him lay a hand on you ever again." As I caressed his back, I moved my lips closer to his ear and whispered, "Just breathe with me, Michael." I inhaled deeply before forcing air from my lips loud enough for him to hear. My breaths soon developed a rhythm. His once convulsing chest soon slowed. "That's it, Michael, we're almost there—just a few more deep breaths."

Michael's weeping eased. "Phillip, I was begging Mom to do something, but she just stood there watching him kill you." My brother sat up straight and rested his head against the wall. "It was awful, man." He ran his fingers through his soaked hair. *"Mom just stood there!"* Sweat rolled down his face like raindrops on a window. He slammed his fist against the wall, causing several pictures to drop to the floor. Grandma buried her face into Grandpa's upper arm. I heard her mumble something about possibly calling Pastor George to come over to the house. I was hoping they wouldn't, because I didn't want him to see Michael that way. Michael reached out and pulled me toward him once more.

"They're never gonna go away! I can't keep living with these dreams, Phillip. *I can't!*"

My mind was being crushed under the weight of my guilt. I knew I was part of the reason why Michael suffered such terrifying nightmares. I had waited too long before protecting him—giving Dad all the time he needed to inflict as much damage as possible.

Later that night, as Michael and I rested on my bed, I whispered, "Hey, are you okay?"

"Yeah," he answered, "but now I'm worried about Friday with those jury people."

I gazed upward, feeling smothered by the oppressive darkness pressing down on my vulnerable body.

"I understand, Michael."

"Phillip, I have to tell them, don't I?"

"Yes, Michael, you do. But remember, I'll be there with you. We can't let Mom and Dad get away with what they did."

An eerie silence filled the blackness.

Michael rolled onto his side—his breaths growing quieter as he faced away from me. "I'll tell them, Phillip. I'll tell them what they did to *both* of us."

CHAPTER THIRTY-TWO

The Tuesday following the grand jury testimony started out as an ordinary school day. Michael and I rushed around the house getting ready while the aroma of a hearty breakfast wafted through the upstairs hallway, stimulating my senses like a hot shower in the morning. Michael and I had grown so accustomed to having mouthwatering meals that we had forgotten about the Spam that we sometimes fried for ourselves for dinner when Mom and Dad were too incapacitated to cook.

Life had somehow returned to what we assumed was something normal. Grandpa allowed Michael and me to spend a few days a week at his business learning some much needed skills, so personal time was becoming a rare fixture in our lives. We simply found it refreshing when trying to balance our lives between school, working, exercise at the gym, and absolving some of the pain from our excruciating past. Even though there finally seemed to be hope, we still had a lot on our minds. We had no idea about the outcome of the unfolding abuse case involving our parents or the paternity test results. We were also uncertain how to handle our newfound friends at school. Oddly, we were no longer afraid to invite them over, and peers were no longer afraid to acknowledge us at school. Perhaps the strangest thing of all was that Michael and I realized that we needed to redefine our relationship as brothers, because our connection to each other had always been defined by trauma, violence, and fear.

When we pulled into the driveway after school that Tuesday, I noticed some extra cars in front of the house. I recognized one of the cars immediately. It was Samuel's. A quick glance at my brother's face revealed that he'd noticed it as well. My brother hurried from our car, which was barely stopped. Waiting for us in the parlor was Grandma and Grandpa, Sarah, Samuel, and his attorney, Joseph Schell.

I was right behind Michael when he blurted out, "What's going on, Sam? Is something wrong?"

Samuel stood and handed Michael a letter.

"What's this?" Michael asked. Samuel told him to open it and take a look.

"Read the first paragraph out loud," Samuel insisted.

"I don't understand," Michael replied.

"Just open it, and read the first paragraph," Grandpa pleaded.

Grandma Madeline had a tissue held firmly to her eyes, as did Sarah. I couldn't help but yell out, "God, Michael! Just read whatever it is!" He removed the letter from the envelope—which brought back a repulsive memory of another letter—and began reading. I gazed around the room, looking at the animated expressions on anxious faces.

"Final diagnostics results?" Michael asked. "What is this?"

"Just read it, Michael," Samuel insisted.

"Dear Mr. Roberts," Michael stated, *"we are writing to inform you of the results related to case number 08061922GF1581. The DNA samples extracted during the laboratory testing have indicated that the alleged father, Samuel Joseph Roberts (2721-731),* ***cannot*** *be excluded as the biological father of Michael Paul Williams . . ."* Michael's head popped up. "Does this really mean what I think it does, Sam?"

"It sure does, Michael!" Samuel exclaimed.

His voice rattled like he was experiencing hypothermia. With the letter still held firmly in one of his hands, Michael's arms suddenly lowered to his side. Samuel and Sarah stepped over and immediately embraced him.

"Michael," Sarah said, "we are so proud of you, honey. You've been so strong throughout all of this."

Michael cried out, "I can't believe it's real!"

Samuel sobbed, refusing to let go of the child he could officially claim as his own. A stampede of emotions crushed my body, rendering me incapable of standing. I quickly collapsed onto one of the chairs.

Samuel lifted Michael's chin with his finger and said, "Yes, Michael, you're my son—you always have been! And somehow, I've always known it!"

Michael buried his face once more into Samuel's chest and cried, "I can't believe it. I actually have a real dad!"

Samuel's lips trembled—his emotions likely rendering him incapable of uttering another word. They started swaying back and forth, genuinely enraptured by the certainty of their eternal connection.

Sarah saw me crying alone, so she walked over and extended her hand. I looked up—my face was drowning in tears. She grasped my hand. I felt her tugging on my arm, so I stood. She guided me over to Samuel and Michael. My brother looked at me and suddenly seized me around my neck. His warm tears raced down his face. Samuel and Sarah backed away, allowing Michael and me several moments to ourselves. My words were buried alive by the joy that possessed my entire body. They soon rejoined us, wrapping their arms tightly around our shoulders. Samuel tilted his head and rested it against mine.

"Phillip, I gained two sons today, and I don't want you to ever forget that!" he said.

"We really mean that, Phillip!" Sarah concurred. "We are so honored to call you our son as well." I released my arms from Michael as my head lowered toward the floor. Sarah wrapped one of her arms around my back and rubbed gently. "Honey, we are so proud of you for being such a great brother to Michael, and we can't imagine our life without you." Somewhat embarrassed by my lack of restraint, I couldn't resist sobbing while pressing the side of my face firmly into her upper shoulder. She stroked the back of my head and whispered, "It's okay to cry, Phillip. We love you!"

Our grandparents soon joined the four of us in the middle of the parlor.

Samuel stepped away from us and walked over to his attorney, who'd also been wiping tears from his eyes and chin. Samuel took some papers from Mr. Schell and walked back over and grabbed Michael's wrist. He lifted my brother's arm and placed the papers into Michael's hand.

"Do you know what these are?" Samuel asked.

Michael wiped his eyes on his sleeve and glanced at the papers briefly and said, "Oh my God, are these what I think they are?"

"What do you think they are, Michael?" Samuel inquired.

"It says something about custody at the top."

"Yes, Michael, and I would be honored if you would agree to make it legal!"

Michael nodded—obviously unable to speak.

Samuel pulled my brother close again, kissed him on his forehead, and said, "I love you, Michael!"

"It will take some time for it to go through the courts," Mr. Schell explained, "but Judge Betz is already aware of your case, and I'm certain he will push things through as fast as he can. The judge really seems to care about you."

Michael glanced toward my direction. "Phillip, I wanna do this!"

"Do it, Michael! I told you that everyone will always know that we're brothers. This doesn't change that."

It was agreed between all of us that a celebration dinner was in order, and it was also time for Michael to officially meet his other siblings. Samuel and Sarah knew they had to get home to Megan and Paul soon. I also realized something unexpectedly that I hadn't thought about before, but I decided to keep it to myself until I had the chance to speak with Samuel alone.

After Mr. Schell left, Michael and I walked Samuel and Sarah to their car. We all hugged again, and Sarah kissed Michael on the cheek before he and Samuel walked over to the driver's side door. I decided to remain with Sarah so I could open the door for her. I thanked her for including me as a part of their family.

"You know, Phillip," she said, "Sam and I have some big shoes to fill."

"What do you mean?" I asked.

"You've always been there for Michael, and it's going to be a tough challenge for us to live up to what you've already done for him!"

"Thanks," I said, "but I wish I would have done more." I lowered my voice. "Sarah, I'm really struggling to get rid of the guilt I feel from not protecting Michael sooner than I did. He's suffered so much, and his nightmares—" I suddenly stopped.

She rubbed my upper arm and smiled. "Phillip, the important thing to remember is that you did stop your father, especially when Michael needed you the most."

"I guess," I whispered, shifting my weight. "You know, Michael has always deserved to have a father like Samuel."

"And so do you, Phillip," she replied. "Sam really meant it when he said he gained two sons today." She grasped my hand and pulled me close to her. "Phillip, I know it will take some time for all of us to work through this, but I already love you very much. I think I realized that from the very first time I met you in the lobby at the hospital. I bought you that crazy soda, remember?"

"Yeah, it was pretty pathetic that I didn't have any money, and now look where I am." I looked back at the house. "But then again," I said, as I turned toward her, "if I did have money, you might not have stopped and talked to me that night. I guess God does work in mysterious ways."

She leaned over and kissed my cheek before getting into the car.

"Thanks for everything!" I said.

I walked around to Samuel as he and Michael embraced once more. "I'll see you tonight, Michael." As my brother stepped back, and Samuel started to get into the front seat, he suddenly paused and shook his head. He stepped out of the car and smiled. "Let me rephrase that," he said. "I'll see you tonight, *son*." He pulled Michael close again and patted him on the back—the kind of burly series of slaps a father would give to his teenage son.

Michael grinned. "I'm looking forward to it, *Dad!*" Michael headed back around the car toward Sarah.

I stepped closer to the car and helped shut the door for Samuel. I leaned down and whispered, "Can I ask you something, Samuel?"

"Sure, Phillip . . . I mean, *son*."

I grinned.

"When Michael was reading the DNA results, I heard him mention his middle name."

"Yes, me too," Samuel replied.

"Did you name Paul after Michael's middle name?"

Samuel chuckled. He glanced over at Sarah, who fondly gazed back at him. When he turned back toward me, he said, "Phillip, as I said to you the first night we'd met, you really are very observant. Yes, when I saw Michael's birth announcement in the paper way back in 1976, I guess I always knew I was going to name my son—if I had another—after your brother's middle name. I wasn't going to at first, but I felt that if I did use the name Paul, it would feel as though I was connected to Michael somehow. I felt it was the right thing to do, I guess."

I reached into the car and shook his hand. "Yeah, I agree. It definitely was the right thing to do." His grip was taut and sincere.

"Phillip, I'm *very* honored to have you as a son as well. I truly mean that. You watched over Michael when no one else stepped up, including me. I can never repay you for that."

"Thank you, sir, but I'll never feel like I ever did enough for my brother."

"Yes, you did, Phillip. You certainly did more than me."

I started to walk away but decided to stop. "Hey, thanks again for everything . . . *Dad!*"

I chuckled, as Samuel smiled and waved. They soon started down the driveway toward Stewart Road, and Michael and I walked into the house.

"I hope Megan and Paul react pretty good to the news," Michael said.

"They've been raised by great parents, Michael, so I think they'll be just fine."

"Yeah," Michael said, "for the first time ever, I think we all will."

CHAPTER THIRTY-THREE

The restaurant was busy, but Samuel was able to get one of the private meeting rooms for us. Some people still seemed baffled at the appearance of all of us having dinner together. That familiar underhanded whispering and finger pointing had resurfaced, and I was reminded of the insensitive babble I had become all too acquainted with over the years. I knew what the soulless, ignorant people were thinking that night: *Why would Samuel Roberts, a well-respected business man, be in the company of the sons of a sociopath like Tony Williams?* I could almost feel their glares clinging to my body like pet hairs stuck to a black pair of cotton dress pants.

The evening was uncomfortable at first, even though Sarah had called earlier to tell me what they had discussed with their kids. At the restaurant, Megan and Paul hid behind their parents for a while before realizing that Michael and I were approachable. Megan eventually handed Michael a card she had made earlier that evening, and Paul started to ask questions about soccer. The three of them soon bonded, as though they had known one another forever. Thankfully, this eased the tension overshadowing each discussion we tried to engage in during those first awkward minutes, which seemed to crawl along each time I glanced at my wristwatch.

Michael made sure Megan and Paul understood that I was his brother. Their confusing stares told me that they, too, were trying to assemble their own puzzle, filled with unfamiliar pieces. They soon warmed up to me, and I did the same with them. Nothing could have wiped the grin off of Paul's face after hearing how much he looked like his *big brother*.

I had to brush away a tear when Paul looked at me and said, "Phillip, you really look like me and Michael, too. I think that means we really are brothers, doesn't it?"

Michael reached over and put his arm around me. "Yeah, Paul, Phillip's the best brother—" He ceased for a moment. "I mean, he's the best brother you and me could ever have in the whole world."

I put my arm around Michael, and surprisingly, Paul embraced both of us around our waists. Sarah snapped a photo of the three of us together. I knew it wouldn't be long before the photo likely found its way onto a wall with their other family portraits.

Sarah's father and mother, Pastor George and Margaret, arrived at the restaurant almost half an hour later than us. Pastor George was late because one of his parishioners had a family emergency. He and his wife spent a lot of their time talking with me about my feelings regarding the changes happening in my life. They also talked to Michael privately, and I noticed several times that they had their arms around him. I used to think such people were rare—almost extinct—but our association with Samuel and Sarah introduced us to people unlike any we had ever known. It wasn't long before I realized something I didn't think was possible: It was actually safe to love people without first having to filter my feelings through Dad's hatred. I was free to reach into the dark recesses of my heart and resurrect true feelings I'd thought Dad had eradicated forever.

An awesome highlight to the evening for me was when Megan drew a special picture on the back of her placemat before we ate dinner together as a family.

Yes, a *real* family!

When I asked her who she was drawing, she said, "I'm drawing a special picture for you."

To my surprise, she included me in the drawing, which was labeled *The Roberts Family* at the top of the paper. Amazingly, Michael and I battled a spiteful man for many years, but a little girl—with a simple drawing—started to help erase the misery of nearly a decade of our lives. *How was that possible?*

Even though nothing was official yet, Michael and I were welcomed into the Roberts family unconditionally. It was only a short time before that night that I believed my world was coming to an end. However, a cruel prank at a party ended up opening an entirely different path into our lives.

I guess Pastor George was right when he said to me privately that God can find purpose in anything we might have to face in this life.

At one point during the evening, he put his arm around me and said, "You know when you open a box full of puzzle pieces, and they're all mixed up, Phillip?"

"Yes, sir," I replied.

"Well, God reaches into the box and takes all the scattered fragments of our lives, and He eventually puts together a beautiful picture we come to understand as our very own masterpiece. We just have to trust Him. God knows just where all the pieces fit perfectly together, and He even fixes the pieces of our lives that we have damaged, and He makes them whole again. That's what love is capable of doing, young man."

My face was soon baptized in tears.

"Are you okay, Phillip?"

"Yes, sir, it's just . . ."

"It's just what, Phillip?" He soon guided me over to a chair and we sat down. "Tell me what you're thinking, son."

"Sir, I can't believe you just said that to me about life being a puzzle. I've always looked at life as a bunch of puzzle pieces, too. I guess I never thought about God somehow working it all out."

He patted my shoulder. "You know, Phillip, the Bible says 'Love endures all things,' and I really believe that. Don't you?"

I lowered my head in shame. "I'm not totally sure, sir. This whole night is making me feel like I'm hovering up in the air, looking down on something I don't quite understand—and maybe don't deserve."

He rested his hand on my shoulder. "Phillip, really listen to me for a moment."

I was nervous from the directness of his gaze into my eyes.

He smiled and said, "You and your brother are here tonight, with your new family. Did you ever think that would happen?"

"No, sir," I said—my voice cracking.

"I know your father put you boys through a terrible time, but somehow, you survived it all, right?"

"Well . . . yes, I guess we did, sir, but Michael's nightmare are all because of me."

"Phillip, who do you think got your brother through everything he was forced to experience while living with someone like your dad?"

"I'm not sure."

"You did, Phillip!" Pastor George declared. "And what was it that motivated you to get Michael through it all?"

"I guess I just hated to see him suffer for something he didn't do."

"True," he said, "but did you ever consider the fact that it was your love for your brother that helped you endure all the things you both suffered through?" A flood of tears were again rolling down my cheeks. "Phillip, love can get you through anything. That's why you're here tonight! This isn't by chance. You see, it just took one piece of the puzzle fitting into the right place, at just the right time. Now that puzzle is coming together in a way you never expected. Try to remember that God works all things out for our good, but He does it in His perfect timing and in His own perfect way."

I leaned back in my chair and lifted my shirt to wipe tears from my stunned face. Pastor George reached over and pulled me toward him. As he hugged me, he whispered into my ear, "Love does endure all things, Phillip. You just have to stop long enough to realize that it sometimes takes us on a different path than we had originally planned."

The soft laughter and pleasant chatter circumnavigating the room caused me to realize the wisdom in what Pastor George had said. A peace I couldn't quite explain surged through my body, and a joy seemed to radiate outward from me like the sunlight of a warm summer day.

I chuckled to myself and smiled when I realized that Grandma Gladie would have been disappointed that I missed such a vital detail about my life. When I rested back in my chair, I said, "Sir, even Tyler, a new friend of mine at school just said to me the other day how 'God works in mysterious ways.' I guess that's the truth."

Pastor George patted my knee and replied, "He certainly does, Phillip. He certainly does."

Later that evening, Michael and I couldn't sleep, so we decided to stay in my room and talk. It had been in the back of my mind that this situation might pull us apart, but Sarah never let us forget that things would somehow work out in the end, and Pastor George reminded me of that same thought before we left the restaurant that evening. By accepting me, Samuel and Sarah kept Michael and me together. Sarah was also one of the heroes who stepped in and rescued us during one of the worst conflicts we had to endure on the battlefield that once defined our lives.

Before Michael left my room that night, I said, "Goodnight, Michael Roberts."

Michael chuckled before replying, "Yeah, it has a nice ring to it, doesn't it?"

"Yeah, it sure does, little brother."

CHAPTER THIRTY-FOUR

Within several weeks, after finding out that Michael was Samuel's son, my brother and I stood beside each other in a familiar courtroom. It was the same courthouse where we had testified to the grand jury. It was also where Judge Betz had sentenced both of my parents, in separate cases, to prison. Dad pleaded out and received five years for the abuse he committed against Michael. He was also placed on probation for several years after prison and was ordered to have no contact with my brother or the Roberts family. Mom was sentenced to eighteen months, with two years of probation for permitting the abuse to take place. It was a fair deal, according to the limits of the law. Dad was facing up to nine years if he didn't take the plea offered to him. Even his revenge against Mom, and his hatred for Michael, wasn't worth four more years to him.

I always remembered the striped wallpaper in my bedroom at home, and how it manifested itself as prison bars; however, it was Dad's turn to experience the sensation of being a captive in his own barbaric, torturous confinement. I realized in that moment that Dad's hatred had already put him into a hellish prison many years before the one he had been sentenced to by the judge. It was at least some form of justice—plain and simple.

On this new day, Judge Betz glanced over the rim of his glasses at my brother and me in that same courtroom, and after clearing his throat and smiling, he said, "You know, these are the types of opportunities when I find myself serving a purpose far greater than I ever expected out of this career. Boys, I find it remarkable how you two stood by each other through some of the worst circumstances of mental and physical abuse I've dealt with in many years."

I looked over at my brother, who was visibly shaking from the intimidation of being in the presence of what seemed to be a stern-looking grizzly bear in a black robe. Even though this was a joyous gathering, I knew Michael was anxious, so I placed my hand on his shoulder and squeezed. His shoulders drooped slightly. He glanced over at me and smiled. Beads of sweat clung to his forehead.

Michael looked so stately in his new blue suit, which Samuel had purchased for the special occasion. Samuel bought a new suit for me as well. Michael's brown hair swooped downward and curved just over his eyes. Thin traces of facial hair still outlined the contour of his jaw. Combined with his blue eyes, he was Samuel incarnate. I had seen Samuel's graduation photo, and no paternity test could have denied the fact that Michael was clearly his son.

"Mr. Roberts, what you and your wife have done here for these boys is an act of love and courage I've rarely seen. You knew what you were up against with the boys' parents, but you stood by both boys and transformed them into your own sons. And, Phillip . . ."

I stiffened and released my hand from Michael's shoulder.

"I want to commend you for being the best brother possible to Michael during such dark times in your young lives. You are the reason your brother is here today. I believe your father could have easily made you an only child that day in the garage. Not all heroes wear a uniform. Sometimes they wear a business suit like the man standing beside you; sometimes they wear scrubs like the woman next to you who has clearly stepped into the role of a mother for you and your brother; and sometimes, Phillip, they come in the form of an older brother just like you."

He sat back in his chair. "Phillip, your love for Michael is what helped you endure the darker days of your past. Mr. and Mrs. Roberts are the kind of folks you boys deserved long before you met them. It just proves that some heroes appear when you least expect them."

Samuel smiled and winked his eye at me. He nodded his head, indicating he wanted me to say something to the judge.

"Thanks . . . umm . . . I mean thank you, Your Honor," I sputtered.

"Now," Judge Betz announced, as Sarah reached for my hand and grasped it firmly, "it is with great honor that I award sole custody of Michael Paul Roberts to Samuel Joseph and Sarah Katherine Roberts."

Sarah squeezed my hand as Samuel placed his arm around Michael's shoulders and pulled him close.

"And as for Phillip," Judge Betz stated, "I have no doubt, Mr. and Mrs. Roberts, that Phillip will make you two every bit as proud as I suspect Michael will. I am certain those boys will continue to bring tremendous love and joy into your lives."

"Thank you, Your Honor," Samuel replied.

Judge Betz looked as though he had finished; however, he removed his glasses and spoke directly to our younger siblings. "Megan and Paul, I want you two to understand what an important day this is in your lives as well. You have gained two brothers today—older brothers—and I want you to look up to them, because I am confident that they will set great examples for you two to follow."

Paul stepped closer and hugged Michael around his chest. He started to cry. Megan suddenly turned and hugged me.

Judge Betz pounded his gavel and stood. Moments later, he came down from his bench and extended his hand to shake Michael's. "It's been an honor getting to know you, Michael. I couldn't be happier for you than I am right now. You're a true hero to your family. You're definitely a survivor."

He then shook my hand and said, "Phillip, you have a courage that I will never forget as long as I live. You go after that college degree, and keep showing this world what you're made of."

"I will, sir. Thank you," I said.

We went out to celebrate after the custody case had become final, and as I watched Michael interacting with his new family around the table at the restaurant, I thought about how his life was once a picture of misery and gloom for so many years. I soon smiled when I also thought about how Samuel and Sarah came along and started to change my brother's life into what I expected would eventually become a beautiful masterpiece. It's amazing what good people can create in others when unconditional love takes over as the artist. I guess I learned that each person we meet somehow adds the color we need to complete the portrait of our life—one that is uniquely our own.

Samuel and Sarah insisted that I live with them. They knew Michael would make a better adjustment to their home if I was there with him. More than that, they loved me for who I was and wanted me to have a chance at a loving family, too. For the first time in a decade, I experienced the luxury of having some really normal days as a family. It was gratifying to walk through the front door and into a home I appreciated; eating a meal that involved a conversation—not an interrogation; and best of all, seeing people I knew were happy to see me. For once, I loved hearing Michael argue with someone else over personal space, and even watching him do chores without being threatened. It was great seeing the excitement on his face when Samuel and Sarah would sit on the porch and talk about things that really mattered to him. I often chose not to interfere when he was alone with them, but the isolation sometimes made me feel empty—like being stranded in an endless, barren desert full of nothing but sand. Regardless, I knew it was far better to let him experience what it was like to depend on people who weren't going to abandon him.

Samuel, Sarah, and I spent a lot of time together as well. I seemed to partner with them when it came to helping Michael trust people again. When Michael awakened everyone in the house during his nightmares, they allowed me to help him first before Samuel joined me. I secretly wept alone one evening in the bathroom after a terrifying nightmare plunged my brother into uncontrollable hysteria. Samuel was up late that evening, helping me with homework, when we heard a thunderous crashing noise coming from mine and Michael's bedroom. We ran in only to find Michael screaming from inside of our closet. Buried under the clothes he had pulled down from the long metal rod, Michael was almost inconsolable. After several moments of intense fighting, Samuel joined me on the floor as I battled to grasp Michael's flailing arms and legs. His strength was getting much harder to control. Sarah, who had responded to the commotion as well—along with Megan and Paul—had immediately rushed our siblings back to the master bedroom as Samuel and I struggled with Michael. Eventually, we regained control.

"Dad," Michael cried out, "please make them stop!" Michael sobbed as he reached out to Samuel for comfort.

"I'm here with you, Michael, and I'm not going to let anything hurt you. Just calm down! Phillip and I are here!"

Michael pulled him even closer to his chest. I rose to my knees and studied the affection my brother and Samuel were expressing toward each other. I eventually stood and stepped toward our bedroom door. As I looked back, right before exiting the room, Samuel was rubbing Michael's back and reassuring him that everything would be okay.

After entering the bathroom down the hallway, I sat on the edge of the bathtub and cried. I realized that my brother now had someone else to depend on when he was frightened and alone. Like a child fighting to give up a cherished childhood possession, like a soft, comforting blanket, I'd realized that it was time for me to let go. I was becoming nothing more than a brother to Michael—a role I knew I would have to invent with each passing day.

Samuel and Sarah had also been asking me many questions about the abuse Michael had endured. They wanted to make sure their discipline would never be perceived as a threat to my brother. The true test of my advice came one evening when Michael and Paul argued over the use of a video game console, and my brother violently pushed Paul over a chair in the family room. I had always been concerned that my dad's violent temper might manifest itself in Michael's actions, especially when he was angry or frustrated. It was almost as if I was anticipating some inherited disease that might consume my brother's body. Minutes later, Samuel was confronting Michael.

I had been with Andrew that day; however, I learned of the incident as soon as I arrived back at home. Samuel's eyes shimmered with tears as he told me the details while sitting on the front porch. He explained to me that Michael seemed frozen in place earlier that evening, as if he'd been in suspended animation, especially when Samuel took several steps toward him in the family room.

Samuel said that my brother had backed up against one of the walls and cried out, "Dad . . . don't . . . please . . ." He said that Michael cowered from what he likely believed was an impending assault. "I'm sorry!" he yelled. "Please don't hurt me!" My brother buried his face and pressed his shoulder into the wall. "I didn't mean it!"

Samuel had abruptly ceased his movement toward Michael. Stunned by the utter fear he was witnessing from my brother, Samuel said, "Michael, I . . ." Samuel said he stepped backward and sat in one of the overstuffed recliners, appearing as nonthreatening as possible. "Michael, I'm not here to hurt you. I just wanted to find out what happened with Paul."

After several moments, he said that Michael had slowly lowered his hands from his face, but he remained firmly pressed against the wall. Michael questioned, as he rolled slightly and rested his back against the wall. "Is Paul okay?"

"Yes, Michael. He's fine," Samuel told him. "He's just a little shaken up from the shock of being pushed. He didn't expect you to react that way."

"I didn't mean to push him. It just kinda happened," Michael said, as a tear streamed down his cheek. "I better tell him I'm sorry."

Samuel told Michael that he expected him to offer an apology to Paul. That's when he happened to notice another tear cascading down the crevice of Michael's nose and clinging to his upper lip, before falling aimlessly to the floor. Samuel told me that he was still hesitant to approach Michael, so he asked Michael to come to him. I guess my brother said that he would just go to his bedroom and wait for Samuel.

As Michael walked toward the steps, Samuel reached out and rested his hand on Michael's back. He said he could feel my brother's muscles tensing from the contact. "Yes, Michael, I do want you to go to your room, but not for the reason you're thinking."

That's when Samuel hugged my brother. He said Michael's arms dropped to his sides, as though he was afraid to return the affection.

When I talked to Michael later that night, while sitting on the floor in our room with our backs against the bed, he said he was unsure what Samuel truly intended on doing when he hugged him. My dad would often brush his hand gently across Michael's cheek, smile, and then violently slap his mouth, often knocking my brother to the floor.

"Michael, you know Samuel would never hurt you, right?"

"I guess, Phillip, but I just didn't know what to do." Michael leaned in closer to me. "Phillip, Samuel said he loved me, and that he'd never hurt me." Michael said that's when he slowly lifted his arms and hugged Samuel in return. "Do you know what he said to me then?"

"No, Michael. What?"

"He told me that real men don't abuse people."

"Wow, that's so different from my dad," I said.

My dad, I thought. It was the first time I might have said that.

"Yeah, he even said that it's going to take time, but he would have to earn *my* trust! Can you believe that?" My brother's head lowered, and a tear dropped from his face and onto his leg.

I placed my arm around his shoulder and said, "I told you that Samuel was someone special. I trust him completely, and so can you."

"Yeah, they're really great people, and I'm really glad you came out here to live with us. I can't imagine being here without you."

"Yeah, I feel the same way, man." I stood and extended my hand to help him up.

"Maybe we can go see a movie after I'm ungrounded," Michael said.

I chuckled as I started to leave the room to get a shower. "Yeah, that sounds good to me, but I might be too old to see or hear it by the time you're ungrounded."

"Very funny, Phillip!"

"Hey, I'm not the idiot who got into trouble." I snickered. "Seriously, man, I would really like to go and see a movie with you. I hear *Batman Returns* is pretty good."

"Sounds good to me," Michael replied, before crawling into his bed.

I knew he finally understood the real purpose behind discipline. It was love!

CHAPTER THIRTY-FIVE

Mom was eventually released from prison and even a rehab center, but she still spent every day of her life struggling with addiction. After my dad was released from prison, she went back to him. It took a few more years, but she eventually left him after a broken nose and several more emergency room visits. She reunited with our grandparents, and although it was hard to trust her at first, they eventually accepted Mom for who she was and not the perfect daughter they'd expected her to be. That could have been what had driven her into the arms of Tony Williams in the first place.

After our grandparents' deaths, Mom continued to live at the estate until she decided to move closer to where my wife and I are living, which is about a half hour away from Westview. She always tried to get away from her apartment as often as she could. I remembered her saying one time: "I'm so afraid of dying alone, Phillip." Sadly, the constant abuse to her body, from addiction, had become too much, and she developed cancer. Her remaining days were very painful.

Michael and I were at her bedside when she passed. A few hours before Mom got so bad that she couldn't speak, she managed to say to Michael, in a very weak voice, "Michael, I'm so proud of you!" A few seconds later, she mumbled, "I'm so sorry boys for everything. I should have stopped him." As she rolled her head back to the center of her pillow, she whispered, "I love both of you so much." Accompanied by tears, we told her we loved her as well.

Seeing more signs of tremendous pain, the hospice nurse gave her another dose of morphine, and Mom peacefully slipped into a coma. Less than an hour later, she took her final breath.

It was several years into my dad's imprisonment before I was able to write him a letter of my own. I told him everything I thought about the way he treated us, especially my brother. I never shared the contents of it with anyone—not even my wife or Michael. Because of my dad, Michael had to be treated for post-traumatic stress disorder, but he was able to overcome *almost* everything—thanks to the people who loved him. As for me, the unrelenting burden of guilt was the cross I had to bear. I always knew I should have done something sooner to stop my dad. Regardless, my brother's new family gave him back the love and security he'd missed during those dark years, and although some might disagree, Michael's *real* father came into our lives at just the right moment—like a perfect plan of sorts.

Hatred took the life of my father, just like the cancer that had consumed my mother's body. Between prison, addictions, and the combination of one bad decision after another, my father eventually lost everything. With no money to support his habits, most of his friends had abandoned him as well. In a fitting twist of justice, he managed to hold onto his house, the place he called "home." To us, it had been our prison for years. What he hadn't realized was that it was his prison, too. While Michael and I eventually found our freedom, Dad remained a prisoner behind the bars of his own bitterness.

Years after my dad had been released from prison, I received a phone call from Bud, one of his few remaining friends. He told me to get to my dad's place right away. He refused to tell me what was wrong. I hung up the phone and immediately headed to the house—unable to justify why I even bothered to go.

As I pulled onto the road leading to our old house, sweat beaded on my forehead, and my chest tightened, leaving me gasping for air. Some of the houses remained virtually the same, but as I approached the driveway, I was greeted with flashing lights, a small crowd of inquisitive neighbors, and Bud. He was leaning against his car, smoking a cigarette. The sight of the garage caused my stomach to burn. Sweat rolled down my face as I put the car into park.

As soon as I stepped out of my car, Bud pulled me over to a secluded area and said, "Phillip, I was on the phone when he did it."

"Did what, Bud?"

"When he . . . pulled the trigger," he said solemnly.

My emotions withdrew behind a protective wall I had erected years earlier. In a curt response, I asked, "What did he say to you?"

"Well, Phillip, he said he drove to the park this afternoon and saw Michael with that idiot who cheated with your mom," Bud explained. "I guess your old man couldn't take it."

"So, what else did my dad say before he took his life?" I inquired.

Bud pulled out a handkerchief and blew his nose. "Phillip, your dad read a letter to me, and I was pretty shocked by what it said."

"Yeah, I know what you're talking about."

His forehead creased as he asked, "You do?"

"Yeah, the one Samuel wrote to my mom a long time ago," I said.

A line etched between his eyebrows, and his head jerked backward in surprise. "How would that Samuel guy know about the cancer?"

"Cancer?" My nose wrinkled from the shock.

"Yes, your dad read me the report he'd brought home from the doctor this morning before he drove to the park."

"I don't know what you're talking about, Bud."

"I guess your old man decided not to tell you after all."

My upper lip curled. "So you're telling me that my dad had cancer?"

"Yep," Bud confirmed. "Terminal, too, I guess." I noticed a muscle in Bud's jaw twitch. "Phillip, your old man had a short time to live. He'd been coughing up blood for months, but he never told me that until today on the phone. He said, "'I ain't going through no chemo' but I wasn't able to convince him to at least try it."

"Bud, what did he say right before he died?" I asked.

"Well," Bud stated, "he told me he'd also opened that letter you just mentioned—the one he'd been hiding all these years. He told me about it after Michael decided to go live with that cheat who messed around with your mother years ago."

I rolled my eyes.

"I told him to burn that thing a hundred times, but he couldn't seem to do it."

"What did he say about it?" I asked.

"Well, he told me that he had a lighter in his hand and was thinking about torching it."

"And?"

"Well, there was some silence," Bud explained, "and I called out his name several times. That's when I heard him say, 'Now they'll know what you and that bastard did to me!' That's when I heard the gunshot."

I locked my fingers behind my neck and sighed. "So," I said, as my arms drooped back to my sides, "my dad still wasn't brave enough to admit that he was wrong for what he did to us?"

"Phillip," Bud interrupted, "I know you had it hard living with your old man, but he—"

"No, Bud, don't even try to justify my dad's actions. You have no idea what he put us through. He chose to torture an innocent boy for something he didn't do, just to get revenge on my mom."

Bud reached up and tried to put his hand on my shoulder.

I stepped back.

"Look, Phillip, I'm not trying to justify anything, but don't you even care that your old man died tonight?"

"Bud, in case you didn't know this, the man I wanted as a father actually died the day he found the letter from Samuel."

I walked away and headed into the garage where the investigator was standing. The paramedics had already placed my dad's body into the back of an ambulance. The investigator, Mr. Taggart, told me how sorry he was for my loss. I never responded. As the details were explained about his suicide, I became increasingly preoccupied with the sight and stench of death, which was accentuated by the burning scent of gun smoke still lingering in the air.

After we left the garage and talked outside a few minutes longer, I noticed Mr. Taggart removing something from his pocket. It was Samuel's letter tucked inside of a plastic bag, and now, it was stained with my dad's own blood. I reached forth and retrieved it from his hand. I turned it over and saw my mother's name written on the front.

With a serious expression on his face, Mr. Taggart asked, "Did you know your father also found out today that he had a terminal illness?" He handed me the medical document my dad left laying on the workbench.

"No, sir, I didn't know that until his friend told me a few minutes ago. I haven't spoken to my dad since the day he almost killed my brother in there." I pointed toward the garage before looking down and reading the document. I saw the word that likely sealed my dad's decision to end his life on his own terms: *cancer.* According to the letter, it had spread throughout his body—just like his hatred had done over time.

Mr. Taggart said, "Phillip, I really am sorry for your loss."

I gazed up at the investigator and replied, "Sir, my dad would have never allowed cancer to destroy him. It would have been way too humiliating for him to simply languish in pain and die the pathetic, weak man I knew him to be."

A moment later, Mr. Taggart reached into his other pocket and pulled out another plastic bag. It was the lighter my dad always kept in his own pocket. It had his initials *AMW* engraved on it. "We found this close by one of your dad's hands when we arrived. Phillip, the old letter was loosely clutched in the same hand."

After examining both bags closely, I gave them back, because I knew they would be needed for the report involving my dad's death. I never really knew if my dad had the thought of destroying the letter written by Samuel, but then again, was it the source of motivation he needed in order to carry out the cowardly deed? Maybe he thought others would have sympathy for him over the betrayal he'd experienced from Mom's affair. I will never know for sure. The letter had once again become a source of agonizing mystery.

Not long after his death, I had his ashes buried with Mom's. There was no funeral or memorial service for him, because much of my dad's life was a tragedy of his own making. His destructive choices ultimately left him with no one.

CHAPTER THIRTY-SIX

My time spent with Michael was sacred. During our numerous visits as adults, Michael began to tell me many details about the private times he'd spent with Samuel and Sarah over the years. Michael never felt he had a place in anyone's heart until his real dad entered his life. My brother's life was like a ship helplessly tossed about in a strong tempest and Samuel was the beacon of light that pierced the darkness, keeping Michael from crashing onto the rocky shores that he'd encountered on his difficult journey through life. During our talks, my heart was broken all over again as Michael started to open up to me about the unspeakable things he had experienced from my dad.

As adults, Michael and I each purchased homes with properties containing at least a small patch of woods. We had to have an abundance of tree frogs singing at night. One night, I showed up and discovered that Michael had cut down a large tree at the edge of his woods. He said he still missed the fallen tree at our old house, and he wanted to relive that special part of our lives as brothers. We ended up spending many nights talking on the trunk of that huge tree at Michael's home.

As the tree frogs soothed our spirits, we shared details about our new lives—ones we were fully beginning to embrace as our own. The fear of my dad kidnapping our dreams was no longer a threat, and sharing our ambitions no longer seemed dangerous. Michael talked often about Paul, because he was proud of the man he had become. Paul had attended the University of Alabama on a soccer scholarship, eventually earning a degree in business. He ended up taking over Samuel's company. Megan and her fiancé moved near Boston after she graduated with her degree in education. Both siblings are married and have children of their own. We are still very close, even though I don't see them as often as I'd like.

Although traumatic at first, Michael's experiences with the courts stirred an interest that inspired him to attend law school. After successfully passing the bar exam, he started practicing as an attorney in Alabama. After several years of dedicated work, he eventually joined a firm which specialized in cases dealing with domestic violence. Michael explained how some of his cases would trigger remembrances of his own abuse. Even though we tried to stay on positive topics when we talked, our past always seemed to be an ominous companion, waiting to cast a stumbling block onto our road to recovery. Michael often shared with me the different nightmares he was still having from his abuse. I was devastated for him when I learned about the many nights his wife sat on the floor and held him close to her as he cried on her shoulder. My guilt remained in my mind, because I still felt responsible for his lingering nightmares.

One evening, as we sat alone on the tree, I listened as he explained the gruesome details of a recent dream where he'd darted for the bathroom and attempted to wash off some blood he thought was covering his body. Michael also described how embarrassed he was over the way he curled up into a ball in front of his wife that night. Knowing Annie, I reminded him that she would never mention such episodes, even to her closest friends and family members. I was the only one she confided in when it came to Michael's PTSD.

"I know, Phillip, but you should have been there when Sammy found me on the bathroom floor, crying like a baby. When Annie took him back to his bedroom, she said that Sammy told her that he'd pray for God to take the bad dreams away from me." He sighed. "Phillip, it still bothers me that I can't get over some of the torture I went through. It's so hard to be strong all the time."

"Michael," I reminded him, "my dad won't be able to hurt you ever again, you know that."

"I know, but it's just hard to think about the things he did to me," he replied. "There are still things I want to tell you, but I just—"

My heart sank, as if it was being plunged into a watery abyss and drowned. *What else could my dad have done to my brother?* Even my own dreams haunted me with the possibility of things my dad might have tried to do to Michael, especially when alcohol was involved. I occasionally remembered the one nightmare I used to have about being in Michael's room. I remembered him telling me to go away while pulling the sheet up to his neck and whimpering. It only reoccurs when I'm haunted by the stories Michael shares with me.

The thought of what Michael might tell me, instantly saturated my conscious with grotesque images almost too unimaginable to allow into my mind.

"I just have a lot of shame about it, so I never told anyone some of the stuff he did to me sometimes," Michael said. "I didn't even tell the grand jury back when we were living with Grandma and Grandpa. That was why I freaked out when Mr. Busby said I had to testify. I didn't want them knowing about the other things your dad did to me." Michael wiped away tears from his cheeks before begging me, "Please, Phillip, don't let Annie know I said any of this! I don't even want Dad to know—at least not right now."

He was right—Samuel would have been devastated to know what Michael was still suffering through because of the letter.

"Michael," I whispered, as I put my arm around him, "you know you never have to feel shame around me. Get it off your chest whenever you feel like it." Admittedly, anticipating what he had to say was like playing a game of Russian Roulette. Was I now ready to hear about the unspeakable things my dad did to him? "I promise, Michael, I will never say *anything* to anyone. I can already see how upsetting this is to you." I attempted to swallow before I asked the inevitable question he likely suspected was plaguing my thoughts. "Michael," I whispered, "please tell me that he . . . he didn't . . ." My lips quivered as my voice started to crack.

Michael grumbled and pressed his fists hard against his temples. "This is why I never wanted to mention it to you in the first place. I knew it would upset you, Phillip."

"Of course, I'm upset, Michael!" I squeezed my eyes closed, trying to block whatever it was I'd imagined had taken place in secrecy. "Michael," I said more gently, "I hate seeing you upset, so please, just tell me!" I started to cry. "*Please!*"

Michael clasped his fingers behind his head and looked upward. "Dad threatened that he would do all sorts of really sick things to you if I ever told anyone about any of his abuse."

"He did what?" I asked.

"Yeah, and I'm only bringing this stuff up now because of a really bad dream I had last night about it. He tried to . . ." Michael paused. "Phillip, I can't get him out of my head! He won't leave me alone!" He tapped the side of his head fiercely several times as if trying to beat the images out of his mind.

I cleared my throat, and started to open my mouth, but I suddenly broke down and began to cry. After several grueling moments, I said, "Michael, please tell me he didn't . . ." I stood and walked over to another tree and leaned my back against it. The bark was abrasive against my tightening muscles. "Look, I don't want you to deal with this on your own, so please tell me what he did."

Michael paused, which only added to the suspense that had caused images to invade my mind. "No," he responded, "he never abused me the way I know you're thinking, but he always threatened to, especially when he was really drunk." Michael's head drooped toward the ground. "He'd always brush my cheek with his fingertips and smile right before telling me the things he'd do to you if I ever told on him." Michael looked up—his tears glistened in the moonlight. "Phillip, I was nothing more than a scared little kid when he'd come into my room. Sometimes, I'd run to the bathroom and throw up when he'd finally leave."

I leaned my head back and rested it against the trunk of the tree, gasping for air.

Relief transformed into anger, then pity, and lastly the guilt rushed in like a tidal wave, nearly knocking me off my feet. My chest bounced as I inhaled air in short breaths.

"Thank God!" I wiped the sweat off of my face with my sleeve. "Michael, what kinds of things did he do and say?"

Michael's head sagged toward the ground once more. "One time, when I'd finished showering . . ." Michael looked up at me. He shivered. ". . . I opened the curtain and he was standing there staring at me with his hand behind his back. I thought for sure he had a belt. I remembered thinking how much it would sting if he hit me."

"Yeah," I said, "I know that feeling!"

"Well, I noticed my towel was gone, so I had nothing to cover me but the cold, wet shower curtain. He had this really evil grin on his face and asked if I was missing something. He pulled the towel out from behind his back and told me to come and get it. I begged for him to stop, but he insisted I step out and get it." I shook my head and sighed. "When I stepped out and reached for it, he dropped it onto the floor and laughed. Then he walked out. Phillip, I still find myself peeking around the shower curtain before opening it."

"But he didn't do anything, right?"

"No, it was just the feeling he might do something like that to me." Michael paused before saying, "I sat on the toilet and cried once he left the bathroom."

I thought for a moment, and then asked, "Is that why you always tried to get me to stay close to the bathroom when you had to get a shower?"

Michael was silent as he nodded. "Yeah," he finally said. "Other times, he came into my room and sat on my bed. When I opened my eyes, he'd brush my hair to one side and look at me with that sick, sadistic grin. I was always so scared when he was drunk. I never knew what he was capable of doing to either of us!" Michael rested his elbows on his knees and massaged his temples, digging into them with his fingertips. "In my dream last night, I couldn't get him off of me. I screamed for Mom, but she never came to help me. Annie found me curled up in my closet, Phillip. I was screaming for him to stop! I pushed Annie away and she almost hit her head on a nightstand. I'm afraid I'm going to really hurt her someday."

I walked over and sat next to him. I knew how afraid he still was, and I couldn't contain my anguish for allowing my dad to do such things right next door to my room. Those very things often led to Michael's nightmares. At that moment, I sobbed—it was my only repentance.

Michael rubbed my back. "It's okay, Phillip. Please don't. Not now. Remember, it was all about having power over us. It was the best way to control me. He knew how much I cared about you, and he knew I wouldn't want him doing any of that sick stuff to you. That's why I didn't want to testify to the grand jury, Phillip. I didn't know if you'd be going back home to live there with him. I was afraid he'd do those things when you guys were alone, and I couldn't live with myself. I just couldn't let him!"

I pulled Michael toward me and embraced him. I cried out, "I'm so sorry, Michael! I didn't know! I could've stopped him! I know I could have!" I buried my face into his shoulder. "Michael, I didn't know! I really didn't! Oh God, I'm so sorry!"

In my mind, I knew then that I couldn't forgive myself, even if Michael truly forgave me someday. I released my brother.

"It's okay, Phillip, 'cause I—" Michael suddenly stopped. I looked up, not knowing what he wanted to say. After a brief pause, he uttered, "I won, because he never did that stuff to you like he'd threatened. You would've told me."

I took my sleeve and wiped my moist, sticky face. "Michael," I cried, "all this time I thought *I* was the one trying to protect you!"

I dropped my chin to my chest in remorse. As my body trembled from my shame, I realized that it was Michael—and not me—who was the real protector! He suffered in silence for years to protect me from my own dad! Yes, my own evil dad!

My sadness mutated into rage as I bellowed, "It's a good thing that pathetic animal is dead!" I sat silently—numb from my outburst—while I contemplated the revelation that it was Michael who saved *me* from the malicious, torturous hands of my own dad. Michael was the true hero! It certainly wasn't me. Everyone had it all wrong. I didn't save my brother—*he saved me!* I let my dad do *unspeakable* things to my own brother! I was guilty as charged!

Michael hugged me and said, "Remember, Phillip, he can't hurt either one of us ever again!" The warmth of his breath in my ear startled me. "There's nothing he can do to us anymore. I really mean it, Phillip. I won, because I'm the one who is still here, and he's dead. We beat him at his own game, Phillip!"

We said nothing more for several moments as we embraced in the moonlight. The gentle, calming melody of tree frogs caused me to squeeze Michael even harder. I knew that night that my brother had revealed something very personal to me—something that had devastated his life for so many years. Although it was painful to hear, he no longer had to bear such a burden alone. Some of the unspeakable things had been released from Michael's soul.

After several more minutes, we let go of each other and started walking toward Michael's house, knowing enough had been said that night. We stopped only once to listen to the sounds echoing from the woods.

"I always come outside when I can't sleep and listen to them," Michael said. "It's amazing how I can have a terrible nightmare and still find some peace when I listen to those crazy little things."

"Yeah," I replied, "I still do the same thing when I can't sleep." I placed my arm around him and we continued walking. Instead of going into the house with him, I hugged Michael and walked to my car. "I'll call you tomorrow."

I wiped my eyes. "Please apologize to Annie and the boys, but I better get going." I knew I needed time alone to process everything Michael had shared that night.

"Okay," he responded. "Thanks for listening, Phillip. Maybe now I won't dream about it as much."

I quickly walked back over and hugged him again. We patted each other on our backs as I replied, "I'll always be here for you. You know that!" I wiped tears from my chin with the back of my hand. "Michael, I'm so sorry." I started back toward my car and said, "I love you, brother! We'll get through this!"

"I love you, too, man" he said.

I cried most of the way home. I imagined my brother, a fully grown man, all curled up in one of the corners of his bedroom and shaking violently from terrible nightmares while his wife held him in her arms. I also imagined a frightened little boy curled up in his bed, years ago, as he watched the man he thought was his father slipping into his bedroom and closing the door behind him. My wicked dad was intent on dousing my brother with fear, only to ignite the terror with a hatred that could never be extinguished. I realized that the lines in my old bedroom wallpaper weren't prison bars after all; they were actually a barrier I used as an excuse not to intervene in my brother's protection. How could Michael ever forgive me for that?

CHAPTER THIRTY-SEVEN

My brother's passion for defending the defenseless took root one night, long ago, when the young boy was brought into the hospital after he was beaten by his drunken father. Just down the hallway was Michael, who was being nursed back to health after the severe beating my dad inflicted on him in our garage that same day. That was *the day* I picked up a weapon and defended my brother's right to exist. We later found out that the little boy died not long after Michael was released into the custody of our grandparents. Like the permanent mark of branding on a rancher's livestock, the image of the dying boy must have been seared into my brother's memory forever, and because of that, Michael often prosecuted cases of abuse with a determination unlike anyone else at his law firm. He must have seen himself in the mangled faces and bodies of the wounded, and he fought to give those victims a voice that someone evil in *their* lives had tried to silence. Michael shared with me, during one of our afternoon visits at his law firm, how sad he was for the family when they had to bury their young child.

"Phillip," he said, "I saw the kid's picture with his obituary, and I always thought how easily that could have been us. The kid looked nothing like his picture when I saw him at the hospital."

"Wait a minute, Michael, when did you see that kid?" Regrettably, the phone rang on his desk and I never did find out, until later, how Michael met the young boy at the hospital.

Just one week after that conversation, Michael was prosecuting a case for a client who had been attacked and nearly killed by a group of thugs. It was later discovered that two of the attackers were related to a couple of my mom and dad's old party friends. Michael didn't know them personally, but he was familiar with their previous criminal records. He chose to take the case because of the brutal nature of the attack.

After the closing arguments, Michael decided to grab a quick bite to eat with some friends while the jury deliberated. As he stepped onto the sidewalk in front of the courthouse, a rusty, old car slowed down along the street. Two shots were fired. Four people were in the car at the time, but no one was able to get a clear description of the assailants. The full report later revealed that the car was found abandoned after being reported stolen from another man's property.

Traffic stopped immediately after the foreboding gunshots echoed eerily throughout the desolate alleys between the buildings. After the car sped away, frightened people soon emerged from behind any protective shelter they could find. They quickly assembled around the victim lying on the cement. Several people called for an ambulance, but it was too late! The two shots hit their precise target. One bullet shredded one of Michael's lungs, and the other obliterated his passionate, beating heart. He collapsed instantly to the sidewalk. Brian, my brother's best friend, happened to be down the street waiting for him at a small diner when he heard the gun shots, followed briefly by the ear-piercing sound of screeching tires. Brian rushed up the block only to find Michael lying motionless in a crimson pool of his own blood—dead.

An unrelenting determination seemed to force me to visit the crime scene later that afternoon. I often wondered why people did stuff like that, but then, I found myself standing there looking at the cement sidewalk where Michael had collapsed that dreadful day. I felt a sense of obligation to visit the place where I knew my brother's soul vacated his lifeless body. Oddly, I felt a connection to Michael by being there—almost as if I had arranged a meeting with him at that exact location, and was only awaiting his arrival. It was in front of the courthouse where my brother spent valuable years defending the rights of victims who needed someone to guide them through their own battlefields of life.

Through many tears, I looked around for anything that showed evidence that my brother may *not* have been there that afternoon—almost as though I was trying to prove that whole tragedy had never occurred. The bloodshed from the crime scene had long been washed away into some obscure storm drain, flowing aimlessly to some larger source of life-giving water. After looking around for a couple minutes, I sat down on a bench next to a small flowering shrub. I happened to look over, and regrettably, I saw some residue left behind from the terrible, senseless crime. On several of the yellow flowers, I saw dried spots of blood—Michael's blood. I squeezed my eyes shut for a few moments, but when I opened them again, the evidence of the greatest catastrophe in my life was still there. I sobbed when I thought about the mindless act of cowardice that robbed the world of a true hero—*my hero!*

As I sat there feeling completely drained of life, I felt the soft touch of someone's hand on my shoulder. I looked up and saw an older woman who had a slight, encouraging smile on her face. She said in a quiet, calming voice, "Honey, I know you don't know me, but your brother was very special to me, too."

Through a broken voice, I asked, "How did you know my brother?" I assumed she was a client from one of his many cases.

"I remembered him from when he was in the hospital many years ago. It was after your father had beaten him so badly. I read about it in the papers during your parents' trials."

"I don't understand," I said. The sunlight radiating from behind her, gave her a kind of angelic glow. It was as if she had been sent there as a messenger from God. Perhaps it was to help me reassemble the now shattered masterpiece that had been coming together in our lives—yes, the masterpiece that had been obliterated in an instant that day.

"Do you mind if I sit down?" she politely asked. I slid over. "I was at the hospital the day your brother was released. That was so long ago now. Anyway, I was just down the hallway," she said. "You see, it was my six-year-old grandson who was beaten to death by his drunken father." I suddenly remembered who she was talking about. "Sadly," she said, "my grandson died not long after your brother stopped in to see him that day."

"But I don't remember Michael ever mentioning meeting you before."

"Honey," she said, "right before he left that day, he came down to our room. I remember him tapping lightly on the door."

"I had no idea Michael visited your grandson."

"Yes," she replied, "he walked in and just stood there for a moment. I asked if I could help him, but he said he wanted to say something to my grandson, but E.J. was unconscious. His name was Joshua, but we called him E.J. He was named after my husband, Earl Joshua Mason."

As I sat there, stunned by what she was telling me, my eyes shot wide open. "Hey, wait a minute!" I bellowed. "I remember that my brother made us wait for him by the elevator in the lobby that morning. He said he needed to see someone."

After two decades, a mystery had been solved: Michael chose to visit the little boy that day!

"Yes, your brother visited us, and he said something very compassionate, and I will never forget it," she replied. "I think that's why I couldn't resist coming down here, even though my daughter insisted that I shouldn't. She's so protective of me."

With anticipation, I asked, "What did Michael say to you?"

"Well, he said, 'I'm really sorry, ma'am, for what happened to the kid. If he ever needs someone to talk to about this kinda thing, I'd be happy to help him. I know what it's like to go through all this kind of stuff.'" The lady reached over and grasped my hand. "Young man," she said, "it was then that I realized that your brother must have been beaten by his father as well. He sure looked it that day. The newspapers only confirmed it." She wiped her cheek. "My grandson's obituary was in the paper the same day the police reports revealed what had happened to you two in your garage. We knew by then who the report was about. It didn't mention your names, but we knew about Tony Williams, but we had no idea he did that kind of stuff to you boys."

I looked at her and replied, "Yeah, Michael was beaten . . . lots of times."

I was shocked that my brother felt brave enough to initiate such a tender act of kindness, especially toward strangers. I guess Michael saw himself somehow connected to that little boy, and apparently, the conversations he heard in the hallway the night the child was brought in must have touched him in a way none of us had expected.

"Young man, it was the kindest act I've ever seen from any teen boy in my life."

I wiped my face with a tissue I had in my pocket. "You know something, ma'am, my brother ended up helping other kids when he got away from my dad. He did it a lot at his church when he and his real dad worked with troubled teens."

The lady said one last thing before leaving. After we stood, she extended her hand to shake mine. "My name is June, and I know what it's like to lose someone you love. If you ever need a shoulder to lean on, please let me know. Your brother offered us a shoulder to lean on all those years ago, so I think it is only right that I should do the same for you."

I started to weep as I reached out and shook her hand. My voice faded abruptly, so I whispered, "I don't know where to find you, ma'am."

She smiled and lifted her thumb to my cheek, wiping away one of my tears. She politely responded, "I now live with my daughter . . . in your old house. We bought it after it was foreclosed on. We've learned a lot about your family over the years." She leaned over and hugged me. Her soft caress on my back eased some of the throbbing pain I had from so much crying that day. "You know," she said, "I certainly didn't expect to find you here today, but I'm glad I did. It's as if God had arranged this meeting for some reason. But either way, it's been a pleasure meeting you . . . Phillip."

As she walked away, I began to realize that even back then, Michael reached out to others who were suffering. His act of compassion had somehow found an unforeseen purpose—a purpose hidden deep within the grieving heart of a kind lady who would one day, years later, wrap her arms around a destitute man found grieving on a bench for the hero—a brother—he'd suddenly lost.

The first piece of my fragmented masterpiece had been picked up by God and put back where it belonged.

As I turned to leave, I happened to notice the plaque near the place where Michael died. I paused briefly to read its inscription. It simply stated: *In memory of our fallen heroes whose courage and sacrifice helped secure our freedoms*. Even today, I am constantly reminded that heroes are not just those who have fought courageously in some distant war zone, but they are also those who have fought bravely on the battlefields of life that we all stumble onto throughout our own struggles in this world. Heroes sacrifice their lives for the freedom of others. They overcome their own battles in order to give others a greater chance at overcoming theirs. My brother was a treasured hero to me, and I left that place that awful day thinking to myself how much Michael sacrificed to make a difference.

And he died doing just that.

CHAPTER THIRTY-EIGHT

Michael ended up being my anchor, keeping me from going adrift in a life full of storms. I often thought I was the one who held us together, but I eventually realized that it was his strength and bravery that got us through the many problems our parents had caused. They were a tornado that had left a wide path of debris in its wake; however, with the help of loving people, my brother and I were able to clean up most of their destructive influence, leaving us a much clearer path to follow.

In spite of all the horrible things Michael experienced from my dad, he courageously devoted his life to helping others. He truly was a hero to so many people who couldn't fight life's battles on their own. Who would have ever expected that from a boy most people considered nothing more than a throwaway kid? Because of my brother, I've learned that God can use anyone for a greater purpose, regardless of their past.

Because of Michael's impact on me, I've decided to dedicate the rest of my life to telling everyone, including my own sons, along with Michael's, what a special man my brother was to so many people. I was so glad Michael got to do a lot of things with his own boys, as well as mine. He was an awesome brother, son, dad, uncle and friend. No one will ever fill the void in our lives that was left behind after his passing. Michael will always be the miracle in my life.

I'm so thankful we had spent many weekends together on different fishing trips, along with the summer adventures to places like Yellowstone, the Grand Canyon, and the Smoky Mountains. Michael, Samuel, and I enjoyed every minute we had together with our sons. The professional baseball games were especially fun, but the greatest joy Michael and I continued to share with each other was sitting alone, and sometimes with our children at night and, of course, listening to the tree frogs.

Michael was blessed to have spent nearly thirty years with Samuel. It was twice the amount of time he'd lost without him in his life. Because of a *real man* like Samuel, Michael grew into the person he was meant to be. Still, the saddest part of my life is the realization that I will have to live without Michael by my side. Every time I look into the faces of his sons, and their mother, I know what I still have left to do: I have to stay behind to watch over my brother's family for him. I have to fill as much of the emptiness as possible. Michael wouldn't trust anyone else but me to look after his greatest treasures.

After realizing that several hours had passed since I first arrived at his grave in the cemetery, I knew it was time for me to get up from the small wooden log I'd carried from the trunk of my car earlier that afternoon. It was from the fallen tree on our old property. The lady I'd met on the day Michael died was kind enough to give me permission to cut it from the trunk of the tree, which was still at the edge of the woods—decaying. Her daughter understood why I wanted it. After all, it was the only gift of genuine value I could bring with me. The piece wasn't very large, but it contained the engraving he and I had carved into it when we were younger. Our names were darkened by years of weathering, but I could still read the words under our names: *brothers forever*.

I wasn't too surprised that I had taken several hours recalling so many difficult events—likely triggered by my visit. My memories often took me back to that traumatic night in the hospital when I was seventeen years old. The only good part of that whole experience, besides Michael's recovery from the overdose, was the fact that we'd encountered Samuel and Sarah. She had taken a huge risk that night in revealing to Samuel that Michael was in the hospital. Sarah couldn't ignore the opportunity for her husband to see the boy he believed might be his son. Besides, it could have easily been Samuel's last chance to meet Michael.

I stood and looked around again, and I realized that I had to accept the stone-cold reality of my surroundings. There was, however, one object that brought me some comfort. Just a short distance from Michael's grave was a smaller tombstone with the name Earl Joshua Mason III engraved into its surface. Yes, it was the little boy whose life ended around the same time Michael left the hospital to start a new life with our grandparents. I suddenly realized that Joshua and Michael got their chance to talk after all.

As the sun descended into the horizon, spewing forth various shades of red, orange, and purple, I knew I had a short time left to visit with my brother. I decided to get down on my knees and pull a few blades of grass from the edges of Michael's gravestone. I also tried my best to brush away some of the dried, brown grass stuck in the letters of his name. It was the first time I had visited the cemetery since the day of the funeral, and I wanted to leave my brother's resting place in good condition.

As I did my best to clean off the stone, I remembered standing beside Michael's casket and watching Samuel straightening my brother's tie before pulling a tiny piece of lint from the collar of Michael's suit jacket. I now understood why Samuel was so particular about the way his son looked that day. In much the same way, by cleaning off my brother's grave, it was as if I, too, was showing others how much our family loved and cared for him—even in death.

It was also the first time I could bring myself to read the inscription on the headstone. I was honored to have been asked to write it. Although he came into this world around forty years ago, Michael never actually started to live the life he was destined for until his real father, the one who loved him unconditionally, walked into his life and refused to leave. It is still so hard to declare my brother gone when I see him in all of the people he loved here on Earth, especially his sons, Sammy and Phillip.

For years, I tried to fully understand what Pastor George meant when he declared that God was still able to create a masterpiece from the fragments of our lives—much like the brilliant pieces of glass an artist might piece together into a custom-made stained glass window. In like manner, Michael taught me that regardless of our circumstances, we can still make a difference in this world, especially knowing that trials pave the way for patience and perseverance. I would have to say, though, that the greatest lesson I learned from him was this: *Love endures all things!* My brother's life somehow reflected this, in spite of his upbringing.

As I removed my glasses to wipe my eyes, I scanned the beautiful and peaceful surroundings once again. We chose such a place for Michael because of the great care we knew would be given to his gravesite. Admittedly, my faith was shaken by his murder, but I knew Michael was still alive and well, and one day, I would be with him again. Samuel and Sarah taught me how my personal faith could make that happen.

When I put my glasses back on, I looked at the engraving on the stone again. I remembered thinking of the words I might like as a brief epitaph while riding from the funeral home to the intimate, little chapel, which was just off to the right of the entrance of the cemetery. We decided to have a brief ceremony in the chapel, because none of us could bear to have a graveside service.

As I read the inscription before me, I remembered our carving into the old tree, as well as the time I said to him: "Everyone will always know that we're brothers! Hey, if I have to, I'll even chisel it into stone!"

I kept my promise to him.

Michael Paul Roberts
1976-2017
A true hero to his family
And to all those he helped rescue from the battlefields of life
LOVE ENDURES ALL THINGS
"Brothers Forever"
Phillip A. Williams

I took out my handkerchief and wiped a few more tears from my face. I remembered how I once believed that my dad's hatred could easily destroy the ability for Michael and me to love others.

I was wrong.

Love *does* endure all things—you just have to let it work its power by giving it the time it needs to mature. Samuel, Sarah, and our grandparents planted the seed of love into my brother's soul, and we all watered it as best as we could. However, it was God who ultimately caused that love to grow. In return, Michael's love for others produced a work far greater than anyone could have ever predicted. Even death could not entomb my love for him, nor could it erase the great things Michael accomplished in his brief time in this world.

I stepped back and whispered, "I sure do miss you, Michael." I sighed and started to cry. "I'd give anything just to hear your voice once again—just one more time, Michael. I just need to know everything's okay between us."

I sobbed for several minutes before regaining my composure. I looked down at my watch and knew I had to end my visit before the groundskeeper, who happened to live in the large red brick house, closed and locked the iron gates for the night. Even though the day brought about some frightening memories for me, I knew it was time for me to stop breaking our afternoon appointments. Deep down, I regarded my absence as a dishonor to him. After all, Michael taught me to have courage over my fears, but I certainly wasn't doing such a good job in conquering them every day. In fact, I knew there was still one unresolved issue preventing me from moving forward with my life.

Sure, I knew what Michael would say to me if I begged for his forgiveness one more time. "There's nothing to forgive, Phillip. We were both victims. You did everything you could."

Why couldn't I accept his forgiveness?

Then I saw it! It was written on the tombstone right in front of me the whole time. I repeated four simple, yet powerful words: "Love endures all things."

In a sudden flash of insight, I realized I'd come to the cemetery to seek Michael's forgiveness, but it wasn't really his forgiveness I needed. I already had that. What I was really seeking was something I hadn't expected to learn, especially that day.

I *had* to forgive myself!

How could I truly honor my brother's life if I wasn't willing to accept such forgiveness?

When I first arrived, I had wondered how I could move my life forward again? If Michael moved on, shouldn't I do the same? My guilt had held me captive for so long, but if love could free my brother, why couldn't it do that for me? Forgiveness is truly a gift we should offer more often to others, but it is sometimes meaningless if we are not willing to accept it for ourselves. How could I have missed such an important detail about my own life?

All this time, I thought I'd been freed from my dad's prison of hate by the love of my grandparents and the Roberts family, but I had been imprisoning myself in self-hatred and unforgiveness—bound by the chains of guilt. In a sense, I'd become my father's legacy.

At that moment, while gazing at those four amazing words, I resolved to end that legacy. I needed to bury it forever.

And with that one solemn vow to myself, while standing silent before my brother's grave, I felt the ripples of freedom ringing in my heart and soul. I'd realized that it was actually possible for me to move my life forward once again.

It would make Michael so happy to see that I was free.

As I slowly turned to leave, I heard the familiar sounds of some cherished and memorable tunes coming from a small patch of woods near Michael's final resting place. I recalled again how my brother and I would sit for countless hours on our fallen tree at home and listen to "nature's soundtrack." While walking to my car, an overwhelming sense of calm settled upon me. I realized my brother had found a way to remind me of his forgiveness, and that I had also forgiven myself. I looked to the heavens and smiled because I could hear Michael's soft, reassuring voice somehow mixed in with the peaceful song of the tree frogs.

ACKNOWLEDGMENTS

While speaking with a friend of mine one evening, I shared with her my enjoyment for creating stories, and she asked to see a sample of my writing. I was reluctant at first; however, I decided to send the original manuscript of this novel to her. Dottie told me to give her a couple weeks to read it because her dog had been extremely ill. Two nights later, my phone rang around 10:30, and I was certain Dottie was calling to tell me that her beloved pet had passed. She was sobbing. To my relief, she told me that her dog was fine and that she had just finished reading my story. We spoke for over two hours about her love for Phillip and Michael, her hatred for Tony, and her shock regarding the climax and the ending of the story. So, three things happened that evening: I decided to seek assistance with editing, I chose to officially pursue representation, and I formally made Dottie my "book critic." I am eternally grateful for her prayers and encouragement.

Although my characters are imaginary, regrettably there are too many Phillips and Michaels out there, left to survive their own world of hatred, isolation, and abuse. To such victims, I dedicate this novel. Millions of child neglect and abuse cases are reported each year to various agencies, and I wanted to offer readers the opportunity to immerse themselves into the nefarious world of two brothers, each struggling with their own fears, regrets, guilt, and even redefining their relationship after unconditional love found its way through the hatred in their lives.

Life is sometimes like a puzzle, and each piece—whether it's a person or circumstance in our lives—is a vital part of a much bigger picture. When we allow God to take over as the "author and finisher," a true masterpiece begins to emerge. How we respond and grow through life's challenges will determine the final image we leave behind for others to see.

I am so grateful for the people who've supported me along this journey. Without the love and patience of my wife, Connie, and my daughter, Madison, I couldn't have done this. I've also been privileged to work with amazing professional editors. Thank you so much Lara, Brooke, Angie, and Deeni! I'm so honored to call you my friends. I also want to thank my Adolescent Literature professor, Dr. Virginia Horvath, for her tremendous inspiration throughout my undergraduate college experience. I'm indebted to my extended family and friends, my church family, and my professional colleagues for their encouragement, especially for allowing me to bounce ideas off of them, ad nauseam.

Thank you, Tyler, Bryce, Joey, and Tony for agreeing to be a part of this project. You've all made a great first impression on the covers. I also want to thank Annie Theiss-Inge, Visual Design and Imaging instructor at East Liverpool High School, and Josh Menning, director and producer of Menning Photographic Films, for the initial and final cover designs. You guys are amazing! I would also like to thank Tina Goss and Bryan Huff for their professional photos. Thanks again to Shayne and Alan for their help in obtaining images for the covers.

I promised a while back that I wouldn't forget the encouragement of my former Westgate Middle School students in my advanced language arts classes, as well as many students in a creative writing class at the East Liverpool High School—many of whom didn't know I was the author of the book until after they'd read sample chapters. I'm so honored to have been the teacher to so many amazing students who've changed my life in countless ways. This certainly applies to the dedicated colleagues I've worked with in my profession.

Finally, I would like to thank you, the audience, for taking the time to read this novel. It is truly an amalgamation of experiences I've known throughout my life. As a junior high teacher, and a college instructor for over twenty-five years, I've had the privilege of getting to know the dynamics of a lot of students and their families. As I mentioned throughout my novel, our life is never complete without the influence of so many people fitting into it at just the right time. No puzzle is truly complete without all of its pieces, and when we look back over our lives, we will likely have a much clearer perspective on how each person fits into our own masterpiece—teaching us something we weren't necessarily expecting to learn—but needed to.

Along with God's grace, forgiveness is one of the greatest gifts we can offer our loved ones, and sometimes—often through many tears—we might even learn to forgive ourselves. We all struggle at times to survive our own battlefields in this world, but love is one of the greatest weapons we have to conquer difficult events. Let us never forget that love conquers and endures all things. After all, an old rugged cross proved that to the whole world.

ABOUT THE AUTHOR

J.W. Kitson is a veteran teacher with thirty years of experience. Having spent most of his career teaching junior high and college students, he has earned various distinguished teacher and service awards, and has traveled from coast to coast, presenting at numerous educational and technology conferences. An ordained pastor for over twenty years, he has also written several inspirational publications regarding Christian apologetics, along with biographies about local citizens. He has co-produced several faith-based movies with Menning Films, an award-winning company. These films include the following: *Unwavering* and *Gateway to Hope: Overcoming Heroin* (for which Josh Menning was nominated as Best-Director at the International Christian Film and Music Festival in 2019). Kitson, through Menning Films, completed filming this story, *Song of the Tree Frogs*, as a major motion picture. Popular Christian film and movie stars joined them, including such award-winning actors and actresses as Shannen Fields (*Facing the Giants*), Karen Abercrombie (*War Room*), Stacey Bradshaw (*Unplanned*), Meggie Jenny (*The Last Defense*), Richard Cutting (*Order of Rights*), and Cameron McKendry (*I'm Not Ashamed*). J. W. Kitson resides in East Liverpool, Ohio, with his wife (Connie), their daughter (Madison), and close family friend and "adopted son" (Matthew, who appears as adult Michael on the cover).

HOW TO CONTACT J.W.KITSON

I'd love to hear from you! For more information regarding this novel or speaking engagements, contact John at Kitson Books, LLC:

Email: info@jwkitson.com
Online: www.jwkitson.com

Kitson Books, LLC
P.O. Box 2886
East Liverpool, Ohio 43920

Get updates on this and John's other writings at:
Facebook: www.facebook.com/kitsonbooksllc
Twitter: www.twitter.com/jwkitson
Website: www.jwkitson.com

To purchase bulk copies of this book at a discount for schools and organizations, please contact Kitson Books, LLC:

www.jwkitson.com

FREE MEMBERSHIP FOR READERS OF SONG OF THE TREE FROGS

Retail Value of $97

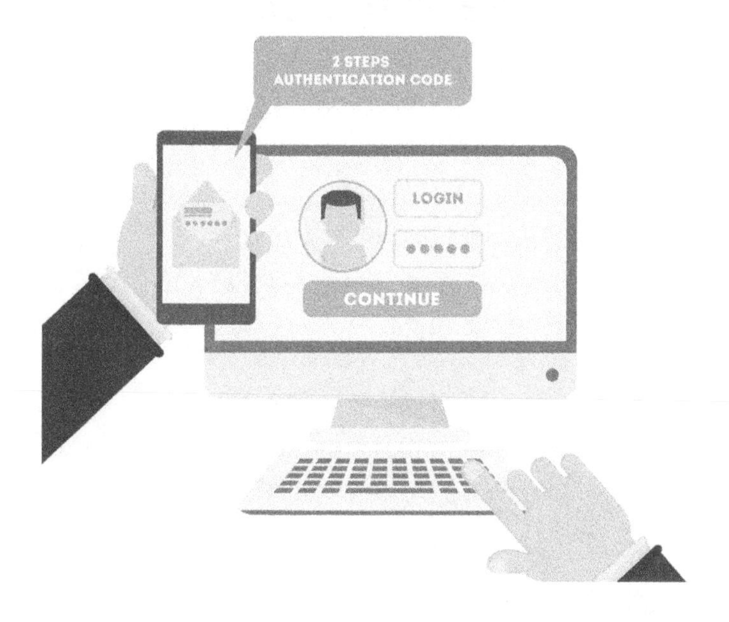

Get access to your FREE reader and teacher membership...

Deleted Scenes (experience even more about the characters' lives you never knew)

Teacher Starter Kit for the classroom (get book club materials and lesson plans to teach the book in the classroom)

Advocacy resources related to themes throughout the story (including child abuse, drug addiction, and the hope found in Jesus Christ)

... and so much more! Visit: www.jwkitson.com

Printed in the USA
CPSIA information can be obtained
at www.ICGtesting.com
JSHW022320140824
68134JS00019B/1201

9 781683 506058